MOTHER

By D.B. Martin

D. B. Martin

EBDB BOOKHOUSE PUBLISHING
A DIVISION OF THE GEORGIA PUBLISHERS GROUP
234 Dogwood Drive SE
Calhoun, GA 30701

Copyright © 2017 by db martin

First EBDB Bookhouse - edition March 2017

For information about special discounts for bulk purchases, please contact:

EBDB Bookhouse – Special Sales – 706.618.4760

www.authordavidmbrown.com

Mr. Martin is available for book signings and lectures. Please contact ebdb Bookhouse Publishing for information.

Cover designed by FLEXDREAMS

Printed in the United States of America

Library of Congress Cataloging-in-Publication Data is available

ISBN: 978-0-692-83861-7

ISBN: - 10: - 0692838619

Author's note

While I have taken many liberties with the geography of Northwest England, Canada, and even the United States, the locations and even some of the events are real. The story THOUGH itself is fiction.

A special thanks to my wonderful editor.

Amber Lanier Nagle

Thanks also to the Members of the:

Calhoun Area Writers – The Dalton Area Writers – The Rome Area Writers.
The Georgia Writers Association - Dogwood Books – Rome Georgia

A special thanks to:

All of those below who read or commented on the pages that I thrust in front of you every month as I worked to cobble this story together.

Paul Moses, Karli Land, Amber Lanier Nagle, Beth Davis, Vickie McEntire, Gene Magnicher, Marla Aycock, Mike Ragland, Millicent Flake, Clarissa Willerson, Ginger Anderson, Regina Wheeler, Clark Bunch, Nancy Ratcliffe, Alicia Alderman, walderman, Sydney Bolding, Meredith Boos, Amanda Brown, Christopher Brown, Bobbi Butler, Jeremy Cantrell, Nicolas Perez-Carreno, Debbie Carter, Chris Collins, Matthew Cowart, Merrill Davis, Alaina Lopez, **Stacie Calhoun,** Ashley derringer, Susan Dillard, Robert S. Evans, Mack Shady, Aseneth Garza, Cathy Holmes, Jennifer Jones, Dave Mohr, Alice Newgen, Sherry Patterson, Caitlin Pyne, Maria Rochelle, Perla Salaises, Con Scott, Kimberly Smith MD, Lauren Sneary, Jim Sneary, Cheryll Snow, George Spence, Liz Swafford, Jane Taylor, Nicholas Tucker, Angelina Vaquera-Linke, Laurie White, Cynthia Wilson, Jeri Zacharias, Nancy Ellen Brown, Joshua Brown / Archer Lewis and Susan Schumacher.

DEDICATION
To the ones who always stand beside me. My wonderful wife Ellie and my amazing son, Joshua.

"Words have no power to impress the mind without the exquisite horror of their reality."
— *Edgar Allan Poe* -

"I just don't understand it, my heart keeps pumping blood, even though my mind has given up so many times. Maybe it knows something I don't."

— Archer Lewis —

"Good things of day begin to droop and drowse, while night's black agents to their prey do rouse."
- William Shakespeare, *Macbeth* -

"When I write it is exciting for me too because I never know how it is going to end."

— *db martin* —

These and more are available at

Amazon.com, Barnes and Noble or your local bookstore.

Titles by D.B. Martin

HORRIBLE SANITY – Dark Tales - Brown

FEEDER – Book I of the Blood Chronicles

MOTHER – Book II of the Blood Chronicles

TERROR TALES – Vol I

Collective Works

World of Pirates

31 Days of October

CAW Telling Stories Vol I

Look for these titles coming soon

Goody

Terror Tales – Vol II

Noah – Book III of the Blood Chronicles

CAW Telling Stories Vol II

CONTENTS

CONTENTS CONTINUED

MOTHER

Book II

The Blood Chronicles

1

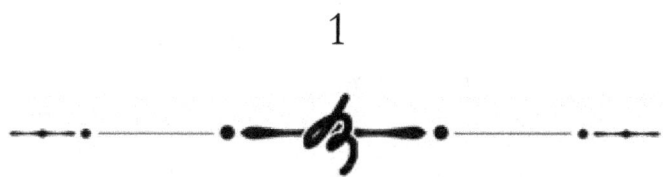

Whatever was out there moved with such calculated patience that she had first mistaken it for the sound of raindrops. It was only after that she could differentiate the rhythm of the footsteps from the white noise of the rain. A furtive movement between the trees caught her attention, and at last, she glimpsed what had been stalking her.

Isabeau's gray eyes snapped open, sweeping in her murky surroundings. A blast of frigid air hit her as she jerked her chin off the mushy grass and peered at the world from the ground. She found herself lying semi-prone on the cold, damp earth with grass stuck to her lips and face. She lay there, her naked body wrapped only in a frayed woolen blanket, secure under the leafy vault of a large, shadowy, sprawling oak tree that was barely palpable in the predawn gloom. Its trunk was black and knobbly while its branches buckled over her as a roof to meet a brick plane and obscured her view of the stars. Water dripped from the leaves, the residual from the rain the previous evening. A heavy wooden wagon stood hard by the spreading tree. The horse gave a quiet nicker, at her movements; its strapping still holding it securely to the wagon. It was still alive?

Isabeau lay there as the glowing light rose within the forest, a new day dawning in the early morning mist, which is how the visual image of the sun rising through the trees translated into poetry in her head. What was the emotion connected to it that triggered that most loquacious and quixotic part of her brain? She had come to learn that emotions are often a poor indicator of reality and in this case, it was no different. For a new day, at least in her mind, was nothing more than a precursor to another night? Night. She figured she had maybe two more hours before actual dawn. She grabbed her crumpled dress lying beside her and rose, letting the blanket slide down her naked body to her feet as she stepped from its confines and staggered wearily toward the nearby lake.

Suddenly she stopped "Damn it," she almost shouted it out loud. Her hands, -they both were covered in blood and with further inspection, looking down her entire body, her breasts, stomach, and legs, were all covered in blood, as well. Dirt and moss clung to the dried gore.

"No, no, not again. Jesus Christ," she said now almost in a quick panic march toward the water. Will this never end? She thought. She tried to think of something else. She just needed to get this washed off her body before anyone saw her this way. She moved quickly and tried to put it out of her memory again. A dense veil isolated Isabeau from the world and without knowing it, an abyss separated her from herself.

If she remembered correctly, she thought she had traveled through Kendal and Grasmere and now believed she was in the Lake District just below Skelton. She should be back home in Ellenborough just in time for nightfall. "Home," now that is a word she thought she had never truly known. She thought of home more as a concept than what she assumed most visualize when the word is spoken.

The forest itself was massive, trunks tall and as thick as corn, barks like rough cut leather towered overhead leaving the pathway between them moist and sheltered from the sun, creating a darkened nubilous environment soft and pungent with decay. Then within moments, she was free of the forest. The cacophony of tree frogs and crickets paused, then started up again as she stepped out and stood upon the bank, listening to the nearby stream's flow, feeding the lake with a soothing rhythm.

The lake was a welcoming site. The moon laid its light across the water, like a golden road, calm and quiet. The hint of pine mingled with the night air along with the scent of the water. The chill of the night crept into her bones and made her shiver. She could see the warmth of the early morning causing tendrils of steam to slide and curl, rising off the surface. She stood there for a moment mesmerized by the reflection of the moon dancing on the bottom. It looked like a living crystal.

Bathing was one of the few things she had left in life that gave her some solace and a smile played around her lips. For some odd reason, it was indescribably satisfying to be the first to break the calmness of the surface. She peered down into the cold blue waters, hoping to locate her supposed beautiful side within the rippling reflection that gazed back. But it was still the same girl. There was something different about water. Isabeau wasn't sure what it was, but somehow in the whole scheme of things it was the only place she could see her reflection and in that she found comfort for if the water could hold her, then maybe, just maybe, she still had a soul. And if she still had a soul, there was always a chance for hope and forgiveness.

She looked out, then down and dove into the cool water. She washed the night off her young body then pushed herself through the water enjoying the motion as she began to porpoise with each kick. She floated there for a while gazing up into the early sky watching the stars and moon slowly fading into light.

Once she felt she was free of the roughness of the previous night, she rose from the lake and adjusted herself lying prone on the grass facing the water's edge, letting her hair dry and enjoying both the coolness of the air, the call of the loons and the chill of the morning dew. She reached over and tossed a loose limb onto a cornice of moss that dipped out over the bank and watched as it broke away and fell into the water below, the soil dissolving slowly into the depth, leaving the mossy sinew bobbing within its ripples. She had made ripples of her own in this life; God knows that. She just wondered how long it would be until she was caught in them herself. How long indeed? She knew that someday there would be a night of darkness and sleep. She passionately believed this with all of her heart, a night where the moon would be in season, and yet she would return to what she was before all of this. It would happen. It had to happen. Otherwise, she'd lose her mind. With every good there is bad, so if something starts, something must end; this had to have an end. She had worked it out so that it had, at least, the semblance of logic and truth but in all probability, it was more of a dream. The fact that she lived on it, and lived for it, caused concern that it, maybe the nightmare, more than the one that raged inside of her, and the reality of what she had, though, unfortunately, to back up this dream wasn't even enough to fill a bandbox. She turned back to the pool of water and stared into its now murky depths. A vision of herself, with deeply etched lines upon her face, her arms wound around herself, eyes swollen and red, staring beseechingly, sorrow emanating from her ever being. Then it was gone. She never expected those times when simple things opened the door to memories of things she'd worked hard to forget. She felt the small pang of hunger. If she only had time she would eat, she could almost taste the brown trout she was sure that lived in lakes dappled depths, but she must move on.

Her attention was drawn to large black crow perched

on the bough of a nearby branch. It's cruel avian eyes were fixed on hers. An eerie sensation began to steal over her, then suddenly the bird took flight, fractionally before she heard the sudden sound of movement in the trees behind her. It pulled Isabeau from her thoughts and caused her to spin around. Something was moving and sounded as if it were moving in her direction. She rolled to her right into a crouched position then moved, taking refuge underneath an area lined with golden blossom-covered clumps of rabbit-brush. She could hear footsteps, working their way through the forest, but she couldn't see much further than the clearing at the lake's edge from where she was hiding. She lay there deathly still. It sounded as if it were many men working, moving all toward her. Then just as she was on the verge of a panic, there emerged from the forest a group of deer slowly walking. They surrounded her, some even installing themselves mere feet from her haven before suddenly darting away at her movements within the brush. She collapsed in relief and berated herself for being so paranoid. She then climbed from her refuge and brushed herself clean.

Isabeau looked out at the morning sky. There was something in the first gray streaks stretching along the horizon and throwing an indistinct light upon the face of the world, which combined with the boundlessness of the unknown world around her. It gave her a feeling of loneliness and dread, and of melancholy foreboding that nothing else in nature could give. Somewhere in all of this, there was hope, a new beginning a rebirth if you will, and this is what she desperately clung to. For

Isabeau, this now was all she could see, for behind the orange and cinder glow that would follow, the sun would arise, and this, sadly, she could no longer see and had not seen in what seemed to her forever. She turned, walked back to the wagon, and dressed, pulling her long gloves and boots on then pulling her oversized hooded clothing up and over her head. She then put her foot up on the running gear and pulled herself into the seat, stopping to check one more time that she was completely covered.

She sat there and waited for the sun to rise. It seemed like she had just done this, but it was necessary. She must be sure of where it was at all times; just a slight miscalculation could cause serious pain or even death. Then it came as it always did, screaming across the horizon burning a trail right to the rim of her hood. She then stretched and switched the reins, and the horse moved forward with the wagon bumping and popping behind in tow. She hadn't gone but maybe a few hundred or so yards when she suddenly stopped.

She just sat staring; in front of her was something lying in the path. No, no, she said to herself knowing what it was. She resisted the birth pangs of panic that gripped her in the moment. It was a body. Isabeau leaped from the seat, climbed down from the rigging and cautiously walked up to it. There beneath her lay the body of a dead woman sprawled within the wagon's path.

Isabeau stood over her; the woman's dull brown eyes stared up at the morning sky as a gentle wind ruffled the dark hair on her head and sent a small wave of motion over the darkening pool of blood that encompassed her upper half. Expensive perfume wafted up over the metallic smell of blood. Her hair was, she thought, shoulder length pulled back into a neat ponytail. No eye paint, no blush; a simple pale red lip rouge which had bled into the soft skin around her mouth, where little hairpins had sprung out. She had been beautiful in life, she thought, as she kneeled down and touched her hair, noticing how the blood was fusing the strands together.

Isabeau suddenly tore her hand away, stood up and stopped, remaining motionless and pensive, her eyes fixed on the horror of what she now knew she had done, and this was not a subtle nudge. No, it was clear, and now it lay there openly, nailed at her feet. She turned away shuddering inwardly then began to cry because she wanted to right her own wrongs, just to live a normal life, but she knew as soon as she saw the body this was never going to happen. There was no going back. The longer she was this way, she thought, the more chaos and the more bodies that would ultimately line the roadside. With every death, it was getting harder to cull any meaning from all of it. She needed to at least believe there was a reason; hell, she needed it just to remain sane. For once, she would no longer feel like a weary soldier wandering, seeking some stability and order in a disordered world.

She possessed no recollection, only a sudden, overwhelming awareness of the image that had come to her during the night. This, honestly, was the first body she had ever seen that she knew she was responsible for. She was cognizant of the murders. It was just the others, well the others she had only read about or heard through the sweeping fearful hearsay from those among the streets. Each of these was sad, but she had never looked on any of them, not honestly, she thought, as real. Not until now. She'd always just seen them as more of a testament to her failure to control this rage that was inside of her, and, of course, the weakness of her fortitude, rather than the truth that a life had been lost. Even at this moment, she felt anger toward this poor soul as she lay there simply to torment her for her cowardliness for not ending this herself. She justified it in the way some do, that bad things were just drawn to her the way iron shavings were drawn to loadstone.

Like a flourish made after a signature she had made her distinctive mark on this land and it was certainly one not to be repeated. She didn't like the way that she described that, even to herself. It had a bit of arrogance about it, something in the bland tone of the words sounded almost proud, and of that, she was not, nor shall she ever be. She truly hated what she was. Despite the scorn that often issued from her own mouth, it was in the nature of this particular shade of red that her eyes and her heart could express only a limited set of emotions: anger, resentment, and antipathy. All toward that one-that one who without her consent made her what she was, and she cursed its soul as it had cursed hers. She did these things, not that she was evil, or impervious to emotions, but because of pure misfortune, of being what she was, and over this she held no control.

She turned and looked once again at the woman lying there in the middle of the wagon's path as dead air hovered over the body in shimmering curtains. She felt as if she should do something: move her, bury her, take her away; she didn't know what, just something. Then she decided the best thing was to do nothing, so she backed the wagon up a bit and went around her, attempting to close the book on this, and continued toward Ellenborough.

As Isabeau rode along, she thought, Life is unpredictable at best. Just to make it through to a decent age is an honor, sometimes it is sheer luck, like getting across the street. I must keep in mind that I am, or should I say I have become, more of a hybrid persona, one part human, and one part whatever the hell else this is. But foremost, I must do my best to remain human, to try to keep that part of me, even though I am to dwell in perpetual darkness, like some creature out of classical mythology. I sometimes feel, though, I am losing this battle, losing myself, and in this, it staggers my faith regarding who, by what I can remember of the former me. For in those times, they seem that I do not have one drop of humanity's blood left in my whole carcass. It is within those moments that I am the most frightened, for if I lose that, I lose me.one text here. Insert chapter one text here. Insert chapter one text here.

2

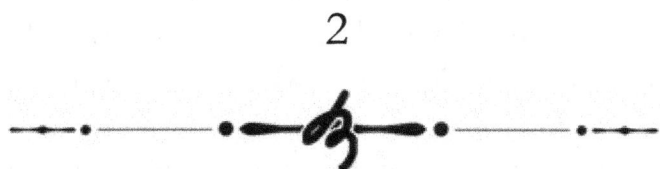

There are among us a darker breed. They gaze into the deeper darkness of the soul. They may appear normal enough, but their outward appearances cloak the horrors happening inside their heads. Their uncontrollable drive that takes them places. Most would never dream of going, pulled by an affliction most never asked for.

Even though it was something she didn't want, nor was it anything she had personally ever sought, she felt as though she were a thief - a thief clinging to this curse like a stolen precious article, not knowing what to do with it now that she held it. All she knew was she just wanted it gone. She wanted to go back to the way things were - the way they were before all this, pain. Twenty-eight years of nighttime sky were enough.

Isabeau wasn't even sure what exactly she was for a long time. She knew the rumors and the words used like; "vampire," "Nosferatu," even "werewolf." These she would not nor could not allow herself to believe. Those are mere characters in a child's fable, some distant bestiary, not reality. But whatever it was and the way it changed her, now that was real and had a purpose. What purpose she was not exactly sure of, but it must serve one. Everything has a purpose. It wasn't an aleatory change; this was definable by design, this perverse expansion, this painful metastatic growth as well as the abatement that followed that her body was forced to endure on an almost nightly basis. She had to stoutly maintain the belief that beneath this sometimes execrable and ogreish exterior there lay a simple girl where inside there beat a heart of gold. Well, maybe not gold, but, at least, kindness, though this was something she had to force herself to do. The idea that she was execrable or even ogreish all the way through was just too grim to contemplate. It had not always been this way; it had begun as something so simple.

As she sat there on the buckboard time unspooled.

When Isabeau left home, it was by her choosing. It wasn't any one thing that led her away but a combination of things that made the choice for her. To all that met her after she'd left, she appeared nothing more than a waif. They all stood in judgment of her - these strangers who knew nothing of her, sometimes quite harshly in the beginning, and perhaps maybe even now, maybe she had just become in a way oblivious or even immune to it. They made it seem a disgrace - a shameful thing to be a waif, but in this misguided title she was also mysterious and a thing to avoid, this perversion of the truth of the word she used and profited from. Now that she was older mentally she had been forced to become wiser in her antics and her outward persona.

People tend to turn away from what they perceive as trouble, they don't want to get involved. In a way, it was like those who grew up hiding what their home life was like, but the fear was omnipresent-particularly when that home life was scarred by physical and emotional violence. Just as we know if we say what we see in a work of art we end up revealing more about ourselves than the artist. So when they see me in the street the image of a homeless or terrified girl, they know to mention why I might be terrified or why I might be homeless would be a breach of social etiquette. The world requires that such children not be mentioned, even when they are looking directly at me. So they ignore, and their ignorance for a while I found my camouflage out in the open. But a homeless child or vagrant will be tolerated to a point, but vagrant adults most just want them to move along immediately and are more likely confronted on their actions. Although her appearance has not faltered and she still looks no older than perhaps twenty, physically, mentally she was mature well beyond her apparent years. In the long run of things, it became just easier to change her outward appearance to appear older than to play the child

Going back to her home again filled her with trepidation. Time and time again she would recognize her extreme honesty and even the seductive paradox full of dreams, sorrow, irony and skepticism. Even after smiles, tears, rage and laughter, she might find herself lost within the blue thoughts. It had been almost twenty-eight years since she last saw even the city, and it seemed like an eternity. Would she even be able to find it again, and if she did, who would be living there now? Would anyone remember her? Her whole reason for waiting was that she hoped not. She was not sure why she had convinced herself into going back. It was a crazy, miserable, strange time of her life. Filled with many times to remember but there was much more she longed just to forget. But she had to go back one more time.

Ellenborough wasn't where she was actually born, but her father had moved them there when she was just a child of three, so as far as she was concerned, that was home. Her life, it seemed had never been an easy one; a primrose path was never for her. No, her road had always been strewn with rocks and large obstacles that she had to work around or in some cases even chip away a path through the center. But she was stronger for it.

Ellenborough is in the northwestern part of England, just southwest of Scotland. Her family, like many others, came along on the hopes of striking it rich mining gold, the same mines that took her father. She didn't wish to return there, but something drew her in, something pulled at her brain. Her memories were a gnarled mixture of nebulous thoughts both good and bad and the one commanding exception, which haunted her most, was that this was the region where her nightmare began. What she had held as the low point in her life was the passing of her mother on May 4th, 1832, from the plague two days following her ninth birthday and near enough two years after her brother, Tom had become a casualty of the Surge in Scotland. Tommy wasn't even in the war, being just a civilian blacksmith working to help restore the resistance. But that didn't make him any less a target. Isabeau's father followed six years later dying in the mines, and without his protection within only three days of his death, two men came in, and her innocence was murdered, torn, ripped from her body in her own house. However, she rallied and only hit rock bottom when seven months later she lost the baby. Her death wasn't something she liked to think about, but of course, she did. In some room in her brain, the images were constantly running. A girl child she had already christened Anthea. She was beautiful, dark skinned, full lips, with eyes as black as a dove's. Her poor Anthea, the young fledgling who never even got the chance to fly. Her daughter had lived less than an hour, yet in that hour Isabeau had become a mother.

Isabeau's life had seemed over; it was like slow motion surrender, her epitaph already written. Here lies a one-time sister, mother, daughter and one–time innocent girl who became nothing and had nothing. She was even a bit surprised never to see her name in the monthly death announcements. A lot had changed in the years since. When her baby died, that should've killed her; it should have been the final nail in her proverbial coffin. But back then, she didn't give a rat's ass whether she lived or died. Isabeau remembered as a child looking at the world with wonder and in any or every observation that she may see in epitome what she would afterward find in the world at large. She was wrong. She could find no true right in this cruel world, certainly nothing to consider as the epitome of anything.

The house was still hers, but she walked away, tossing the key into the bin as she left. After several days travel she ended up in a dive of a tavern, across the moors in the village of Camerton to the south of Ellenborough, and to be honest, she had no clue as to why there or how it was better. Perhaps it just seemed like far enough away to escape her nightmares, but, of course, it wasn't. Thirteen months later, she returned. She only came back down because she wanted to see the garden, the border, the place that cherished her daughter's body, but she didn't want the questions from those that she knew within, so she chose to travel at night. If she had only known.

Many small connections are evident of the whole. She had never believed in religion, in the afterlife and all that - well, not really. She'd been through the motions of bowing to Jesus, without her faith growing any substance. In fact, when Tommy was killed she had lost any vestige of the mystical. And Anthea's death, well, that just somehow made it all that much more vivid. These reminiscences would hack at her at night hideously after a chance term struck her in the random sightings of objects that had bored into her subconscious during the day's travel. She often would wake in a drenching sweat, shaking uncontrollably like a small child with a fever.

Sometimes when Isabeau would think back, she felt like life wasn't worth it. Really, what was the point? The way she had to hide all the time was as if she were spending her life like some arenicolous worm - living, growing burrowing into the sand at the slightest hint of sunlight. She just felt like her existence was gradually becoming a monument to entropy. There had to be more. She just had to find it.

Looking out she could see she was getting closer to Ellenborough, being this close to people, her nerves were a swirl. She had been in the woods and on her own too long. She had to retrain herself, change the way she acted, and speak if she were going to make it here. She needed her outward confidence to reflect a difference in both attitude of mind and the ability to act between individuals.

3

A layer of dust-furred the shelves and countertops, and she drew a line with her fingertip along the edge of the mahogany mantle.

The number of people along the roadside began to grow consistently. The odd transient soul here and there grew, to small carts and wagons moving along and through the pathway - each one giving her a curious glance. She hated being near them, and her nervousness was warranted. There would be at times long lulls in her appetite. She would often stare, looking out at the people each and every time it was gone from her, wondering when it would reappear to wreak havoc on their lives and hers once again. She considered it separate from her because it wasn't anything she wished to do. When it did overtake her, and, even though sometimes she had a semi-conscious knowledge of what she was doing, she truly had no control over it. Isabeau longed for it to end - to find a cure - but there was no alchemy or incantations to induce immunity against this bewitchment. No, this was wicked, and it was in constant devilry.

Riding along, she found an old inn built out on the ridge in a vicinage that overlooked the city of Ellenborough. It was just far enough from the main population that she felt she might be able to get a few hours' rest in a real bed and maybe not be a threat or be exposed to pillory. She went past, waiting for the shadows of the night to be cast. Once the sun was behind the mountains, she returned. She pulled the reins, and the wagon came to an abrupt stop alongside the stable area of an old Inn, and she sat there clinging to her seat until the dirt road's easily - airborne dust wuthered past. She settled once again before attempting to disembark, but before she could even think and almost immediately out of the shadows, a beautiful, bright-eyed girl came running up - rosy cheeks and between the hem of her worn coat and her knee stockings, her bare skin flushed a salmon pink in the cold.

"Take care of your horse, miss?" she yelled.

"You're awfully small little one. You sure you know what you're doing," she said with a grin.

"Of course, miss. I'm much stronger than I look," she replied.

"Alright then," she said flipping her a copper coin. "Be off with you."

"Thank you, miss. Thank you" she replied.

The young girl grabbed the leads as Isabeau grabbed her bag and left the wagon making her way in the direction of the proprietor's desk. Suddenly, she stopped and turning toward the young girl admired her, for, in her face, she saw the sweetness of the world, the fun and happiness of life, and the yearnings of a child. She turned back and was kissed by a gentle breeze. She breathed in deep. Rain was in the air. She could sense it as she walked on toward the desk.

She walked into the proprietor's area of the inn. The door opened, and a loosely suspended brass bell rang triumphantly over the loud creak of the rust-covered hinges. The room was just growing dark, but Isabeau could see everything quite clearly. The desk area was fusty and more like a tavern. There was an old counter with beer kegs and taps loosely laid behind it. There were a couple of dilapidated old chairs, dirty tankards and a rusty bell, placed beside a worn and dog-eared log. The room was oddly and completely devoid of human activity. For this she was thankful.

Isabeau walked up and rang the bell. She couldn't understand why they had two bells. The bell over the front door jingled lightly every time a gust of wind blew, and she stared round, her glance darting from the door to the hands on the carriage clock resting on a small table in the corner. Almost half past seven. Staring, the black arms on the dusty clock seemed to slow. And yet, the sound of the ticking became louder with every passing second. Tick. Tock. Tick. Tock.

Suddenly, as if bursting out of thin air, it seemed an older gentleman came to the front. Without a word he walked around lighting candles and looked at Isabeau almost angrily as if relishing her apparition coming at the gloaming when to him the day's darg was done. He moved back, his unbathed and unlaundered bulging figure now pressed firmly against the back of the counter, and his paunchy mouth shook as he spoke.

"Yes, madam can I help you?" he said with a heavy sigh moving from behind the counter once again to now uncomfortably close, looking her over, up and down quite intently. She knew it was wrong to judge so quickly but even at this first moment, there was something about this man, just the way he looked at her, it was difficult for her not to feel a shade of contempt for him.

"Yes, I'd like a cabin," she announced pushing with one finger against his chest edging back from him.

"How about a nice room?" he added.

"No, I want a cabin, something secluded, but with a view. You will rent me a cabin!" she said abruptly. He should have smiled politely and done as he was told. However, the man was not used to being told what to do by a woman. Everything he said and did reflected the appearance of unbridled avarice and one who is bent on power and control. He hesitated again and was slow to seeing things her way.

"You want a cabin. It all be a pound a night he barked and an extra farthing if you be wanting a bath."

"No, no bath. Just a room," she added. He gave her a displeased snarl and plopped the paperwork on the chest high counter in a huff. His fingers and palms were shattered with filth. Every crease and line was brown. His hair crawled past his ears and down his neck, which blended with the buildup of grime on his skin. She lay a quid on the counter. His double-jowled countenance shook as he coldly ushered her about the bar area. He gestured for her to move closer as he forced a pen into her hand. His pudgy fingers running across her fingers as he lay the instrument in her hand. This sent another run of a twinge up her spine and goose pimples danced across her arm. She signed the register, signing her name as she always did "Isabeau" with a circumflex over the "u" to show it was to be pronounced as an "O." It always irritated her when her name was misstated. She then dangled the pen between two fingers in a disgusting manner as if it were dirty before letting it drop onto the counter.

"Emm - Lee," he suddenly screamed out, and almost immediately, a young girl emerged from the back and rounded the corner. As she walked into the room, Isabeau could see it was the same beautiful child from the stables. She had finely pierced features, pale, opaque skin, which was in stark contrast with her deep green eyes peering through her waves of beautiful red/auburn cascading hair. She was dirty but cute in that tomboy sort of way, her hair was up in the back and held with a gauzy snood (a beautiful handmade piece constructed of bits and pieces of odd cuts of cloth). She walked toward Isabeau then stopped and raised her green eyes in her direction. Just as a small smile was cracking the corners of her mouth, then came the grating voice again of the man Isabeau assumed was the girl's father.

"Where in the hell have you been? What have you been doing?" the man carped at her insistently. She never spoke. His face hardened further as he gripped the key in his hand so hard it looked as if he could squeeze a glass of juice right out of it

"Show this lady to her room!" he barked at her, flinging the copper key in her direction across the wooden counter. The key slid and fell to the rough lumbered floor, and the young girl I now knew as Emily stooped to pick it up.

"This way, miss," she said quietly. Emily turned toward Isabeau, raised her eyes, gazing at her through the sweet tendrils of her soft adolescent hair with a broken smile. She took her bag which was obviously much heavier than her small frame should carry, and she awkwardly walked out of the bar area toward the rental cabin. Isabeau longed to take the bag from her but was afraid to get the girl in trouble with her father. Besides, she seemed to want to prove she was strong and resourceful.

She wondered as they walked along what the mother of this child was like. Such a pretty little thing, she thought and wondered was it necessary that the active gloom of such a tyrant, horror of a father, should commix with such a passive sweetness, to produce a constancy, an equanimity, a steadiness, which never a woman before could boast of. She wasn't sure, but still, she was there, and she seemed as near to perfect as one could achieve. There was no comparison - the contrast between her and this man was unmistakable. The rain was falling heavy now as the two figures made their way boldly silhouetted against the darkening skies. Skies black and angry shaken only by the broken inn signboard banging in the October wind.

The child Emily appeared first lacking in intelligence,

her pale tensile features pulled themselves tightly with the exception that she had a tiny scar just above her lip on the right side. She wore her style beautifully, held up in the back, which exposed the round soft nook with a few little clinging circlets of soft, auburn hair now wet and even darkening still with the rain. She seemed rather well kept and assumed it was all the girl's doing after meeting her father with the small exception of her worn and wet shoes like two abandoned sparrow's nests strapped about her feet. But what stood out most was this young girl's sweet almost columbine demeanor.

The cabin was much larger than Isabeau expected, two-storied and backed to the edge of a cliff that overhung the city below. Entering, she saw a living area, kitchen, and bathing room. She followed Emily up the stairs to a large room that covered the entire second floor. In the room, there were heavy velvet curtains drawn across tall windows to keep out any early light in the room. Water began to drip and gather at her feet as she looked out at the large faded and tarnished but stern portraits marching along the opposite wall - soft pools of yellow thrown by oil lamps set between the paintings were the only illumination for the furnishings. Besides Emily, there was nothing inviting about this place at all. It was, even though larger than expected, oddly enough, a bit cramped. Filled with a miscellaneous collection with not much forethought, cluttered with the paraphernalia of poor daily living and bad house cleaning, but all in all, it would do.

Emily once again looked up, and Isabeau saw her face was studded in the cutest freckles. This child enchanted her. She smiled as Isabeau walked over and pulled back the heavy curtains and stood there. Her face contorted by the recent memories. Her back was to Emily as she looked out the open window at the passing lives of sparkling Ellenborough below her as if lording over it all, yet trying both to remember it clearly and forget it completely. The sun had gone down, and it had begun to rain hard again. Intermittent lightning lit up the room, and trailing thunder rattled the walls and shook the clear pebbles of rain from the glass of the oddly large cabin.

"Will the room do, miss?" Emily asked as Isabeau continued to stare out into the night.

"Yes, it will do fine."

"This used to be our house," Emily stated.

"Really?"

"Yes, before Momma died."

"I'm sorry."

Isabeau replied without turning. Emily laid her bag on the bed and decanted some water into the washing bin. Isabeau looked back at Emily, thinking about how she had just torn this house apart with her mean ridicule. She then noticed how Emily lingered within the room. She turned and walked over placing a copper coin in the child's hand.

"No, miss, you do not have to do that," She said quite sincerely. "If you need me, miss, just yell, I'm…"

"I know, Emily!" Isabeau said smiling.

"Yes, miss, the name is Emily," she said cutting her

eyes and smiling back seemingly proud that someone remembered her name as she backed through and out the door.

Isabeau returned to the window, looking back out toward the valley below the adolescent symmetry of the city and the long clear-cut commissure of earth and sea there in the far distance. She thought I have told myself many times before I am not immune to emotion. I am not cold and heartless, as some may perceive me. There is still a human side to me. I know it. Sometimes, with drink, more times without, it overtakes me. I find looking back at my life from childhood is much like peering into a child's kaleidoscope. At one angle, there are only hues of off-whites and grays. But then at another, there is red, a deep, deep blood red that emanates from the symmetrical images radiating only the death and dismay that my life has brought, not only to my own world but the many others that it has touched. I try to disseminate and obliterate the ones I chose to discard, but they remained even though I understood the images as they appear may be only truths as I perceived them. My dear God, What if I have watered them down?" What if I tamed them, so to speak, within my mind's memory? There is truth in this I am sure; these little pearls of wisdom scare me, and make my mind dance and question itself to what true hells I may have wrought? The memories always playing over and over in my mind, though silent to those around me, they are unforgiving. The thoughts that twisted in my head so tight, wanting to stay stuck. The screams, the profanities in my ears and the smell of blood that filled the air. The vomit that hits my feet. I scream and feel sick. I yell to God, "Please, quiet these things in my head," as I fall to my knees with my head in my hands, and I weep. "I weep for those that have sustained me, for those that never wronged me, yet I took the husbands, wives, and children of those that did not and will not return, and for myself for the hell that I live and for the weakness of not being able to end it.

Somewhere within the town below a clock struck the half hour, and it brought her back to herself. She pulled the thick curtains shut and turned and looked about the room with a bit of a frown, then moved her bag on the bed about an inch to one side and lay back upon the bedding beside it and closed her eyes.

***

When Isabeau awoke the room was dark, and it took her a minute to just remember where she was. She climbed from the bed then noticed there was a soft glow coming from a crack in the curtains on the other side of the room. She cautiously pulled them to one side and saw it was actually the horizontal window showing a myriad of tiny gold, orange and other colored lights that were the city below. She looked out toward the sky. Was it night again, or was it still night? Hell, she thought it was always night, even in the day. The night was out there hiding, waiting, waiting to torment her. There is, of course, she thought, my unremitting aloneness. I am in every sense an isolato, and if this state is elicited by my impertinence and my refusal to conform, it is brought about as well by the inability of all those around me to perceive either my uniqueness or my pain. Her head suddenly snapped around to the sound of the door closing behind her.

"Oh, miss, I didn't mean to startle you," a female voice moaned, "It's me, Emily. I thought I heard you up. I've brought you something to eat. I hope it is okay that I came in?" She brought Isabeau a tray with black bread, wine, a small punnet of dried fruit and single wilted flower in an old brown preserves jar.

"Yes, it is fine," Isabeau replied, stretching and rubbing her eyes. "What time is it anyway?" she yawned.

"It's nearly four, but I thought you might like a snack, being on the road as you were?" She set the tray down on the table by the window and stood there shuffling her feet to and fro, coyly looking up at Isabeau with her big green eyes that seemed to dance in the lamp light. She was a nervous, excitable young girl. It was easy to tell she tended to fidget when she was under pressure. Even her clothes seemed to be on edge. They shifted and slid and drooped and were never still.

Four, huh she thought, she had slept almost an entire night, and she never slept at all at night.

"Oh yes. Thank you," she said as she looked at young Emily and sat down at the little table closely examining the food as she picked up the glass of wine.

Emily began to speak and tried to explain herself and maugre her plain talk. She came across as quite knowledgeable but overly complacent. One apparently beaten down through the years to the point where the sweet, childlike demeanor you would expect nothing more than a sparkle in the night. Isabeau had just met her, yet she felt a fondness for her and longed to see that sweetness shine through. She tried to see her as she should be rather than she was. A trait she wished others would see in her. Isabeau had watched as her father, or the man she assumed was her father, treated her like a slave, and a rube, an easy target, which seeing her now more clearly, she guessed that she was, but something made her that way, and that curiosity plagued her. Isabeau smiled at her innocence and in her glass a dream she left for her in her eyes.

While Isabeau was busy re-examining the paltry tray, she noticed out of the corner of her eye Emily standing in front of the mirror prinking and preening like a pouter pigeon. She caught her stare and turned away from the glass, blushing.

"You're quite pretty," Isabeau added.

Do you really think so, Miss?" she replied with a cooing.

"Yes, I do," Isabeau said walking over to her bag, which now lay open on the bed. Isabeau pulled a short dress from its confines and offered it to her,

"This ought to fit you." Emily looked at the garment like it was made of pure gold.

"Oh, miss, I couldn't."

"Go ahead try it on."

"Father will be looking for me."

"Go ahead; I will tell him you were helping me - let's say unpacking," she said with a wink.

Emily's face lit up with a smile, and she turned

around, holding the garment in front of her in the mirror. The dress was black silk, with dull, prismatic sheen of oil on water, finer Isabeau guessed that she'd ever worn.

"Oh, miss, I would love it. Where should I change?"

"There's nobody here but us girls." She gave a wincing giggle. Isabeau still sitting with a glass of chartreuse spun the green liquid in the glass watching it ride the rim as Emily began to disrobe. She was cute, how she put the dress on over her clothing then worked so diligently to disrobe beneath it, a way she felt Isabeau guessed to keep her modesty intact. Emily smiled while at the same time biting her tongue as she reached behind her neck, fumbling with the clasp. She was very smart in the way she carried herself, even though Isabeau thought she could be even as old as she was when all of this began for her. She had a soft but professional sternness to her voice and demeanor when she was working. Isabeau thought she believed it was much more lady-like than it really was. But once she questioned her if she would like to try on the outfit her entire demeanor changed. Her dolce voice tried to turn away the other more saccharine voice that again sonorously said, "Oh, yes, miss, I would love it." And even though coming across as a bit shy the entire time she was trying on the clothes, Isabeau could easily tell she loved to prattle. Isabeau always had this preoccupation that she was being watched. She pushed back a fleeting impulse to check the wall behind her to see if there might indeed be a hole, filled with a single eye peering at them. Instead, she let her eyes wander over Emily. Her beautiful hair now down and cascading over her thin shoulders, her eyes bright with wonder and questions.

She watched the young girl over the edge of her glass. She admired her innocence, being that she was no more than a child; she had no preformed thoughts on life, no divination. She lived as all children do, for the day at hand and nothing more. Not like Isabeau, she had developed her own bizarre cosmogony theory and strange and curious views about the construction and meaning of life and the universe. Now some days are filled with a longing for death, but it is not true, she just wanted free of this curse, nothing more, amazingly life was something she cherished and held in high regard.

Once she felt comfortable getting undressed in front of Isabeau, Emily quickly became bolder and asked to try on something more daring - a nightgown. It slipped over her young girl pointed breasts and shoulders, supple as a garment of heavy water, and now teasingly caressed her, egregious, insinuating, nudging between her thighs as she shifted restlessly in her new narrow berth. Emily stood there in the gown in old-fashioned awe of her presence and her room, by tacit consent, was treated as an adytum into which no one else dared to penetrate. She had no knowledge of the evidence of indiscreet, criminal, and in most all cases undeniably felonious behavior. To her Isabeau was a lady, a sex she was apparently missing from her upbringing and someone to look up to and to emulate.

"Well, how do I look, miss. Do I look pretty?" She

asked twisting and turning in Isabeau's sheer gown. Her young figure silhouetted within the candles light, the translucent fabric clinging to her bottom half and hanging unfulfilled on the latter. Emily tried on four outfits in all and spoke continuously. Her words came forth with an almost cadence so splendidly stilted the words both slowed and varied, bringing them more closely to a lilt and Isabeau came to realize in that moment where the term a dance of words was born and was immediately taken with her. They exchanged swift percipient glances, talking and laughing as the early morning wore on. Isabeau learned that Emily was sixteen, not much younger than Isabeau had been when all of this began, and that her mother had died when she was eight of consumption and that it had just been her father since then. Just before sunup, she left for fear her father would find out where she had been the main length of the night. She hadn't been gone long, and even though Isabeau's room was across the courtyard behind the office, she could hear Emily's father yelling threats and curses as Emily helplessly ran to fulfill whatever her father's wishes were.

4

There is only one way to free yourself from guilt - you must embrace your sins, for it is our memories that make us monsters.

Isabeau had given Emily instructions not to bother her during the following day as she was going to sleep.

The rains had finally ended, and the bright stain of moonlight lengthened little by little over the lawn, climbing the wall of the little house, making the Ivy glisten in a thousand dewy lights. It found an opening - the window. It penetrated and suddenly took possession of the room, slipping through the tiny gaps in the curtains waking Isabeau for her nocturnal life.

She dressed and left the cabin making her way

toward Ellenborough. She thought it appeared as if there were no lights on in the city tonight, nothing discernable anyway, just an ominous glow. It was one of those nights when the Ellenborough city fog got thick. It got so dense at times you couldn't cut it, not even with a razor. By 6:30 in the evening, this brume would have already blanketed the docks, creeping like the evening shadow it trailed, working its way up from Maryport then into Ellenborough and slowly engulfing the city. The mist made nightly commutes very dangerous, and it's not so much the fog, but that which prowls within, that made it so.

Walking along the dark labyrinthine of streets seems ominous with the houses leering over Isabeau like ovated giants as she navigated her way down through the city. The uneven verge of crude gray stones once taken from the ballast of ships within the harbor jutted out of the ground like the hands of the dead reaching and grabbing at her feet. Each stone laid in good faith and each stone now broken and moved from the constant pounding of the heavy wagons and seasonal flooding on the non-irrigated grounds. At the foot of this anfractuous path which leads through Ellenborough lies the port of Maryport, in the Allonby Bay, which leads out to the Isle of Man within the Irish Sea. Here the world was indeed excluded, here the sides of the mountain closed the valley shutting it off, and, therefore, fenced it in from the keen and biting winds, and only those from the sea were drawn into the city. Isabeau began to frown as she walked past strangers on the streets. Once in a while, justified melancholy would darken her face, a dull and incomprehensible nostalgia for times never experienced would invade her. Meanwhile, the people around her carried on serenely, their foreheads smooth and unworried. A jealousy overwhelmed her for a moment that receded from her as if drawn away on a string, like a child's toy.

Ever she delved deeper into the dark, walking without fear for she was again new to this area, as far as those within this city were concerned. It had been many years since she had even been this close to home, even though her movements, acquaintances, and even lovers came and went like fleeting clouds. Her virtue remained untarnished as she spent all her time on the move and no one was the wiser of the new girl upon the moors. So as a lady she was treated and worked to remain so, keeping the ruse intact until she chose to move on again. By day, who could be more respectable than her? But, unfortunately, that was not all she was. The woman of the daytime bled into the creature of the night. Her pleasures were not of the ordinary kind. Though she would drink and laugh with those she met, those who dabble at the foothills of vice, their simple and innocent improprieties bored her, for the beast within her demanded more. So she left them. They would often joke that she could not keep pace with their games while she set off into the darkness.

Like most cities in this time, at midnight, the streets of Ellenborough pulsed with the drunk and dissipated, gentlemen adventurers, students learning the somewhat necessary mysteries of manhood, as well as the lonely, desperate and deformed. There were singers, tricksters, artists, actors, and actresses all looking to claw their way up in the world as they inevitably all sink to the bottom. There in the depths was her vice, her need, her requirement to her way of life. To discover the deepest pinnacles of vice, you need to roam those back streets and alleyways where the gaslight does not reach, where tall tenements keep the sun from ever penetrating the shadows, where church bells are only heard as muffled hollow echoes through the fog.

The smells of this vital wasteland excited her soul; the foul miasma of the rivers flowing slowly into the Irish Sea, the whiff of the opium den as the door quickly opens and shuts, the cheap perfume of the streetwalkers in their garish dress and makeup, their expressions of blank indifference as they pursued you with lewd shouts and gestures. She has ventured through all of their tricks and secrets, yet always at night. She longed to move on to further exaltation in degradation and would do so until she found what she was looking for.

It wasn't far from here that she had taken her first. She hadn't realized for some days that it had even been her. News of the death had run through the streets like a whirlwind. She had cut her eyetooth on this child without even knowing it, and before long she had moved onto new and sometimes larger prey. But tonight wasn't about feeding, she came here for a reason and wanted it done and behind her, but at the same time, the excitement and the tension of it made her pulse race. She struggled, in searching to remember the way. The crooked dog leg cobblestoned alleyways of the town seemed familiar but also new at the same time. There had been changes to the landscape over the years, yet the familiar rise and fall against the grid formation of the streets somehow made the search seem clearer. Even over the short time, once fairly nice were now ruined buildings with sagging, swaybacked roofs, some leaning precariously. Their stone foundations split and cracked from neglect and stolen stones. Isabeau realized she was a stranger now and felt no warmth from the tight rows of sawn wood homes and aging businesses. There was hardly a light on anywhere. Their roof lines looked like night-blackened claws against the moonlit mountainside beyond.

Isabeau understood that everything God creates is a miracle, individually and unto itself. She also knew there are men and women alike with such characteristics and deformities that they choose not to look into mirrors and must hide their faces in order to pass simply through the streets unmolested. Some were even paid paltry sums so people could stare at them in a surrounding that they felt superior in and gawk at their oddness. She could, on the other hand, could at least walk the streets at night but never in the day; that was part of her deformity, and it seemed a bit trivial in comparison. She wondered if people out there would sit and stare to catch a glimpse of the marvels of her in the dark?

It amazed Isabeau, that this part of town was even still here it had been dying for years, just never pronounced. Then turning down one street she found what she had come in search of - her home. It looked so different. It was a pockmarked and pitted thing. But the rutty smells of the area seemed recognizable. It stood there almost foreboding, drenched in the darkness. It wasn't as large as she had remembered; just a small tenement house shoehorned between two larger ones. It was completely dark; she wondered who lived there now and if they were at home. Would she even be able to enter and if she did would she gain the solace she seemed to think she would find? Suddenly, a man appeared out of the house beside it, and Isabeau approached him.

"Please, sir, can you tell who lives in that house?" she said, pointing toward her former home.

"No, no one lives there, miss," he said, "and no one would live there. You're a bit out of your element ain't you miss?" he added looking her over closely.

Ignoring his glances, she continued.

"Can you just tell me where are those that used to live there then?"

"They don't live there anymore; they are gone," he said.

"I understand they're gone, but where?" she went on.

"No one lives there," he said, raising his voice, the stench of ale pronouncing each syllable as he moved in uncomfortably close, "and no one would," Isabeau tried to remain pleasant and smile through her thinning lips, teeth grinding behind them. He turned and walked back into his house, slamming the door behind him. Every word he had spoken carried an implied meaning that carried more significance than his precisely placed words could provide, and she couldn't grasp all that he wasn't saying to her. It just came down to the fact he wasn't giving her straight answers. He kept the facts from her like he was not at liberty to disclose information, though she personally believed that he was not just keeping it to himself. No, it was more born out of a fear of speaking of the family's name. She had seen this fear before. If he were to know that she was the one he was afraid to speak of, he would run from this place screaming and wailing. But if this was true, but how she thought, how was it they were able to attribute her to the killings, and if they had, wouldn't she have heard of it? Maybe she was just making more out of it than there was.

Looking around, she found a piece of candle on the neighbor's window sill and walking back to her old house lit it. She sighed thinking how her family had died and left her a legacy of tears that had never quite dried. The door wasn't locked but blocked with a wooden board with odd markings painted on it, and it laid crossway to the door. She glanced around then slid it up and moved it out of the way. Cautiously she walked inside, her shadows lurched and seesawed up and around the dim room from the candle's light. Gazing about, it appeared it hadn't been lived in since she had left twenty-eight years ago. Oddly, it looked as if everything was still there, still in its place. Why had no one overtaken this house in all those years and why was nothing even stolen? She looked around, the reality of it all inevitably sinking in; that everyone and everything she had ever known was truly gone. The shadows of their former lives now but a faint shimmer through the gloom of the front window and a mere flicker of the candles flame. That former life now a mouldering dark expanse. The candlelight illuminated all of their little relics, the tumbled garments she had left behind for which there had been no room in her trunks. The room was filled with sadness and in the midst of all of this, she felt a pang of loss. Her father's pipe still lay resting on the old cherry wood desk. Her brother's books still lined the bookcase and Mother's silhouette still hung upon the front wall (smiling unknowingly that in a mere three months from having it made at Ellen-fair, she would be gone.)

Everything smelled musty, vaguely ruined, but for the most part, it was the way it was before, save for dust and the fact that the wallpaper now hung off the walls, like torn pieces of skin. The floor was all but buried by the detritus of years black with mold where the derelict light had penetrated. Then she saw and a single burst of color in the corner, like a hastily planted flag. Isabeau moved closer. It couldn't be, but it was. It was the blanket, the blanket she had made during her pregnancy. She had made it for Anthea and when she didn't make it she had wanted to bury her in it, but she couldn't find it that day and now to have it lay so blatantly in the open? She stood frozen for a moment, clinging to her spot, like a bit of lichen to a stone. Her hand moved to her chest, hovering for that moment over the image inked there. Then bending, she shook it, to free it from the dust and parts of it fell to the floor. "Damn rats", she said out loud. Still, she caressed the knitting, her heart hammered as she held its tattered strands to her chest.

She took a few steps back and laid her hand upon her father's dust covered chair. She touched the old iron oil lamp he had used every day as if to confirm for herself that the uncanny persistence of half-forgotten objects, all in their old places, was not some trick of the mind. She walked around and dug through the dreck in hopes to find something from her childhood, something, anything with meaning. She beat the seat of the old chair, and the dust burst into bloom. She backed away and waited for a moment for that effloresce to settle. She then sat down thinking of the good as well the bad times cradled within her memory of this place, as the candle's light continuingly danced about the room until it finally landed upon Isabeau and it found her crying.

She sat there thinking of her sweet Anthea, her beautiful child. Her soul was lost as she desperately missed her. She'd never stopped thinking about what happened. The one good and beautiful dream, which had walked away never to return, leaving only the fondest memories of the time they had. She had talked to Anthea every day while she was carrying her. It was like she knew her. She had always known it would be a girl, but now she's gone and Isabeau was lost, and her life was torn without her to hold her hand or kiss her goodnight. Lost within those memories that she would never have.

"Mother?" The voice snarled in her ear; she jumped, knocking a drinking cup on the cupboard next to the chair and it shattered against the floor. Like taking a drink after years of thirst.

"Anthea," Isabeau said turning and looking. Ah. She was later than usual, this most favored figment of her too-long grieving mind. She had never been one that had the ability to sidestep reality except when it came to Anthea. Forgotten thoughts of yesterdays, through her eyes, she saw the past. She would often when alone, hear the voice of a daughter never known; maybe it was this that she needed closure on. It would approach with small steps; then, like a guest long awaited, it arrived all at once. She sometimes thought she invested too much emotional energy in something she couldn't change, but it hurt, and she guessed it always would. She stood up and looked around but the moment was gone, and she clutched the blanket a little harder and walked out. She closed the door and replaced the lumber. Isabeau then blew out the candle and tossed it toward the neighbor's house. She looked at the tattered blanket and slowly walked around to the courtyard behind the house. There was an access lane between the gate of the yard, which no longer stood and the gate of the garden and Isabeau walked through into the dysfunction of this decaying yard.

There in the dark was a large rose bush growing wild and untamed; it was beneath this very bush she buried her dear Anthea. She climbed through an opening in the old broken fence and sat beneath the dead blossoms, holding the stale smelling blanket to her cheek. There was her name, Isabeau had scrawled on a rock those many years ago. Not much of a marker for this beautiful child, but it was all she could do. The words were fading, but her memories of Anthea were stronger than ever. She purloined a small piece of the blanket, tucking it inside her bosom before burying the rest of the blanket beneath rose bushes. She stared watching as the vapor from her lungs gathered in a pocket of stillness before the breeze found it.

Her mind wandered, the indelible memories flashed upon her consciousness as the dark currents of memory washed her downstream again. She looked down at the infant swaddled in her arms, it's beautiful soft auburn hair, but there was no life, no breath. Isabeau wondered what it would have been like, was she capable of loving this child-this child conceived in terror and pain, fathered by a monster. A man who had broken in, beaten her, raped her, cursed her and left her for dead. Her soul felt shattered, like a million shards of glass inside of her. A deep sob swelled in her chest.

She saw a crossed piece of steel, and on her hands and knees she stabbed at the earth shoving it into the ground beside the stone and gazed at the thrusting steel spiral. Better. She sighed and shook her head. This sad accident that took away her peace of mind, her health and some might whisper her sanity. If only Isabeau could travel back in time, maybe something could have been done, at the very least she could have warned herself about the one day that would lead to this moment. She had an ongoing imaginary conversation with Anthea that had gone on for years in her mind. It was easier, more comforting to go on talking to Anthea in her head. She bit her lip and wondered, what her life might have been like if Anthea had lived. But it was only speculation and self-torture, she was gone, and Isabeau was left at the very least, broken inside.

5

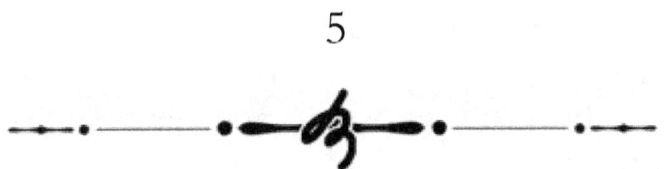

I knew what I had done. And I just wanted to hide. I just wanted to hide, everything, I wanted to hide, me! I couldn't fix it; I couldn't get control, I couldn't...

Twenty-eight years ago.

The road back home was lonely and long, much longer than she remembered when she had left. It was nothing more than a murky pool of water lined with tall trees that split along the twisted trail in front of Isabeau—their leafless branches silver in the moonlight. Her breath misted. It had to be eleven or twelve at night and the rain, although light, was relentless. Isabeau knew that many mysterious things happened when the darkness consumed the light. It had always been so. Here, of all places, the thoughts of what might be, haunted her. Above her, the great arching trees gave little to no cover, and the path ahead—in the lapse of ages most of it had sunk, and every here and there as far as the eye could see, it was filled with water where it lay submerged. She could do little but remain drenched while the earth spat mud at her with each and every step. On one side of the path, a sheer cliff descended into a dark rapid and boulder-strewn river, some few hundred feet below, and water ran over its jagged edge like a river in itself. The other side rose above her into the dark, ominous wood. In these forlorn regions of unknowable dreary space, this reservoir of woods scared her. For what lurked within was unknown and unseen and rumors and tales ran amuck. Walking along, the umbriferous trees stood towering—casting down the shadows of fate upon her, and the strangest sensation had crawled over her as if she were being watched.

Then the noises began. A simple crack of a branch, the rustle of wet leaves. She stopped. Listened. Nothing.

Then with each and every step she made, there was a mockery of movement, something would move, something would crack. Whatever it was, it was behind her, but well within the wood. Her pace quickened along with her pulse. Her nap sack hung heavy over her shoulder, she began walking faster, trying to move along and descry the noises over her now deep and heavy breathing and constant rain. She was moving now almost at a run, she looked back over her left shoulder and saw it, the shadowy silhouette of a person just at the edge of the wood maybe a hundred or so feet behind her.

Isabeau screamed and threw the nap sack onto the path and ran headlong withershins into the woods. Faster and faster into the darkness as limbs clawed and grasped at her from all directions. She felt the horror of the gossamer-like threads dangling from innumerable twigs that lined the branches from the spiders that inhabited the trees, weave themselves across her face and hands and arms, as she blindly ran hands out in front of her deeper into the wood. She wished she hadn't taken her shoes off to keep them dry for her bare feet bled. It was as if each step was a search for the hidden debris which might impale her soft soles and further cripple her escape.

She could see the figure through the trees rushing after her, moving in and out of the shadows like a fiddler's elbow. Faster and faster she ran, turning and twisting up one rise down another, then up and there she lost her footing tumbling and sliding head over feet down into a trench-like ravine. She lay there only for a moment before quickly sifting through the leaves and debris of underbrush for a place to hide. Far off she could hear the approach of footsteps. She could hear it working its way just over the last ridge, moving, searching for her. She could hear it, she began to crawfish her way back, but its sound sent her into a large swivet as she frantically turned, grabbled with her hands, then to her feet and decamped into the cover of darkness. She wove deeper and deeper into the labyrinth of endless identical woodland alleyways, slipping in between the trees and brush with an almost serpentine ease that masked her increasing panic. After a while, she realized she had gone to great lengths and breadths in her struggle to lose whomever, or whatever, it was that was following her, and she felt as though she were going to flounder. In spite of the cold, sweat ran from her hairline and into her eyes, blurring her vision. She blinked, once, twice, then used her dirt encrusted fingers to rub away the sting. She clutched her chest trying to capture her breath and began to shake as she became weak with fatigue. She stood there war-torn and wet, shaking from both fear and cold. Shivers ran the length of her body like a cramp from her head to her toe. Then THUD! It hit her, slamming her back against a cold hard tree.

As she searched for her breath, grasping hands tore at Isabeau's clothing and scraped her skin as she pushed against it, forcing her forward. She swung around flinging the creature from her body only to have it leap and reattach itself. It pulled at her, one taloned hand holding fast to her shoulder, another pulling at her hair as it sunk its teeth into her neck. She screamed again and pushed herself and the creature against a tree, just hard enough to dislodge her from its grasp. Isabeau fell backward and crashed through the brambles to land on her back. A branch now clutched in her hand punched at her stomach, driving the thumb size stalagmite of dead root she had landed on further between her ribs and into her back. Isabeau reached back and grabbed tighter to the branch. She looked up just in time to see a predatory grin flash across its darkened face a second before she threw her weight forward as the creature once again lunged at her.

Swinging it with all her might, she howled with pain as the bark scraped against her frozen palms. The limb caught it square in its chest, sinking deep within its skin and the creature screamed in agony as it fell only a few feet from her.

It writhed there on the ground at her feet as she lay at the base of the tree. Screaming and pulling, clawing desperately at the wood lodged within its chest as Isabeau pushed her back against a tree trying to back away, her eyes never leaving the beast as she screamed in horror. She watched in amazement as the deformed creature slowly transformed, its fingers and claws cracking and popping as they retracted into hands. Its twisted body bending and wrenching. Its face slowly contorting to a blur before becoming a recognizable figure.

In mere moments what lay before her was what appeared to be a woman scantily dressed in a tattered nightgown. It turned and sat squatting there, dirty feet a quivering mass, blood running down her cheek, with the piece of lumber lodged deep within her chest. Blood ran from the wound as she sat there, shaking hands pulling and tugging at the wood, muttering as if there was something to say, something that would or could make any of this alright. Her lips moved, but Isabeau couldn't hear what she was saying. Isabeau watched as she fell to her right, still pulling at the wood protruding from her chest, shaking and quivering, then one final kick and she was still. Her mind went kind of fuzzy for it seemed as if the woman's form simply dissolved before her very eyes. She reached up and felt the bite on her neck, then pulling her hand back, saw how much blood there was and knew she was ripe for death, and worse within the woods. If she fell there, she wouldn't last long, not with the animals in these parts.

A paroxysm of coughing shook her body. Bright red blood sprayed from her mouth onto her hands, but she continued to pull herself along the forest floor. She stood as she could pulling herself through the Cimmerian land of darkness trying hard to remember the way she had come. Then, after what seemed an eternity, finally found her way back out to the wagon's path. She stumbled forward the blood oozing from her wounds and looked out into the darkness and saw amazingly a wagon coming down the path—its lantern's glow dancing in the mist, then everything moved to the left and went dark. The strange blackness had come like a dark wind. It oozed through every crevice until it filled everything around her —a suffocating blackness that was as ominous as the thunderhead that had stretched before her the night she had left Ellenborough.

Isabeau thought it seemed as if it were a dream, as if it happened to someone else and not to her, but still it played over and over in her mind. When she opened her eyes, unknown to her, the poison was circulating through her blood irremediably, its power already ancient. She awoke to small round-faced woman staring inventively at her. There was no noise. She moved slowly trying to adjust to her unfamiliar surroundings. The room was dark, curtains drawn, the only light from the candle the woman was holding. Isabeau pulled at the curtain's edge and looking through a crack to her right, she could see outside the glass. It was daylight muddled by the clouds, and shadows of the landscape but it was daylight, and it was still raining and much harder now. She could see within the rock and mud enclave a large waterfall, murky and spumescent as it apparently cascaded outside its normal boundaries and ran off beyond her view.

Just how long had she been there? Was it the same day? She closed the curtains back tightly, just as the woman began waving her hands in front of Isabeau's face. Suddenly her voice burst through the silence, and Isabeau jumped.

"Are you alright dear?" the woman asked.

"I think so. What—where am I—what happened?"

"Carl and I found you lying out in the middle of the trail last night, and bless your heart, it looked like you and been bitten by something. Don't you remember?"

"No," Isabeau replied, starting to sit up.

"You just stay put. You've had a bit of a time, but we patched you up, and Carl took Ethan, and they have gone into town to see if anyone can identify you. My name is Rose. What is your name dear?"

"My name? My name is Isabeau."

"Isabeau. Why that's a lovely name. What is your last name and where do you come from, dear?"

"Isabeau Barnum. My name is Isabeau Barnum, and I was coming from Camerton going home to Ellenborough."

"Well, my goodness. Are you saying that you came

through the Broughton moors, a little girl like you all alone? My word. Well, this is Dearham. You're still a little way from home but don't you worry your little head. I'll have Carl run over when he gets back and get your father."

"My father is dead."

"Oh, I'm so sorry, dearie. I'll have him get your mother then."

"She is dead as well."

"Oh, my. Well, what family do you have, dear?"

"None," she said as her eyes welled and she rolled over, away from the woman.

"Well, that's enough for now," she said, patting Isabeau on the back and shoulder. "You just lay there and rest. Carl should be back soon. After all, it is almost sunset. We'll talk more then."

She then left a small tray of food by the bed and left the room quietly, closing the door behind her. Isabeau sat up and looked around the room. She was apparently in the couple's bedroom. It appeared to be a simple house, although still much nicer than what she was used to. There were real paintings on the walls, and the room was furnished in beautiful, hand-carved furniture, and there were even carpets on the floor. She had to get out of there. She grabbed some fruit from the tray the woman had brought in and wrapped it into the quilt that had been lying on her and moved toward the window. She reached out to open the window, and her hand felt suddenly as if it was on fire, the skin abraded and blistered in just a few seconds.

"What the hell?" she screamed, pulling back in

horror from the pain. The woman came running into the room. Isabeau quickly put her arm under the quilt.

"What are you doing, young lady?" the woman said as she forced Isabeau back into lying down on the bed still in a constant under the breath berate.

"You're in no condition to be up and about."

This time, when she left the room, she left the door open. Isabeau pulled her arm out from under the cover and examined it closely. The burns seemed to slowly heal before her eyes, turning first red, then brown which slowly faded to a yellow like a bruise before completely dissipating. What the hell caused that? She decided after a few experiments with the sunlight coming through the window that it was the sun. Somehow it burned her, and badly. She decided to wait until dark to make her escape from the woman's care. She closed her eyes and lay there thinking of all she had been through, trying to understand it all, and then she fell asleep.

Isabeau awoke again later and noticed that the light had faded. She sat up and pulled at the wrappings that the woman had put on her wounds and found a bedash of blood on the fabric but nothing beneath it. What the hell was going on? She had been bitten. Why were there no wounds? She slipped over to the woman's dressing table and looked into the mirror. She stifled a scream. "Where the hell am I?" She stood full in front of the glass and everything behind her was clear within the mirror, but there was not a sign of her. She had to get the hell out of this witch house. She moved quietly over to the window and began sliding it open. It squeaked and moaned as she moved the old frame. She did this while constantly looking over her shoulder for the old woman. She slipped through the opening and stood up just as a wagon pulled up in front of her.

"Hey where are you going, young lady?" the man exclaimed from the wagon. It must be Carl, she thought. She looked at him. He was carrying a small child with him.

"Don't run, little one. I won't hurt you."

Suddenly, she felt fire on her skin. Pain, intense pain but not like the burning of the sun, no, this was much worse and different as it was over every part of her body. She fell to the ground writhing within the madness. She trembled as she felt her bones moving, twisting snapping like twigs in the fire. She screamed from the pain. The man cautiously descended from the wagon and walked uneasily toward her.

"Are you alright? What's wrong?" he asked, holding the child tightly against him.

Isabeau crouched on the ground. She pulled her arms out in front of her and screamed in horror. Her skin was pulled taut against her bones and had grown pale to the point of achromic. Her fingers, and arms no longer in proportion as before and her nails now elongated and curved, her knuckles overly pronounced and everything in the darkness around her suddenly became bright like the sun was shining brighter than it ever had. She turned toward Carl, and he screamed falling backward into a shrubbery, dropping the infant as he fell. Isabeau grasped the child within her talons, pulling the child tightly to her breast and ran deep into the shadowy darkness of the night.

At seventeen, she had been confident and strong—at least, she felt she was until this horror entered her life. Then everything she thought that she knew, or dared to believe in, was shattered. She found life as it had been shown to her was a lie and began living away from others, she thought being a recluse had its benefits. As I seem not to age, shall I, like so many others, turn to wine or will I live eternally as a child?

It was hard to piece together the events in her mind exactly as they had happened. So many, many years had passed since then. But it did happen, a long time ago, a lifetime ago, but still it happened.

Violent red hair. She remembered violent red hair on the woman in the carriage, the one who found her and who had lifted her head and peered deeply into her eyes, inquiring. "Are you okay, Love?"

"What? I think so, where am I?" Isabeau asked. "Why, you're on the road, in the middle of it, to be exact. What happened? You're bleeding. Are you indigent?"

A question so bold it struck her like a punch. No, she wasn't so much coarse about it, it was a direct and extremely honest question posed to a woman before her in an obviously questionable state.

"Am I indigent? Am I?" She said, repeating it out loud as the woman continued to ask her a series of questions, like where she lived, what was her name, why was she there? Isabeau did not even think that indigent was even a word used any longer and now how did it belong to her.

"No," she suddenly announced, attempting to sit erect. "I am not sure how I came to be here," she added. "Carl, lift the child into the carriage," she demanded of her husband standing at her side. Isabeau passed out after that. It is amazing how quickly the infection of a bite can take. In some, days. Others, weeks. Isabeau's was mere hours. She had cut her eyetooth on the child before eventually moving onto larger prey. She had always felt guilty. They had been so nice to her.

6

My weaknesses torment me—a simple step off a ridge, a dangling noose, a sip of poison from the amber bottle. There are ways out of this. I'm sure that there are. But yet, I do nothing. I console myself and justify my weakness by questioning what peace can there be without atonement? How does one even begin to atone being what it is that I am?

Isabeau was as quiet as she could be during that first year after the attack. She guessed somehow she was perhaps processing it, for she spent many a day in prayer then, screaming into the heavens as she inveighed against sin and hell, trying anything to gain favor with a God, which seemed to have turned his back to her. She felt she was a person of good repute and could not understand why this hell was thrust upon her. If it were a test, surely she had failed. Over time, she slowly grew into herself. In the beginning, she learned to stay within the shadows. She wasn't sure exactly how to fit in. She didn't know how this nocturnal beast, child form, fit with these the mortals, the normal, the beautiful, that lived beneath the bright and vaulted skies. Isabeau discovered early on that she had a singular affinity with the outcast, the derelict, the unloved, the broken things. No matter where she drifted, there they invariably lay within her path, the odd guttersnipe, working to leech off what little she had.

So, Isabeau changed her outward appearance, in an attempt to wash away these parasites. To alter their perception of her position in life so she would now look within a station that they inevitably would fear upon approach. Once Isabeau had done this, she found to her satisfaction that it put her in a place where she could mingle, within the affluent and the connected. So life as a whole, became, let us say, more lucrative.

Isabeau slowly walked the streets of Ellenborough, working her way back up toward the overlooking inn, trying to remain anonymous, keeping to the shadows when they were available and moving away from anyone moving in her general direction. The moon was not in season so she was favored by not being forced to change. In those times, she could choose her form, and in that at least she felt some small reward of independence, although the hunger often forced her otherwise. Each morning Isabeau Barnum would wake excited in the hopes that the mirror would finally tell a different tale. A sign perhaps, something, a shadow, an aura, anything? Of course, it was always the same, nothing more than a futile exercise as perfunctory as her daily hope that something would find a way to reverse the misery of her accursed life. Isabeau arrived back at the inn just before midnight that evening and stood within the room looking out across the yard and evening skies.

Isabeau suddenly saw Emily's father coming around one of the buildings in the back with little Emily in tow. Tugging and pulling at her small thin bruised arms, telling her what she should be doing and what she was doing, how inadequately it was being done. This was only Isabeau's second time in the view of this man. Each time he grew a lesser character, this lunker that reeked abhorrently with his thin but fat laced arms and falcate digits that hung twitching at his sides. Body to snout this man was detestable, offensive, all in all, he was an egregious horror. So how could this child, who could not sort her own, have made anything at all of the jumble of mixed motives and crossed purposes, that had grown as ordinary and routine as a day at the market, or seen design in his snarl of wills, feelings, and intentions. She could not, she thought

Isabeau, as an outsider, could see with clarity what was held within his design, the bending of her will, that he worked so ardently at, to the point that he had but to say boo to the child and she would jump. She knew she shouldn't get involved—she should remain in the shadows as insurance to remain oblivious to the world and not bring attention to herself. But she couldn't just sit idly by. She just couldn't.

Isabeau had not always been as careful and cunning—no—it was time that had made her what she was. She had even once had a narrow escape from being captured and killed, for in the beginning she had been plagued with habitual carelessness. It was nine years ago. It was early in the evening, she had attacked in the middle of a fish market with others much closer than they should have been, and the girl had screamed. She had run, and in seeking refuge she was forced to spend more than two weeks wading in the nauseating stench-filled cesspit sewers of London. The stench permeated the air and leaked into her subconscious, and she realized then how careful she had to be in the way she chose her victims. For if it were a test, then she surely failed it and paid the price. Isabeau had thought the coal smoke, noxious fumes, and sulfurous fog had been bad upon the surface. No, down here when the fetid Thames was at high tide, the foul miasma that she was living in rose to well above her waist. The sewer casing being no more than fifty-six to sixty inches in most areas meant Isabeau had to travel bent over, her face mere inches from the thick mass of human excrement and hospital wastes. She would find small rooms within the sewers as they were, that she could stand upright and even some, where there would be small outcroppings to where she could climb from the sludge to rest.

The streets of London as they had been designed, lay thirty feet below the surface of the Thames at high tide. When the cesspits filled to overflow, they were built to drain to the streets, so there were times she had to seek refuge in upper carved out areas of the sewer trenches, crawling on her hands and knees through the mire. It had only been a few years since the city had installed the trench covers and caps. Large concrete caverns with iron disk caps that were designed to keep the locals from searching for night soil, excrement harvested from the cesspit and sewers and sold for fertilizer, but in truth they did nothing but hold the stench in that much more. The waste soaked the walls, and foundations around her and above and for the entire two weeks she waited cold and wet. This would have killed her if she were not what she was. Even above, the situation was deteriorating—epidemics of cholera, typhus, "consumption" and other undefined maladies were taking their toll on the population and they were not sitting in the cause as she was.

Two weeks in those damned catacombs trying hard not to vomit is a long time. She spent most of her time hiding beneath the Templar's sanctuary. She figured they didn't want to be caught any more than she did, and so if they felt safe, maybe she could as well. She had been bade in the darkness for so long that any time a shaft of light came into the sewer, she was almost overcome with agony. Her time was absorbed in thought and filled with worry. There was very little air there, and what there was rancid and stale and did little to cool the sweat and filth that plastered the rough homespun to her back and chest.

Not long after her arrival she was awakened by a noise, the sound was like an animal's cry. She tracked it through the tunnels and tubes. There she found a clearing beneath a vent. From above she could see the night sky, and she pressed her face against the iron vent and breathed deep. Suddenly she heard it again below her, she rolled her shoe against a bundle, and there swathed in an old bit of sailcloth, was an infant. It apparently had been tossed like a bit of rubbage, which unfortunately wasn't strange. It was still alive and as horrible as it may sound, she had found it a blessing as it nourished her enough for the stay.

Isabeau's standing within the tunnels, even though hellish to think of, had its brighter moments. It gave her a chance to think—to evaluate her life, so to speak—what life it was. She decided that the one thing she needed to do was to return home to her daughter. She had to go back. She had to see where she was buried to make sure that she was, well, just make sure.

Isabeau grumbled to herself for letting it take nineteen years to abandon this self-imposed exile in London and return home. Roughly two weeks or so after her arrival in the sewers she heard the sounds of digging and worked her way through some small openings, moving up and across into a large tunnel. There she found it full of digging workers. They were dirty and nasty, working to create new trenches for the ever growing population of the city. Even the women workers that were there to do nothing more than to tend to the men struggled their way through muck and mire.

Isabeau hid behind some stonework and did her best to clean herself. She had a plan. Then even before she was ready to put it into motion, a bell rang, and the entire population began to move away from her. She ran from behind trying her best to blend into the faction and work her way toward the stairs that led up and out of the tunnels. She was noticed but only because of her state, no one could say a word as the group moved in one motion toward the exit and out of the tunnels, crowding her quickly within their rush. She was glad she apparently was blending, but she gnashed her teeth, irritated by the slow pace of those preceding her up the stairwell, then suddenly she burst into the swarming city streets into a drone of voices—a mishmash of English and French and the sounds of the wagon wheels running hard against the stones. It all seemed to diminish the anxiety that dogged her these past two weeks.

Finally, she was out breathing clean air, but now she was in the open, exposed, and a woman who had just spent the past two weeks living in the sewage tunnels sticks out physically and embarrassingly aromatically. She moved quickly into the ominous shadows in and between the large buildings, searching for water and clothing. She had learned a lot from that experience and even more since.

Humans, for the most part, angered Isabeau, she had witnessed little to no compassion in her travels. She sometimes wondered if she used that as an out. Could it be because she was in ultimate denial and unconsciously craved for a real-life theater show full of humans turned into vicious tigers wanting to attack each other? If only they had that immense thirst for life. If they were but a youthful population in its entirety, a new mankind, inspired with an eager appetence for knowledge and truth, then perhaps, the guilt, her guilt might be more. They didn't pass from one another self-confidence, or even kindness for the most part. No, they lived their lives self-consumed, unconcerned, and lacking in moral restraints as they worked to kill one another, steal from one another and tread on them as if everyone but themselves were but doormats. Isabeau felt she had more compassion in her heart than most of them, and she had killed more than most of them, and yet it was as if they were going at the same rate.

7

It is said that within all of us there is a flicker, a flame, that light, that makes us who we are, that cauterizes us and makes us pure in the beginning. It is also said that same fire can smolder in sin and be set ablaze to incinerate us.

Isabeau was dreaming that she was falling in darkness. Emptiness surrounded her and below her only black. Nothing to grab, nothing to hold onto, no way of knowing when it would finally end and in struggling she found there was no way of stopping it. There was an intense vulnerability to it all, and she awoke—breathing deeply and bathing in a sweat. Then it was over as quick as that, and for just a single moment she thought of the stress and panic that should be, in all rights, smothering her at this moment, but instead there was a strange calmness to it. There was a relief, if you will that the dream was over and life now had, although it might be minute, some control to it all. The essence of calm in the moment had lent itself to the gathering seconds of clarity as a storm of emotions brought together the fabric of the night's weave. As though a sigh had escaped the earth that solemn nightfall, the wisp of breath that had coursed the land had stilled, and within all this something was wrong. She could feel it, like a dither in her being and she could not jilt it. This feeling stirred her from her meditation, her dream, and she yawned and inhaled the stale air of the old inn.

Isabeau rose to her feet throwing her long coat around her shoulders and passed through the faded double doorway, then walked out upon the ragged porch. Gazing out into the night, the sky appeared as if it were straining against swollen clouds. There was a dark silence and it was as if all of her senses were electrified. Then breaking the silence was a single blood-curdling scream, the direst cry she had ever heard, and it echoed into the night. Isabeau's mouth had dried. She squeezed the balcony's banisters so tightly that her knuckles turned white. Her mind, shocked and panicky, struggled to pull information together.

Isabeau jumped the railing and dropped the twenty odd feet to the ground landing firmly on her feet, then moved quickly over and across and out along the front of the inn. Once she had reached the cornerstone she turned, and as she walked out along the side of the building, blouses and pants hung there in the dark from the laundry wire flopping in the breeze like nervous specters frantically trying to locate their bodies. She loved the night. It condensed into her and allayed the bonds of her abhorrent blight. Her new life seemed to seek moist shadows underneath the bridges and quays, in marrow-darkness.

This was different, though. This was not her hunt and she amazed herself by feeling uneasy, and as she meandered toward the unknown sounds, the night seemed to get darker, and she became acutely conscious of all that was around her. As she crossed the windswept courtyard the peplum on her chambray jacket flapped like the dark wing of an injured bird. The stars and the gibbous moon demanded to be looked at as they waved gloriously through breaks in the heavy clouds. She was certain that this was the direction the sounds came from. She noticed she was getting farther and farther behind the inn than she had ever been before, and then she saw it, it's soft citrine glow there within the darkness. Slowly, she approached the tattered building. The site itself was edged right to a small boscage off the main wood just ahead of her.

This was a structure she hadn't seen before. There was what appeared to be a single lit candle within, casting odd shadows through the somewhat toile curtains that danced wildly from the flame. Panic beat in her chest like a bird trying to escape her rib cage. She pressed a hand to her chest and came away with a wetness. She was nervous. From this distance she couldn't hear much. She heard nonsense, incomprehensible noises, and words without form or definition attached to them. Her hair whipped against her as the fury of the night's wind grew. The ground was wet and springy underfoot and she could hear the gurgling of water somewhere off to her left. The noises inside were now quick and plangent, like someone was being thrown again and again against the wall, then everything went still. She could just make out the shadowy silhouette of the top of a head of what appeared to be a man against the curtain. She idled over the area for a moment before easing her way cautiously up each of the three steps than in onto the narrow porch. As she moved closer a strip of light slid through the door crack and cut across her arm as she turned her head and her hair dusted the screen separating her from those within. Here, she cautioned herself. Weakness had led her to the boundaries of this place.

Curiosity? A weakness she was unaware she bore. There was something... Then she saw them, and her lip curled. There, within the small one-room cabin and even in the half-light, she could descry the rough forms and vague outlines, to where suddenly everything was at once coldly precise, voluptuously real and strangely horrific. It was a destructive picture to see. Isabeau, a person not easily moved, was now shaken suddenly off the trammels of reason and anger grew within her, swaying back and forth and intensely building just beneath the surface. There, within these walls dappled in gray his foul grunts and his shoat like moans became more intense as he thrust himself upon this gauzy thin form of a girl. Isabeau watched Emily's relentless struggles beneath her father's slovenly body weight, bleeding from her eye and mouth from his obvious heavy hand. Isabeau stood there frozen in place her focus never leaving Emily's eyes as her mind did furcate as it will. She was proud of her at that moment that even though she was going through the unimaginable, she remained recusant, fighting all the way, never fully submitting to his wants and wayward desires. No longer screaming, not crying, just fighting. Her torn nightdress wrapped precariously around her waist as his foul bulbous ass rose and fell, seething as he took from her, her pride, her dignity and, most horribly, her innocence—something Isabeau was quite sure he had done many times before; removing a little more each and every time.

What kind of man could desire an unwilling woman, more a child, his child nonetheless? A sick one. A lot about little Emily now became crystal clear. Grasping hands tore at Emily's clothing and scraped her skin as he forced her back pulling her legs higher as he pressed his heavy weight down on her. Isabeau felt the burning and tasted the vomit rising into her mouth. Then he let out another pig-like grunt, and it was over. He then lay his large hands against her small chest and pressing hard, lifted his massive body and rolled, flopping his corpulent flesh off her and onto the remaining portion of the old brown mattress. Just as soon as she was free of the weight, she leapt to her feet, stumbling and falling, pulling at her tattered gown, tears finally erupting as she left, slamming the door as she passed Isabeau there without even seeing her.

Isabeau stood there waiting in the shadow of the doorway, watching as Emily ran out aimlessly into the night. Isabeau's drawn out growl through her clenched teeth was the only response she could give herself after Emily passed. She stood there for only a moment before turning her attention back to this callous bastard of a human being. Oh what to do, what to do? She knew what it was that she wanted to do. What the hell was she thinking, this was not how she worked, so why was this any different? Why was she so nervous? Wasn't the outcome to be the same? Her mind which arranges that wisdom to do shall come at an equal pace with the departure of zest for doing. But this was not just to do, it was without thought, it was that God-given morality, which was still within the human side of her, and for once, she just embraced it.

Then there across the room Isabeau saw it. Lying alone beside the candle on the small table next to the window, was a knife. It's blade calling out, sparkling, shimmering, beneath the dance of the candles flame. She imagined its reason. It must have been a tool, its mere presence another assurance of poor Emily's submission. This apparent revelation only further sickened her, and she could take no more.

Isabeau smashed through the door in an explosive carom, sending billows of dust and wood splinters into the air. She leapt through the opening, grabbing the knife and pinning the beast to the wall, shoving the blade to his throat. The sheer strength of this frail figure of a woman standing before him, holding his weight firmly to the wall caught him off guard.

"Ah! Oh, Jesus, what the..." was all he could muster at the moment of impact.

"You, sick, twisted, bastard! How could you!" Isabeau cried out, moving her face uncomfortably close to Carter's. Pushing the tip of her blade tighter against his skin as he flailed about within her grip.

"You? Get off me, you bitch," he screamed in his feeble male attempt at courage, as he squirmed beneath her hold.

"Shut up! Shut up! You, you disturbed, warped, horrible excuse for a human being. Shut up, before I, I gut you like the pig you are," she said shaking him and then smashing him hard against the wall again.

"I mean it," he said through airy breaths. "Get off me," this threatening tone waned dramatically, and his breathing raced hard like his heart.

Isabeau finally devoured the last of his masculinity, as she shoved him harder against the wall, lifting his feet now fully off the floor. He hung there like this hulking parody of a rag doll in her arms.

"What are you?" were all the words he could flutter past his unsuspecting mind and flaccid, corpulent lips as Isabeau's grip tightened further. His faced bled sweat, like an open vein, his eyes bloating within his head and his lips quivered like

"I should gut you, right here, right now. Isabeau said. "Or, maybe, yes, maybe, divide you, from what you seem to hold so dear" as she moved the blade down between his legs.

"Wait, wait, what is this, can't we work something out?" he begged.

Isabeau stared at him crossly as she slid the blade from his groin, slowly up his distended perspiring body, raising it back up to his throat.

"Do I look like I'm negotiating?" she said as she tightened her hold and pushed the blade firm now biting his skin. He looked at her with shock and fear in his eyes as they darted repetitively from her face down to the poniard in her hand. He felt helpless. He didn't so much want the blade for he wasn't sure he would have the willingness to use it, but he longed to possess it if he could just grasp the handle then that empty feeling in his mind would not make him feel so cruelly helpless. The outward surface of it was extremely slippery, and the edge and point so very sharp and cold withal, that if he endeavored to take hold of it, it would glide through his fingertips like a smooth sheet of ice. She could see it in his eyes, the confusion. She pushed the knife hard against his throat. Sweat began rolling down his face.

"Do you know what your God hates worse than a pedophile?" Isabeau asked. He looked up at her, squinting, his pleading eyes burning holes in the wall behind her.

"No," he answered in a staggered out a whisper.

"Neither do I," she said as she sunk the blade to the hilt into his throat, twisting and pushing it harder, holding his twisting, twitching frame beneath her, until it finally stopped. Isabeau sat back and let the body slide the rest of the way, slumping to the floor. She crumpled to the ground just after he did. As she leaned there against the bed frame she heard a rapid, overwrought breathing, then she turned and as she pulled the blood soaked poniard from his throat, there hunched in front of her, peering terrified through the nasty marbled glass of the window was Emily. She had seen everything, her eyebrows raised as she suddenly became attentive to what she saw was madness, and it emanated in her expression.

Jesus! Isabeau didn't want to hurt her. She seemed so innocent in it all. Isabeau knew the increasingly frequent, everyday cruelties that she was imposing upon those around her but never had it been directed at someone this close to her. Someone she had come to know and even possibly care for. Emily had reminded her of herself in some strange mutated way, but she couldn't take any chances. What must she now think of her? The thought that it mattered caught her by surprise. She only loathed herself the more, as the foul course was borne beyond her kin, that her lot was not even that of him who lay dead beneath her.

She stood and stepped from the room out onto the porch, then down and out into the courtyard beyond. Isabeau stood there as the wind would wuther around the building's cornerstone howling across the small porch ruthlessly sculpting itself through her subservient hair as it passed. She couldn't see Emily, and had she not seen her with her own eyes she wouldn't have known she was even there, but she had been. Where now would she have run to? Isabeau yelled out for her, "Emily! Emily!"

Her voice was strong and carried easily against the wind but still it was lost within the night's storm.

Lightning flashed again, throwing shadows across the courtyard as it ran closer, fulgurant brilliance striding the fractured landscape like the stilted legs of some ominous spider. The thunder growled as if in anticipation of the next flash from the heavens above. The trees undulated to the winds beckoning, like a cobra swaying to the lute of its charmer.

Isabeau turned and walked back into the room and his eyes were open, staring blindly at her. Dear God, the bastard was still alive, even after he had been lashed by her fury. Hushed lips parted slowly, and his voice came out as if it was to be a whisper, but he just gurgled and spat blood. She stood there watching his body, blood bubbles still breaking at his lips, twitching, just not enough to allow that death rattle to overtake him. His eyes ever watchful of her movements as he lay beside what had become his sacrificial bed. Now it was more a task, the fun was gone, Emily was upset, so it had grown like that of one disconsolate, so before putting a blade to vein, before watching life seep away, drop after bloody drop into a rank, transitory sepulcher, she needed to know what she should do.

Isabeau watched as his eyes strayed from hers and turned. There was Emily. Like moonlight on daisies, she stood glowing in the doorway, paint peeling, one hand resting on the frame for balance. Her red hair was in tangles. Her lips were trembling—eyes so wild with fear, Isabeau thought they might gobble up her face. She had on her tattered night-dress that shimmered in the moonlight. She stood there, white with fear, the horror crippling her momentarily. Her eyes flickering back and forth. She weaved a bit as she became almost unstable. It was as if all the breath in her chest, was literally torn from her body. Her hand found the knob on the door and tightened, her other hand unconsciously clenched tightly into a fist. Emily's heart froze, as she watched the red vermilion blood running across and down her father's body, a shade that contradicted the color of the fear upon her face. She shook violently as she felt the fear pour from her body, and run down her legs, a bastion of warm comfort born in a moment of primal terror.

Then, her face washed of all color, suddenly regained its youthful glow and her expression no longer strained in fear. No, it changed to almost a smirk to the recollections. A devilish gleam filled her green eyes, making the scattered golden flecks stand out more than usual. Her hand moving to cover that grinning mouth as if aiding in the stifle of a giggle, her heart pounding, lungs heaving for the breath to feed the moment. His eyes narrowed at the attention, as she walked past Isabeau with that evil little girl grin, moving closer to his mangled frame. She stood and watched as he clawed at the pillow at the edge of the bed lifting, and then falling, struggling to pull his bleeding body away, but to no avail. Her widened eyes focused, never straying from the dark beast of a man that lay before her.

She looked down on her father's broken body and boldly spat upon him. There was no fear in her now, the beast was broken, her bindings loosened and here Isabeau thought she must be a gorgon to her and yet

Emily seemed to embrace the momentum of the moment. It amazed her how Emily had grown, and now seemed to have the power to lacerate him, inside his bowels, not only his mind and spirit but right in his belly, to tear him and make him feel that he bled inwardly.

"Hello father," she said, her long vowels moaned like the wind in the pines.

He in a vacant muse turned and flinched away from her, from the mere sound of her voice in sudden terror.

"Oh God in heaven, he said as if invoking protection against her."

"There are only two ways to die, father," she said staring into him as quiet tears licked at her face, wide-eyed and emotionless.

"We either go, or we're taken. Consider yourself taken old man," she said through clenched teeth as she stomped onto his crotch and belly over and over, twisting and crushing with her small feet, laughing, crying and cursing, spouting the traumas and horrors, that his existence had caused in her life. Each and every breath she took in she exhaled the hells of her childhood. She kicked him from head to groin over and over. It sounds horrific, but it wasn't, it was beautiful. Like the blooming of a rose. Isabeau watched as this meek, innocent little girl grew before her. Finally able to release a lifetime of anger, brutalization, and abuse, both mentally and sexually as she baste her oppressor over and over and over again, until she finally collapsed onto the floor, blood-soaked, her body covered in gore, exhausted and overwhelmed.

She then raised her small arm and removed the bit of candle from the stand on the table near her and raising her eyes to Isabeau's, smiled as she extended her arm out to the curtains and they went up in a flash. In what seemed only a moment the room was engulfed in flames. They licked the walls and ran quickly up toward the ceiling, where smoke swirled searching for air. Tiny as she was Isabeau struggled to lift Emily's small frame off of the old wooden floor. Her arm cradled her shoulder in a bear-hug position. Her feeble legs flailed about, but her hands managed just fine in finding security at the grasp of Isabeau's shoulder and breasts, as Isabeau drug her from the flames out into the night.

8

Life is unpredictable at best. You never know how long you have or when it all will just end. Not until it is too late. It is at that moment that Christians begin to curse God, Atheists start praying and the dying display their true colors. Then there are those moments when it comes truly without warning and there is no time to repent.

They stood there together on the short rise behind her home, watching from the overlook. The cottage Isabeau would find out later that Emily was born in, some sixteen plus years ago, burn as if in a funeral pyre for her father—smoke boiling up into a caliginous sky. Sooty tears rolled down leaving pale tracks upon Emily's cheeks. Isabeau didn't know if she was crying for him or joy, and she didn't ask. Hatred branded Isabeau's heart but now within the warmth of the fire seemed to sooth the burning, and she felt some minute justification for her actions, not that she needed it.

Emily's screams and the grunts of her father as he raped and beat her almost to death reverberated through Isabeau's head as it had earlier when it had inflamed her rage into an inferno that would have consumed her until justice had been done for little Emily. Revulsion filled her for the man who had done this and for herself because she had not stopped him sooner. She stood there lost in a vague emotion as Emily reached over and placed her small hand in Isabeau's. When she touched Isabeau's hand, on her face there was a kind of peace, and she gave a sigh from the bottom of her heart. A slight frown marred Emily's features as she began to cry again.

Isabeau reached out and wrapped her arms around Emily, pulling her shaking frame to her. Predictably she resisted, moaning complaints even as her fingers knit in Isabeau's blouse. She pressed her face against Isabeau's body. Her head lolled against her like a broken flower. Everything about this moment felt right, and yet so very wrong. Emily shook her head against Isabeau's chest, burying her tear streaked face away from her eyes. Isabeau dropped an arm and tucked her hand beneath Emily's chin, pulling her head up toward hers.

"There's no shame in it, Emily. He can't hurt you anymore.

Emily shook her head, huddling her hands to her chest.

"What do I do now, though?" She said in a breathy whisper.

"Now that?" she began to cry again.

A large lump forms in Isabeau's throat and she

brought her gaze down to meet hers.

"I guess you're with me now."

"What do you mean?" Her slender features tilting toward Isabeau as she met those gorgeous green eyes. She draped her arm around Emily's shoulder and looked down at her with a smile.

Now, here she was, lost in it. This was exactly what she had feared.

The lump in Isabeau's throat burned. She crossed her free arm over her chest to coax the sensation away, and then placed her fingers to her mouth, willing the congestion in her throat to ease. Yet it didn't, it grew and grew. Isabeau focused on not showing it, on hiding the pain welling within her.

"Just what I said, just what I said," Isabeau replied, turning her head back toward the flames. Suddenly Emily grabbed Isabeau, and she held her so, very, very tightly as the tears continued to flow. Isabeau wrapped her arms around her as she turned and looked up at Isabeau with those big green eyes. Isabeau brushed the tears and hair from her face, and she smiled.

Now Isabeau was this person Emily held in such a high regard, and in truth, Isabeau felt the same toward her, but Emily had no idea of what Isabeau truly was. It was like a millstone around her neck. What does she do with her now? Does she just leave her? Isabeau even thought about changing her, and she knew it sounded absurd that someone such as she would hesitate to act on moral grounds, but to simply take the child and turn her into such as she was, it would be an abomination, and she wasn't even sure it would work.

"No, no I can't and I won't," she said to herself, yet still she sought to draw her in—to make her and keep her a part of her life, but what kind of life would that be? But to lose her now for some reason would be more than Isabeau could take.

Isabeau looked out at the fire, then back at Emily. Was this but the foreshadowing of their great and glorious life together? The thought scared her, in more ways than one. She had lived all over Britain, Wales, and Scotland during her lifetime, sometimes staying only a few months and even days before relocating. She had no living friends or family, no genuine connections, and no sense of belonging. But this is how it should be, for her to remain in the shadows. Emily was the first shadow who visited her for Isabeau's benefit, and not their own and was, therefore, precious to her. She arrived like a shade on a sunny day and it gave her hope. Filling the gaps that she wasn't even aware lay open, her pale green eyes held precious wisdom, innocence and shone with equal parts hope and sorrow, with an enlightened, round face, and all of this framed by a halo of curls and she admired her.

The house behind the inn was mere timbers now as tendrils of smoke slid and curled up off the surface and gently rose into the pre-morning sky. A gentle morning breeze crawled down the lush green hills and tenderly stroked the leaves of the trees as it cooled the quiet country village, where most were still oblivious to the horrific trial of the night.

Amazingly, no one even came to the fire. It was

strange no one even questioned it. A fire like this situated high above this cold little town that shivers on the edge of the wild should have brought the entire population out. She put her arm around Emily and walked her back to her room and put her in her bed. She sat there stroking Emily's hair and watched as she drifted off quickly. She had admired her bravery through all of this. She looked so beautiful, and the one thing she would never forget was Emily's expression, her look of unflawed fulfillment, of beatitude, as though at last she stood tall and could finally be herself without the fear.

Due to the lingering confusion over the effects of the evening, Isabeau felt it was time to move on. She had to find a new balance, otherwise, what little she had built would quickly fall like a house of cards. The problem was she needed to feed, but it was too close to morning now, and so she closed the curtains and crawled in beside Emily. They both lay within the shadows of that rustic bedroom the entire day. When Isabeau awoke she found herself in intense pain, her leg was burning, and she pulled it quickly beneath the covers. She realized that the curtains were now open. Jesus, she was exposed.

"Emily! she screamed, Emily!"

"Yes?" Emily replied from across the room. "Oh, good you're awake. Come I've made you something to eat."

"Close the curtains! Close the curtains! Isabeau bellowed from beneath the covers.

"What?" Emily replied.

"Close the curtains!" Isabeau screamed again.

"Okay, okay," Emily said as Isabeau listened to her moving within the room.

"Okay. They're closed, Jesus." Emily said.

Isabeau slid a hand cautiously from beneath the blankets and then peeked out from under the covers. Isabeau looked up at Emily as she stood there with this puzzled look on her face only inches from the bed.

"Emily, listen, I should have told you I have a very bad allergy to direct sunlight. It, ah, it causes me to get a, a bad burn and rash."

"Really? Oh, I'm so sorry," Emily said plopping down on the bed and giving Isabeau a conscientious hug.

She then sat back and looked Isabeau over with this curious expression.

"You mean you're really allergic to the sun? How is that even possible? You mean you can't go out in the daylight? At all?" she inquired further.

"No, I can't," Isabeau admitted.

"Ever? Why?"

"Look, it doesn't matter. It's okay, just don't, don't do it again, alright?"

"Alright, I won't." Suddenly Emily's cheery disposition returned.

"Come eat. Look, look!" Emily said, jumping from the bed to show her the meal she had so carefully prepared and decorated.

Isabeau smiled, admiring Emily's innocence once more.

Night was once more. It called out to Isabeau like

wild geese – over and over again, announcing her place in this world. Isabeau stood watching as Emily sifted through the embers as the gray smoke curled and rose from the remains of what was once her home. Isabeau looked out at the fireflies sparkling like gems in the lingering light. How she had loved them as a child, she could spend hours watching the insects disappearing twisting this way and that, dancing with the nuances of the wind, dotting the landscape as if they were playing a rhythm to the sapphire sky. But this was different, life was different now.

Isabeau remembered when the dusk used to be a magical time when the violet and plum shades coaxed the burning orb out of the sky and turned distant clusters of trees into silhouettes. Isabeau looked ever skyward as the pale moon began its nightly climb into the copper green skies. Even now within the shadows of the clouds, it struck her like lightning to a tree. Almost immediately the fight began to whipsaw Isabeau like a sharp stone cutting through her flesh as she stood struggling to keep herself true. We all have claws for a reason, they are real and true enough, but for her the dark side of herself was strong, and she worked fighting within her mind to quell itself from the rebellion running thickly through the course of her. I just have to get through this, she thought, always grasping for tomorrow.

"Emily." Isabeau struggled with a pitch that would make a boy in the midst of puberty proud. "I have to run to town for some things, stay here, I will be back soon."

Emily rose from the ashes and stared at Isabeau.

"But…" Emily started.

"Just stay here," Isabeau said slowly with a tone deeply submerged in irritation and pain.

Emily stood slowly wiping the ash from her hands as she watched as Isabeau quickly ushered herself out of sight.

Once within the walls, Isabeau moved about the city, still maintaining her person—looking, searching. Somewhere out there within the tangle of streets and alleys there was someone—someone who would quench her desire. She hated this and had to force herself to move forward, knowing it would not cease until it was satisfied, coaching her movements as she went.

"Have patience, enjoy the hunt," she would tell herself. God, how did she become this? Something had whispered, and she listened. Perhaps it had always been there, this thing, this demon inside of her, waiting, just waiting for her to turn around. It was that possibility that this had always been within her that haunted Isabeau—that it wasn't the bite that changed her. If it had, then this is what she was. Then there was no returning, for there was nowhere to return to.

9

A fallen soul lets the rain into my dark den. It puddles at my feet.

In childhood, they say all those things that mark you when you're young, make you who you are. Perhaps it is the reason she casts no reflection within the mirror. Isabeau wondered, could it really be that simple? Is it all merely psychological? Is it that her image is there, but she simply refuses to see it? That the truth is just that she cannot face herself? If so, she was much weaker than she thought herself to be. She knew that she could not unmake the past and that she would have to live with the guilt. She knew she should, but she didn't lie around thinking about it, dwelling upon a past that could not be altered. In fact, there is little to no guilt Isabeau felt, except maybe just after the moment that it has happened. Then it was gone, seldom to return. She considered these moments, weaknesses, nothing more, for the alternative would be more than Isabeau could bare. She had to put her soul aside, buried it somewhere deep in the cold, gray clay on a forgotten hill, entombed it there until she could find an answer. For now, the only torment was the one she dragged across her own heart, for she dwelled more on the fact of what she was than what she had done.

The town was busy, and as a whole, there was a subtle spirit and cumulative force to them all. Isabeau needed somewhere quiet away from the masses. Normally, when she was on the hunt, she moved like a ghost, traveling where she liked between the walls, there she would find the things that occupied her mind, but it was different, more carnal and hurried.

Then she saw her, a flash of form and eyes. Her name was Abigail—a beauty. She was young, perhaps just under twenty, delicate and stately in design, dressed mature for her young age, and Isabeau was immediately drawn to her. A gentle breeze brushed against Isabeau's face. The breeze felt like a sensuous massage and the cool evening air imbued with the sweet scent of anticipation. Clandestinely, she followed her and marked as she turned and went into a doorway. Isabeau paused before entering and gazed up at the old iron pump handle post with a roughly painted piece of timber dangling beneath it. It read "Ambassador East's Pump Room."

She looked both left and right then walked inside. It was an odd place—an alehouse in the front but also within the back what one would consider to be the local library—large and airy. The room, misty with smoke from padron cigars and the candles and gas lights that lit the establishment. They cast eerie shadows through the ambient glow caused by rays of light that shown reflectively in through the small colored glass and mirrors oddly placed within the walls of the large labyrinth of rooms. Those within talked and drank as Isabeau wandered around in the shadows of the back, trailing her fingers over the spines of books, on a shelf. Books written by those who man, as a collective, decided mattered—the great minds of the day, all these that will be left behind by those that build upon the foundation laid and written in the future, with only a trailing few to be quietly remembered.

There at the end of the room was a raised platform, as if for a lectern and it is there that she stood, her Aphrodite, whom Isabeau followed from the streets into the depository and who now apparently became aware of her gaze. She turned, smiled and walked through the door behind her. Isabeau followed closely through and up a turnpike stair. Already she had the melliferous taste of victory on her tongue, but she mustn't be too eager lest it show. By happenstance or design, the girl was beautiful. She walked as if she had been coached in her movements of preposterous effeminacy. Isabeau's own movements, graceful, smooth, were ones that had become a philosophy of life and ones that over time had transformed themselves into instinct. The last of the day's light had faded through the windows as the evening moved to its gloaming, casting ominous shadows throughout the chamber, shadows that they would soon embrace.

Isabeau closely watched as she turned and walked down a row of shelves then stopped and smiled back at her then she turned again down the third column within an area both closed and concealed. This was a look Isabeau knew as an agreeable one—a come hither if you will, and there were no pauses in her advancements.

She bit her lower lip, then moved to the side to let Isabeau in.

"I don't believe I'm doing this."

"That's a good girl. You know I was lucky I followed you in here."

Isabeau leaned in as she passed. An electric jolt moved through her and this angel as her arm rubbed against her breast. This was her favorite part. No more had Isabeau turned down the third column than they locked in an embrace, one that, for her part, lasted far longer than she anticipated for she was pleasing. She grabbed Isabeau's breast and kissed her deeply, pulling her closer and rubbing herself against her, with one leg up and wrapped around Isabeau.

"I am Abigail," the girl cooed. Isabeau said nothing. She pushed her hard against the bookshelves and brushed her hair back from her neck. Abigail turned her head at a sharp angle and offered it up to her, a movement Isabeau was not used to but willing to embrace. The kiss, though, she was obviously expecting came in a different form, but unbelievably, she struggled very little beneath the bite as Isabeau sought the center of her fading warmth.

Once Isabeau had her fill she pulled back from

Abigail and watched as she went completely achromatic, her eyes staring, vacuous, vacant, growing amber then paling to a faint dry steel gray as a perse washed beneath, hollowing her eyes, as the life left her body. Isabeau listened as she expired to the hollow call from a strange bell ringing in the distance on that overcast night in Ellenborough. She felt little to no compassion for the girl, for taking a life, to her, had grown to be nothing more than tossing a coin to a beggar, a detached and superficial act, but not one without its rewards. Her body now hung limp and flaccid in her embrace as Isabeau ran her tongue glossing the last of the liquid from her lips. It never dawned on her until later that she had seen the outcome of this act. But it is with the later evolution of her own theurgy, this power that she alone wielded, the taking of lives that she was mainly concerned, and it is here she found some compensation for the lacunosity of her mind.

*

There was not a word from Ellenborough's Viceroy about the death of Marsh. This worried her, surely they would have heard something, with the mindless blather that branched its way through the masses of this city, unless they were…, no, no, they didn't know, not with the search going on for little Abigail from the Ambassador. They would have made their presence known if they indeed suspected anything of her.

It is strange she never worried about things such as these. Why now? At times, she'd go about her day like there was nothing egregious in her life, that everything was well. It was like sometimes she'd forget, over and over that she was awake, that this was not a nightmare, that this was real. Other times in her mind it was as if she separated the two, the dark from the light.

Comparatively, she guessed, that was okay, being mindful is a process of forgetting, and then remembering, repeatedly. Just as breathing is a process of exhaling and repeatedly inhaling, at the very least it means she was alive and conscience. But was a mindful life worth the effort? It's a life, where she would awaken from the dream state, she was most often submerged in, the state of having her mind anywhere but the present moment, past recollections blocked from her subconscious and locked in thoughts about what is going to happen later.

Being awake meant she was conscious of what was going on inside, as it happens when it happens, and so in all rights, she should be able to make more conscious choices, rather than acting on her impulses. But unfortunately, she, being what she was, wasn't always offered that conscious choice. She did though sometimes wonder, was she consciously making the choices she was acting out, and simply pointing blame anywhere but where it should be directed, which was at herself? There were, though, the blackouts, which in some strange way gave her some solace. Moments where life was, for the most part normal, then she would awaken with blood on her hands and body and have no recollection, of what she had done or where she had been, sometimes for hours on end. Since she had no memory, she had never seen herself in this state, so as far as what she would become or what she even looked like, or even if there was a physical change to her being, she just didn't know or didn't remember. She had only the stories of those, who say they had seen the beast on those nights, where death screams echoed beneath the lamp lights.

Walking on, Isabeau began to wonder why it was that she was worried now. Was it Emily? She knew her relationship with this child, was at the very least cancerous, but just maybe she thought this relationship could create an instauration, which she could proclaim, and conceivably could change her in ways, in a way that nothing else could. She viewed her emotionalism with ironic detachment and needed to, in order to just function. But fact be known, she was beset by guilt because of her desire. She walked aimlessly to the end of the civilized part of town, where it turned to a disused industrial section. The old canal lay still and half frozen over before her. There she stopped and stared for a moment before she sidled down to the canal itself. Isabeau then idled over to one of the bridges and stairs below. You could say that when she descended those rarely used steps to the small, usually deserted shoreline, she felt confident in her actions. She knew she had kept her obscurity.

Looking out, stretching along the shore, illuminated by the moonlight an occasional lantern flashed, there were groups of people. Men and women, young and old. They were bundled up in layers of shapeless clothing against the cold. They worked on into the night. They stuck to the areas they knew to be safest.

They avoided the channels and the mud sinks in search for the missing girl. A thin wind brought with it a scent of brine and the distant hissing of waves. They were working against time—the tide was coming in. Another two hours and it all would be under water. Then there was a thunderous cry that cut the air and ping-ponged ahead through the formless shadows. One of them, a young lad, had drifted away from his parents and siblings to just below where Isabeau was standing. Head down, he had wandered off unknowingly. He was bent over, digging out cockles from the cold mud when his gaze lit upon her body. "Here, over here!" he screamed, backing away, pointing into the shadows in front of him. Slowly, people moved in his direction, then they began to run as screams and cries rang out into the night. They all began to gather below her. Several of the onlookers turned and looked up at Isabeau from the sand, there was nothing left but to retreat against the railing, and with her back turned to them, she was sure it was quite a noticeable sign of guilt; at least it seemed so in her mind. Why was she there? She knew where the body was, but why come here and place her face at the scene of the crime? She turned and made her way back toward the heart of town. Then she heard the horse and turned and watched in horror, as the thundering hooves dug deep into the wet marshland soil as the swarthy rider hunched into the beast beneath him. The girl's mud soaked lifeless body draped across the saddle's pommel in front of him. Passing brush swung back in rebellion as the maddened horse careened through shore side toward town, awash with eerie darkness, silhouetted only from the occasional distant glow of burning torches from the searchers which only served to heighten the rider's grim resolve.

The next evening curiosity—that foul tormentor—pulled Isabeau back to the city streets again.

Turning and in a turn of irony, there plastered on the outer wall of the building next to Isabeau was a vicious lampoon of the creature that was there to emulate her an obvious obloquy for the deaths within the region. A hideous interpretation not at all a glorious image cast of one's true self, but if any of us were truly represented in an image of our true selves would we be proud? She thought not, maybe not to the point of this, but still. There scribed upon this broadside "Bounty for the Murder of Abigail Walker."

Murder. That one word—that one singular word that held so much power that if added to any sentence it came screaming out like someone whose soul just left their body. Isabeau knew how the implausibility of all this would raise cause to a creative outlet, which can only lead to a myriad of ludicrous stories. She could just imagine the dissilient pod of rumors the non-creative Bureau of printers and writers might hatch. Stories once sprung, would snowball out of control, growing more damaging with each repetition these tales would soon be embroidered with the fleur de lis of fiction. She understood, but it still angered her that someone was out there scribbling stories extolling the real and fictional exploits of Isabeau Barnum. She knew that she was news, the papers always hailed her as male, which she took as a compliment to her skills and obviously was taken and used to her advantage. It was hard to tell at times from some of these placards if she were being feted or feared. Still, it crawled beneath her skin. It wasn't that she wanted credit for these horrific acts, it just breached her mind and was a consistent reminder of her actions, and for her, she was the victim, an innocent woman, declared guilty by an affliction, enslaved to a hunger of violence. Cast on barren shores, bound and burned for something beyond her control for the monster was not in her soul, but in her biology.

Everyone had heard the whispers, rumors of these creatures, called back hungry from the land of the dead by the ones who made them. Most were certain they only existed in the stories old women told each other while they folded laundry or children in the evening by the fire – something to pass the time, or to make other children want to hurry home before the dark. Everyone had been so sure up to now, before they were sure that God in his infinite wisdom would not have allowed such an abomination.

Suddenly a shadow cast across the sign and as she turned she saw a pale half-moon peeking through the clouds and found herself standing in front of a large, heavyset man, who had moved in uncomfortably close, well within her bubble. His face was darkened by the night at first, distorted by the flickering flames of the group's torches. Then it became clearer in his movements, even though bearded, was worn, torn and battle scarred from a youth, ravished with extreme acne and appeared as he'd shaven it with a rasp every morning for the last forty years. Then he spoke.

"Well, I do not believe we've met, madam," he said hat in hand and hand out. "I am the new Viceroy; Viceroy Burton Kessler is the name. And you are?" he asked.

"No, I do not believe we have," she replied with a gentle curtsy and offering her hand to him.

"I am Isabeau Barnum."

"The pleasure indeed is all mine." He went on pressing his plump lips against her hand. "Are we just passing through or are you moving to our fair town?" he said coyly, looking up at her from her hand.

"No, just passing through. I am staying at the Inn up the hill there." Shut up Isabeau, do not offer information no matter how trivial. She knew she was not invisible, but eyes of the world were so used to looking at her without seeing her—one person mistakes her for someone else and another could distinguish no more than her outline. She had become accustomed to this and built on it, to now take that for granted. She shed identities like a snake leaving them shriveled and pale behind her to blend into her environment. This she had nurtured to a fine wine, and now to make simple mistakes like this?

"May I ask Mr. Kessler," she went on, "But have you caught this terrible creature?" pointing toward the broadside.

"I'm sorry to say no, Ma'am, I'm told, oddly enough, that this kind of attack is all too common in this part of England, but I am new to this area, and I do share your concerns. But now that I am here you can rest assure, that I will get it. You may feel comfort in walking our streets day or night," he said, patting her hand.

"That is reassuring," she added, nodding.

"Well, my dear, while you're here in our Ellenborough, do feel free to call upon me for anything, and I do mean anything," he said with a devilish twinkle in his eye, again moving in uncomfortably close. "Anything you might desire."

Isabeau's eyes hardened, and her mouth twitched.

"Thank you," she replied. "I will be sure to keep that in mind, but, unfortunately, I will be leaving in a day or so."

"Oh, what shame, and us just getting acquainted. Well, this has been a pleasure, Miss Barnum. I do hope we shall meet again," he said finally releasing the grip on her hand.

"I'm sure of it," she replied, smiling.

He popped his hat back on, smiled at the Lampoon and turned toward the crowd.

Even in her intense discomfort of being held and touched by this beast of a man, Isabeau felt even stronger resentment toward herself for making this moment memorable for him. She was either growing too bold in her movements or too stupid to realize how she was not blending. She is, she thought, what she has been told by men and women alike as beautiful, and by all rights and with the knowledge of common sense she should be better at the ruse. Unfortunately, common sense is something she seems to have run a bit short of lately and scolded herself for being careless. I may be getting too nervy and just a little overconfident. She should have made sure that she was, well, deliberately plain looking. She could then more easily lose herself in a crowd, a doorway, or a wall if need be. Everything about her should be described as average. However, her attire was very distinguished, her person, very clean and perfumed, all well-kept to the point of not a hair out of place—one of her passions, a weakness really and one she knew that could have repercussions someday.

Suddenly, a voice called out over the crowd behind her. Isabeau turned to see the Viceroy working to balance his stout frame on a makeshift podium, screaming out to the people below. He started on about the girl, Abigail, and the terrible act committed against her, quickly gaining the attention of those within the village square. She stood there while the Viceroy did his glib and rapid office. Isabeau looked around at the faces, young faces, old faces, those who represented the village and they were all the same. They all had the same stone carved horror etched into all of them. The speech was intoned by the be-whiskered Viceroy, in a deep sonorous voice. Looking around, it was obvious to see some were there for the right reason, but most were the very dregs of English peasantry, and they reveled to view others' misfortune. His speech was a mishmash of words, some without a point, others just misplaced. He stood there making a semi-jocose speech at a most inappropriate time. Then he suddenly went serious, his face went blank with an almost gaunt appearance, he straightened his back as he prepared his words carefully in his head. The crowd saw this and quieted.

"It is time," he said, "Time to flush out the beast once and for all."

The crowd cheered. He had told them nothing. He had given them nothing, but in their minds it was action. He was a true politician, one who quickly stepped down from the podium on this last hurrah. The crowd around him moved in patting his back and shaking his hand. They knew nothing, for they only knew what was told to them of the deaths. I am sure those that were witness to her attacks, be their witnesses, could see the strangeness of the creature before them, and hear the scissor sounds Isabeau's gnathic movements had made. Sights and sounds that were sure to haunt them the remaining days of their lives. Isabeau felt sad about what she had caused, but almost found all this cheering and jeering and the fact that she was standing safely in the middle of it all a little bit humorous.

10

In her short time, she had stripped the glorious blaze of color from the faces of the small seaside town, casting a dark and foreboding shadow that ensured she would forever be a fixture in their mythology.

This, like each and every evening, Isabeau would gaze into the nearest available mirror, in hopes, it would finally tell a different tale—a sign perhaps, something, a shadow, a glimmer, an aura, anything. But each night, like the one that proceeded it, nothing had changed. This futile exercise was just another perfunctory act of her daily hope that something, somehow, would find a way to reverse the misery of her accursed life. Again she turned and walked away.

Isabeau hated what she was. Still, she had become quite deft at what she did, and even though it was to her and the entire world, both horrible and damning, she still had a strange sense of pride in the way she did it. In fact, her curious justification for the way she felt was that if she didn't take some pride in it. She might, in fact, be caught, or who knows what, and then she might never find her way back from this nightmare. It amazed Isabeau, for she knew the truth. Yet, the lies she continually told herself and the false hopes that she bore and used as excuses still existed, and even gave comfort. All those words that she should be in all rights-holding some devastating contempt, directed solely at herself for even uttering, are repetitively prostituted, year after year in some twisted and vain attempt to gift herself some spark of hope at possible forgiveness and peace.

***

The silence mingled with the sound of her racing heart as Isabeau stepped away from the door and onto the porch gazing out into the night. Then there she perceived what she had been too busy to observe before—heavy black clouds were rolling in from seaward. Suddenly, the clouds broke and God-like beams of light shown down from the heavens, and the land seemed to open up into a huge lyceum. There in the center's far end, you could see a stump as a pulpit to admit a thin figure which held back for a moment in the shadows then stepped forward where he now stood. This one, was self-appointed to represent God—facing his demon. Off in the distance, there was a triumphal clangor of bells swept along by the wind from the church towers, summoning their flocks to the fold. Isabeau sighed.

"Apparently it was time to move once more."

She now stood swimming before her exulting

pursuer. It seemed that every apparent symptom of alarm had eluded her. Apparently, she had not been as smart and aware as she thought. The ruse to appear as nothing more than a traveler moving through the area had not staved off the coming of at least one's silent religious revolution, and he now stood bearing down upon her. Isabeau wasn't certain that her secret was completely out, but on the other hand, they had now brought God into the mixture.

"Come forth demon beast," the exhorter shouted toward her. Isabeau didn't move at first. She just watched and listened as this man spout.

"Bitch from hell, I call you out."

She moved forward only slightly onto the first step off the porch, as he began to read scriptures.

"Yea, though I walk through the valley of the shadow of death, I will fear no evil; For thou are with me; your rod and your staff, they comfort me."

Isabeau took one step further down and calmly interrupted.

"Father, surely you do not expect me to simply climb into a confessional and narrate my crimes to you, do you?"

"You cannot resist. I command you, come forth demon beast," he repeated holding a rosary in front of him, now reading some ancient Latin incantation from his book. Isabeau thought he had this pernicious theory that whatever it was that she is, was afraid of the cross. She had heard of this before. It seemed that anything that the people deemed evil, they tend to throw crosses at it. Isabeau turned and walked back into the room and closed the doors. This one-sided rendezvous showdown that this rail of a man had envisioned was not going to come to light.

Isabeau turned again and, through the awkward cadence of the shadow outside, pulled her rucksack from the floor and lay it on the bed. She began packing her few items, searching drawers, and tables, just as Emily came running into the room. Isabeau looked up, at the moonlight through the lace curtains stippled the far wall and danced across Emily's small frame as she entered.

"Where are you going, what are you doing?" she screamed, throwing her body across the bed and Isabeau's bag.

"Listen, Emily, I have to leave," Isabeau said.

"Leave? What do you mean you have to leave? You can't leave me," she cried. "I, I love you," she said dramatically in her first declaration of feelings for Isabeau.

"I am sorry Emily, but I have to go, so move your body."

"No, no you can't," she said, rising from the bed and confronting her face to face. It was amazing how this tiny willow of a girl, once meek and shy only hours ago now stood with such determination and fire. Isabeau, even being a venerable woman, found herself summarily set aside by this child who proceeded to continue to shock her.

"You just don't understand," Isabeau went on.

"Yes, yes I do," she said.

"Do you? I mean, do you really, Emily?" Isabeau

said, grabbing her by her arm and leading her, pulling her along the way to the double doors. She flung them open and pushed her out onto the porch.

"You see that man out there?" Isabeau screamed.

Emily just lightly nodded.

"Do you? Do you see him standing there? Do you hear him?" she said, pointing out into the yard. "He is only the first, the first of many to come. Many I say."

Emily just stared up at her with those beautiful eyes. Isabeau tried to explain but her words came across more apoplectic than she planned, but Emily had to understand. The point had to be made.

"Oh, I can't debate about this, I have no choice. You'll just have to understand, or don't. I don't care at this point, I have to leave, and you have to move on with your life," Isabeau repeated walking back into the room, returning to her packing.

"If you have to leave, then take me with you," Emily said. "There is nothing more for me here. You know that. I won't be any trouble, I promise," she said, pulling on Isabeau's arm and pleading. Emotions Isabeau thought dead in her long ago now swirled and eddied within her head.

Isabeau laughed rakishly.

"Emily, you can't, you just can't go with me."

"It's nothing to laugh at!" she screamed defensively.

"I wasn't laughing at you Emily, I understand, I just meant it wouldn't be safe for you to travel with me," she replied caressing Emily's hair and dragging a loose strand and tucking behind her delicate little ear.

"Please, Isabeau, I want to be with you," Emily

begged, rubbing her face against Isabeau's hand and staring into her eyes. Isabeau sat back onto the bed, placing her head in her hands and she breathed a heavy sigh.

"I'm sorry. I can't. I just can't."

"I don't understand. Isabeau, what is it that you fear?"

Isabeau breathed deeply, dropped her eyes then sat down. She slowly raised her eyes to Emily.

"What am I afraid of? I'm afraid of those things of which I am capable, of which I have proven myself capable of doing, and that it might affect you. That is what I fear," she said.

"I don't know that I understand, but I am here for you, and I'm willing to take whatever the risks are to be with you," Emily said sitting down next Isabeau and resting her head on her shoulder.

"Emily, I just," Isabeau stammered.

"Please, Isabeau, please, you're all I have."

Isabeau raised her head and looked down at Emily's tear-filled eyes gazing up at her.

"It's against my better judgment, but okay," she whispered.

"Really, really?" Emily screamed, bouncing off the bed.

"Yes. Gather some things together and meet me out front in five minutes, and I mean five minutes. If you're not there, I'm gone. I mean it.

Emily grabbed Isabeau and kissed her cheek and ran from the room. Isabeau placed her head back in her hands again and shook it displeasingly. What am I doing, taking this child with me? Isabeau worried about the optics of moving on with Emily. It wasn't smart, with that constant monster whispering in her ear, but she did think the perception problem could be to her benefit. I mean no one would be looking for a woman with a child. Isabeau was again amazed minutes later when she made her way out front. She found that Emily was already there holding a small knapsack with Isabeau's horse, and wagon hitched and smiling from ear to ear. Isabeau cut her eyes at Emily and smiled.

As they climbed on board, they could still hear the priest's cadence behind the cabin calling out to the empty structure. Isabeau turned to Emily.

"Now listen, Emily, and I mean listen well. You have to understand that anything can happen, anything happens all the time," she said, pulling her face close to hers. "You have to do whatever I tell you, at the moment I tell it, without question, without thought, if you're going to come with me. Do you understand?"

Emily didn't say a word, just nodded excitedly, still holding that enthusiastic grin, gripping her knapsack tightly in her arms.

"I mean it, Emily. Immediately and without question," she repeated as they made their way through the back lots of the property and out onto the trail Isabeau had originally arrived. Emily seemed to be quite giddy with getting to come along and her love for Isabeau now not being denied although not embraced as it were. It appeared to Isabeau in Emily's eyes as an espousal in the literal as well as in what she assumed the Christian sense?

***

The two traveled most of the night, then, suddenly, a hard cold rain came, pouring down. Isabeau, luckily, came across an old abandoned cabin just fifteen miles from Ellenborough and the two set up house for the day. Isabeau again explained to Emily about her allergic reaction to direct sunlight and together they secured the cabin before sun-up. Suddenly, Isabeau heard screaming outside. She looked around. Emily was nowhere to be found. Isabeau ran in a panic out the door and there out in the dark, cold downpour, naked as the day God made her, arms outstretched, dancing, laughing and staring into the night skies, was Emily. It was ennobling, as well as invigorating. She was… incandescent. Her eyes like fireflies in the night, she felt alive. No skirts to hold up, or to draggle their wet folds against her ankles. No stifling veil flapping in her face and blinding her eyes. No corset. No umbrella to turn inside out. But instead, the cool hard rain driving slap into her face… and Isabeau again, was lost in her.

Later Emily dried off. They sat in the makeshift bed Emily innocently wrapped in only a sheer sheet, her hair still slightly dripping from her escapade. The lightning flashed, lighting the room like the flickering candle. They listened for a while as they could hear the thud of the storm sometimes, echoing through the corridors, or the creaking of the building's very structure as it protested against the abuse. Emily moved closer to Isabeau, laying her head in her lap. Isabeau stroked her damp hair as the skies outside continued to grumble and growl.

"I do so love storms," Isabeau said. "They're so, so primordial."

"I never liked them before," Emily said looking up at Isabeau.

"You don't fear them now?"

"Not now," Emily said. "Not while I am with you."

Isabeau bent forward and hugged Emily, and together they laughed and talked for a while. Then Isabeau got up and undressed for bed, and the two lay together side by side. Sometime in the day while Isabeau was sleeping Emily crawled under the sheets and snuggled up beside her, their cold naked bodies intertwined together.

Isabeau awoke feeling Emily next to her, embracing her warmth, her trust and she lay there thinking.

Here was this child, a rose grown in a concrete garden, beautiful and forlorn and Isabeau was afraid, yes afraid. Her mind cautioned her against this, for not only were there the moral implications to deal with but the precipitancy with which she would be allowing them to rush into this. Was this right or was this just thoughtlessness on her behalf, with the wanting of the animal gratification that this was sure to provide? Yet, to be with her was a benison, curiously exhilarating an anarchic experience, and she didn't want it to end.

Isabeau felt Emily stir and closed her eyes, slowly Emily crawled from beneath the covers and stood, leaving Isabeau balled up and sleeping, she threw on something and then went downstairs to the washing room and stoked the fire. As in all such houses, the grand difficulty of hygiene was the insufficiency of water. Emily went out to the well, filled two pots then brought them in and hung them on the chimney cranes to warm, then repeated the process. She hated the water took so long and stood there shivering in her jumper in the narrow room. Thinking of all she now knew and the excitement of the future with Isabeau as she would decant heated water from the fireplace as it became ready into the big tub.

After a while, she had enough to immerse herself in and just as she began to undress completely she looked up. Isabeau stood at the threshold of the room. Some unspoken rule forbade her from going in, especially without permission. The gap in the door allowed her to see more of Emily's body than she wondered if she should, then she cracked it a bit more looking in on her. Isabeau could see the illuminated form of Emily touched with a faint yellow and red halo from the flames that flickered within the fireplace beside the tub. Emily had been so sweetly bashful the first night she had met her. Isabeau had first looked upon her almost as a child with pigtails and grazed knees, but somehow overnight she had grown. No longer that innocent and shy girl too afraid to try on a gown and unveil herself before Isabeau. No, now in a matter of only days she was someone who had done her best to promulgate her affections toward her without being completely blunt and outright attacking her. Isabeau had overlooked them for the most part, pushing them off as merely the adolescent wantings of a child. But now standing in front of her as she was, she was no longer the child. No, she was a woman. Emily raked her fingers through her shoulder length red hair, and Isabeau just watched.

Emily's wants and desires seemed bolder, even brazen about them, and now, it was as if she bore a saintly aura around her, lighting the pale, serene face that so stirred Isabeau. She reached behind, never taking her eyes from Isabeau's and loosened the clasp. She then allowed the jumper to fall, sliding the length of her legs and come to a billowing rest upon the floor. A faint smile twitched at the corners of Isabeau's mouth as her eyes dropped from her stare following the form of her body. She had expected her skin to be fair and youthful instead she found her annulated legs covered with whip-like bruises from waist to ankle. That bastard of a man, she thought. She never noticed them in the rain. Emily saw the look in Isabeau's eyes which ignited the shame in hers, and she attempted to cover herself. Isabeau smiled reassuring her, and then she smiled. She then shed her shielding garment and stepped into the tub. Isabeau watched as she leaned over to wash. Emily's shapely wrists and fingers moved over her small frame and as she became clearer within the twilight. The horrors she had faced, Isabeau thought. The murder of her father which she more than participated in, no one would believe, for one so pure and lovely could emanate nothing but what was innocent and good. That innocence she would covet as it would shield her for now. For the moment, Isabeau could do nothing, nothing but deny her heart's desire and try to start again. She turned and walked away.

Emily saw the shadow as Isabeau left and angrily slapped the water. She sunk beneath the rim and screamed within the waters depth. Emily lay in the water feeling the warmth circulate around her, pulling the frustration and anger from her body, watching as it rose in small tendrils to carry them all away. Why did she not want her? Emily thought. She lay there silently proclaiming her love for Isabeau within her thoughts. The water slowly began to chill, and Emily rose from the tub and stepped onto the cold wood floor then threw an old shirt around her naked body and went in search of Isabeau.

Emily found her lying on the makeshift bed on the floor when she got to the top of the stairs. She quickly crawled beneath the blankets and snuggled up to her in attempts to warm herself. They lay there together for a while then Isabeau slowly rolled onto her side and faced Emily. They just lay there staring, neither one saying a word, yet so many passed between them. Isabeau raised her hand and slowly stroked Emily's still dampened hair brushing its strands from her eyes and tucking them almost individually in behind her ear so she could see her beautiful face. She softly rubbed her thumb around her eyes and across Emily's nose, touching the little freckles that she loved so much. Then she leaned forward and kissed Emily on the end of her nose, and Emily smiled, and she smiled back. Isabeau backing a little stared into Emily's eyes biting lightly on her upper lip, thinking intently. Then again she leaned forward, but this time, she angled her head to one side as she moved closer, then she kissed her on her lips, and Emily kissed her back. Isabeau adjusted herself and took Emily's small face in her hands stared at her for but a moment then kissed her deeply. There was no resistance from Emily, only submission, surrender, and desire. The passion and thirst that emanated from her lips pushed Isabeau onward. Isabeau went at her with a voraciousness that surpassed the craving that held her; it compelled her, this overwhelming edacity for, for, Jesus, it was Emily, and it was for Emily. It no longer was just the appetite, it was Emily who held Isabeau, and now that which so consumed her, she held within her grasp.

There was an electric charge as Emily's teeth raked against Isabeau's ear. She wanted her more than she had ever wanted anyone or anything and this scared her and excited her all at the same time. Emily's smell permeated the air, her neck constantly rubbing against Isabeau's face. She felt the urge, but she dared not taste her, but the control it held, she feared, was far stronger than she was.

Isabeau would pull back at times moving quickly in an attempt to divide and gambit. They were poor attempts and desperate countermeasures and the results shown as they stayed close upon her. Isabeau saw the sexy curve of Emily's small breast overflowing the shirt, and she moved down Emily's body diverting her unwanted desires kissing and licking her. She pulled at the old cotton shirt that was separating her from Emily's skin and feeling the deepening breaths of Emily's desire ruffling Isabeau's hair as she caressed her breasts within her lips. Isabeau leaned back and tore the shirt from Emily popping buttons around the room as she moved in and delved deeper down her body.

Emily looked down admiring the beautiful breasts of Isabeau lying on the round sleekness of her own waist and smiled.

Isabeau was flooded with euphoria as she explored every inch of Emily's body. Emily's hands gripped at Isabeau's hair, and she pulled for a moment then pushed directing Isabeau where she wanted her.

"Lower, Deeper" she gasped in anticipation. Isabeau gripped her small frame hard as her lips inched farther along the smoothness of her skin.

11

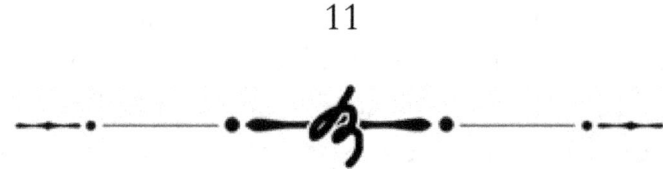

These are all the things that walk in your nightmares.

Just after the sun seated itself behind the mountains, Isabeau lay watching as the meager light from the fading day clawed through the cracks in the makeshift shielding and freckled across her bedspread. Tiny dust motes rose slowly in the air and then vanished. She reached over and pushed the curtain aside looking out the window, embraced the eventide as lighter dark clouds gathered, casting shadows against the war-torn cottage and creating a checkerboard pattern on the wall. Isabeau pressed a kiss on Emily's hair, rose and picked up her clothes from the floor, where she had dropped them the night before. She turned and looked back and saw the last of a slow lingering sunset, the light slowly dying in soft muted shades and her love's sleeping face and body in trusting repose backlit in rosé and orange fire.

Her childhood was mostly distant memories, an abstraction of history, yet looking on Emily her dreams playfully flickering across slumbering eyes, she felt closer to it. Feelings she had never felt before now flooded her mind, and she gave herself the trouble of carrying the burden—the burden of what she was and, of course, the subjoined lie that she was keeping from Emily. There should be no secrets in love—she knew that but…Still, she slipped quietly from the room, and the cabin without a word to Emily for the desire was too strong. If Emily remained here, Isabeau feared she would feed on that which is closest to her. Walking with a heavy and unsure gait, she found herself mumbling out loud like a transient chastising herself.

"What the hell is coming over me? This is not smart, and for certain dangerous."

She stopped her chattering as she moved into the next village which was much closer than she led Emily to believe. She looked up at the skies, now cloudless and pierced by one solitary star. The sky was pretty when she was young. Now it was just something to trouble the brain. She stopped, regaining her thoughts to become more focused and poised to search for that which she required. She wanted it quick and over with so she could return to the cabin before Emily awoke.

Isabeau tried to avoid the epicenter of each area she traveled. She kept to the outer lines and only ventured in when it called for nothing less, and this was one of those moments for she needed to feed. Calmly and surely she walked into the busy streets of the early evening. She looked upward as music and large flames rose in the distance from what appeared to be a night market or even some small celebration, and like a moth, it drew her in. For she knew where there was light, there was life. In the distance there came the white noise of many people. Slowly it started to separate as she pushed closer and closer to the gathering. She could hear women singing—old hymns. Their voices made the song round and full. The song's waves rolled over the tops of the trees as the sky sagged low, heavy with clouds, as Isabeau made her way closer.

Soon she found herself standing on open ground—a park or square of some kind within what appeared to be the center of the city. There must have been a hundred, maybe even two hundred people there. Crowds disturbed Isabeau. She didn't do well within large factions especially when she didn't have a chance to do her homework or have a ready backstory, well-rehearsed on her tongue.

Generous fires burned the light bathed the land in a kind of lingering dusk. Kindled at the bottom of deep holes in the ground, big sticks were laid crosswise at the top, and whole wild boars were hung from them and turned on spits. Their greasy, bulky swine bodies distending within the heat and their ungulate legs dangled loosely on every turn. The thought of the boar's meat turned her stomach. The men, for the most part, seemed to be manning the fires and the women, all seemed to gather in their groups or little cliques. There are too many here. I need to find that straggler— that one non-conformist within the gathering. Then far across the lawn, she saw them. Children—children running and laughing in and out of a small wooded area away from the main collective. They all appeared to be playing some sort of hiding game, and she smiled to herself, for children, for the most part, are an easy target, easily distracted, and easily manipulated.

She looked around cautiously, faces off and on staring at her. For a split second, she was there, among those blunt and hazy faces, looking silently and curiously at this stranger they did not recognize, and she realized just how vulnerable they were, for they had no idea of what was in their midst. She then slowly and methodically made her way toward the children, working cautiously in an attempt to make her movement seem natural and that she was just, enjoying the festivities. Trying to be natural is always harder than just being natural. Once you're aware you're trying, you're wondering if you're acting correctly, then you start to question if you're just being paranoid and it becomes a vicious circle.

A small group of four women suddenly stood within her path and began immediately attacking her with a barrage of needless and pointless questions to feed their hunger for gossip. She guessed to fill their empty and pathetic lives.

"Where are you from? Wherever did you get that dress? I haven't seen you before," And so on and so on. It was as if she was either unwilling or unable to speak up at once. They stood there before a blazing fire, the dancing flames casting strange shadows over their pale faces. Then her answer was delivered, muffled but intelligible, she made some small talk and her excuses at the same time warranting that she was in need to check on her child and quickly wandered off toward the small thicket where they were still playing. Her ruse had worked, she felt pride in how she played it off so quickly.

Slowly she walked within the woods, listening intently to the rumbling dirge in the background which seemed to play in harmony as the children ran around. The firelight knifed through the pine boughs in translucent wedges, backlighting the shadows of the children running through the trees. Each one that ran past her, she could smell as the blood coursed its way through its host and thoughts slowly overtook her. She was now in her element, she could hear with eerie clarity her own pulse, and she could hardly contain her excitement as a small child moved closer, and closer. She was good at this. And there within the shadows, the little one never saw her.

12

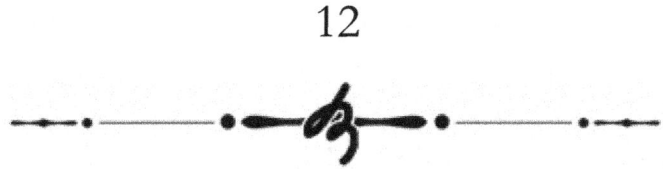

"If emotions were physical, mine would be a tangle of hooks and thorns."

She was just a small thing no bigger than a sparrow, her face now etched within Isabeau's memories, like the others before her. As she cradled the girl's limp body on her lap, she lifted and looked at her lifeless hands, hands more yellow than flesh-colored, veins running down the back like small blue ropes barely covered by yellow parchment. Her fingers were long, and although gnarled like joints on an aging apple tree limb, they were slender, and she could imagine how pretty they once had been, and how she may have grown to play the piano. Her nails were an oval shape and once well kept—that is, what was left of them. Most were broken or torn, red and ragged cuticles covered half of each nail. Four long fingernails—two on each hand—were grotesquely black with layers of grime caked underneath.

"When poets write of death, it is always portrayed as sweet and serene, but as Isabeau looked upon this child, she knew it was not always so. The attack Isabeau didn't remember, but that was not the oddity here.

Why am I still here? Why am I seeing this, never have I stayed the way I am now, and never have I been witness to the during, or the aftermath of the death that I create? No, wait there had been one. The girl Abigail back in Ellenborough. I had been so lost in the moment with her that it never dawned on me. Dear God there's—no looking at this child and saying she went quickly. What have I done to her that would have caused her such pain and trauma?

From the looks of her, she fought with all her might against Isabeau. She had harried this poor girl, and she was not even sure why. Did she get some sickening perverted kick out of this, like a hunter who hunts for trophies or more, was it her body's need for nourishment? No, a child like this she could have taken quietly and quickly. This appeared more like a cat with a mouse. She had played with her—a long drawn out playful bit of torture. But why?

She glanced up and down the street, wondering where exactly she was within this village. The night had moved on. She saw only a handful of people walking slowly, casually talking and looking in the store windows. Surely not hurrying, and most certainly not behaving in any manner that would require her immediate departure, but they would be upon her soon.

She stood carrying the girl's lifeless dangling body, moving cautiously through the shadows of the streets down by the river's edge. She stopped for a moment thinking she had heard something, listened, but in the smallest hours of the night, there was only the wind rustling through the trees and the faint distant sounds of laughter from the gathering across the way. Then reality hit her hard. She thought, No, what if I am. What if I am still? She closed her eyes and lifted one hand in vain and stared horrified. For there before her, were fingers long and gravid, knuckles like knots in a rope, and nails—Dear God, her nails were long and thick like talons of some predatory bird.

"No!" she just kept repeating the word. "No!" She dropped the child and fell to her knees gazing into the reflective water's edge and screamed!

***

It felt more like lace than wool as Emily awoke and shivered as the cold bit at her skin through the blanket wrapped around her. She stood. It was dark—so dark that she could barely see her outstretched hand in front of her face. Her frozen fingertips searched through the darkness for direction. She wished she could remember where everything stood and wondered where Isabeau was. Suddenly, like a dart, wounding sharp and deep— she realized she was alone, or was she? All she knew was that she had an instinctive desire to flee from something lurking there in the darkness. She wanted to call out for Isabeau, but if she did, it would know where she was, or maybe worse, she would know where it was. Emily halted when her fingers touched something, it felt like a person yet hard and cold.

"Isabeau," she whispered. Nothing. She moved her hand left, and the object moved with her. She stifled the scream that threatened to explode from her throat and backed away, and as she did, her back brushed against the heavy curtains and the moonlight through the window exposed her villain. It was just the old dress form that was standing in the corner. She felt childish and a bit silly. The bite of early spring raised goosebumps even before Emily let her blanket drop. She stood shivering in the neutral light, the single window blank as a slate. Her toes attempted to dig into the wood floorboards as she circled the bed, trying to find her garments. Without making a sound, she dressed in woolen drawers and a waist rough jumper. Pulling a scratchy knitted hat over her ears, she flipped her braid-crimped hair, tucking it neatly beneath. She rubbed her fingers together in attempts to force the circulation to warm them. Barefoot, she crept downstairs watching the pool of bottom-dark take form. The saw-hewed floor beneath only imagined in the gloom. She counted each step, left hand on the wall, until halfway down when the wall moved away from her hand, and she was on her own the remaining four steps. She remembered this from her childhood, but then she forgot she wasn't at home, and the bottom step came fast, and she stumbled almost falling to the ground. She regained herself now that she had reached the main floor. Emily stood for a moment allowing her eyes to semi adjust to the night and her mental map layout to work its way into her memory. As she worked her way toward the kitchen area, she heard something snap.

"Hello, is, is someone there," she said as her carefree attitude changed and she nervously reached for a match to light a candle without taking her eyes off the black hole that was the kitchen.

Oh, how she wished Isabeau were here and thought maybe she shouldn't have ventured downstairs by herself. There was a darkly sweet aroma that permeated the air and an energy, dark and ancient, that filled the area around her. As she stepped into the room, she picked up a candle. Cold fingers touched her back. She gasped and whirled around, but there was nothing, nothing but the darkness. She struck the match and no sooner had the flame ignited when she saw standing there, mere inches from her, the face of a woman covered in gore from head to toe, fangs protruding wildly through her blood soaked mouth, and the match was snuffed out. Emily screamed backing away tripping over her own feet in the dark and falling against the entry wall, swinging her arms out in front, trying to push the darkness off of her.

She pulled herself further back against the wall, searching all the while with her hands for the candle she had dropped. A small sense of relief came to her as her hand grasped its waxy surface and she pulled it to her chest.

"Don't look at me!" The voice in the darkness shrieked in a deep baritone voice.

"What? Wait, Isabeau, Jesus, Isabeau is that you? What happened? Are you okay?" she said trying to raise herself. Eyes wide, she pulled the match against the wall, and it sparked to a flame. Her eyes blinked as the flame pushed the shadows from the room, and she adjusted to the new light and saw Isabeau backing away into a corner attempting to cover herself.

"No don't," Isabeau said trying to turn herself away from the light. Emily relit another match and fired the candle and turned it in Isabeau's direction. Isabeau turned her head and looked at her through her boney fingers, eyes glowing within the candle's light.

Isabeau could see Emily, her small chiseled nose, her mouth so delicately curved, which gave a token of taste. In the whole was harmony. The upper part of the countenance seemed to reign over the lower and to even ennoble it, making her usual placid expression thoughtful and earnest. Then suddenly like a wave of cold, her complexion paled, white as the bitten lip of worry, her face muscles contorted in the most unpleasant way and her tumid eyes filled with tears as she backed away shaking her head,

"No, no, no, no!" She kept repeating as she began to cry, the reality of it all soaking deeply in.

"It can't be. No Isabeau, no!" she went on trying to convince herself of anything but what she now knew to be the truth. That the one she was closest to, the one she dared to love, the one she trusted with all of her heart, her soul, and her safety, was also the one she and all she knew feared the most. She turned, clinging to the candle and ran into the other room screaming.

"It can't be!" Emily repeated over and over again. Isabeau rose and moved through the kitchen and into the next room following her closely. The candle caused the shadows to dance across her deformed and bloody body.

Why was I still this way? She had these thoughts, yet there was still another side of her, a side of her very much alive at this point, a side she could not control. Emily had backed herself into a corner now by the fireplace, trying not to look at Isabeau but still watching in fear as she moved closer and closer.

"Stay back! I mean it, Isabeau, stay, away from me!" Emily screamed. Each forward step she moved Emily was becoming more and more distraught. She placed the candle on the mantle, freeing her shaking hands. Isabeau watched as her eyes flickered frantically from side to side straining to find something, anything at all to protect herself with. Then in one move, she glared at Isabeau, her eyes filled with wroth, she reached out grabbing an old fire rod from beside the fireplace, then turning quickly, she firmly gripped the would-be rapier. Emily swung it backward and forwards, trying to widen the space between them and working till she found its balance.

"Stay back!" she screamed again. She lifted the would-be sword in front of her face and then eyed her foe.

"So... you've discovered my secret," Isabeau said. "Forever unchanging. My sins made, manifest only here."

Emily said nothing and Isabeau made no move, no advancement upon her, and even gave her time to feel somewhat comfortable about her choice. Emily then stepped sideways and steadied the poker in front of her body. Pointing the tip at Isabeau, she positioned her feet in her fighting stance and prepared herself for battle. Isabeau watched her bosom rise and fall as she breathed deeply to calm her nerves, and relax her muscles. It was apparent regardless of her efforts every muscle in her small frame was tense, rigid as a corpse.

"So," Isabeau asked, "Are we ready then, are you sure this is what you want to do, Emily?" The deep baritone of her voice running its course through Emily as she slowly nodded. Isabeau, semi-circled Emily, back and forth like a starving dog anxious to devour whatever scrap of attention might be tossed its way, crackling her long clawed fingers at her sides waiting for the slightest misstep.

"Don't make me do this Isabeau, please, just go away, and leave me alone," she said crying, tears running down her face. Isabeau could hear deep down at the center of this intense display, a bit of devotion and maybe even a bit of love.

"You need to stay focused little Emily," she said. Her eyes bearing into Emily's like those of a predatory animal.

"Why, why didn't you tell me?" she asked as the anger, fear, and distrust caromed around her like jagged stones.

"Why?" Emily asked her eyes narrowing again, as she swung the poker back and forth, her back against the stone framework of the fireplace. She stood there staring at this incongruous perversion, this monstrous misshapen, this façade of the one that she so loved.

Even through all of this, she still saw the woman beneath that she cared for.

"Isabeau, you didn't tell me. All this time, you didn't tell me, and I, I knew nothing. Why?"

Isabeau said nothing.

"You're supposed to love me. You're supposed to tell me everything. So tell me. Why?" Emily repeated.

Still nothing

"Why!" Emily screamed at the top of her lungs.

"Why?" Isabeau finally answered. "Why? Emily you're looking at me like that, holding a poker at my head, you see what it is that I am, and you have the audacity to ask me, 'why.'"

"You still could have told me, Isabeau."

"I know, honesty is best, but look at me. Look at me." Isabeau shot back, giggling a little to herself and passing a look only they understood.

"Please, don't give me that morality crap," Emily shouted, "We all know it doesn't apply in all situations, and it's easy for you to say. I trusted you. I loved you. You're the one at fault here, not me. You never gave me the chance to fail."

Sadness once returned to those beautiful eyes of hers, green and bold. Worry lines appeared on her forehead and the area of her mouth for the first time in her life, marking where the finals will carve her memories. The candle Emily had placed on the mantle suddenly, sputtered and sparked, sending momentary epileptic shadows dancing around the room, before resuming its gentle burn. This one act broke the mood, just for an instant but it was enough.

Emily's arms dropped, and the poker tip hit hard against the floor, then she dropped it completely and interlocked her fingers nervously. This conversation seemed to wear her down. She stood up straight regaining some of her composure, but still, she showed fear in her eyes and the tears continued to run trails down her face.

"I think I understand," Emily said softly as she leaned against the wall and slid to the floor.

"No, no, you don't! Telling you would have been suicide, and you know it, you know how you would have reacted once you found out. I am, even though I know what I am, proud, and in love with you and there are—no—there were expectations. Expectations, I have, had to live up to," she frowned feeling a bit dizzy. "Do you really think I asked for all this?" tears now welling in her eyes.

Emily said nothing else, the tenuity of her statement left little doubt, and everything was clearly visible through her words. She waited, though, words coiled for the moment to make her point again, but ultimately she was the one to take the higher ground and just hold it in. Emily watched as Isabeau's quiet, bemused and intent face returned to is normal state as she plumbed her empty thoughts one by one, trying to come up with the answer to make all of this somehow okay. Isabeau collapsed to the floor as her body writhed working to reform itself, and then she was still.

Emily slowly and cautiously worked her way across the boards and knelt beside Isabeau. Isabeau turned and looked up at Emily.

"Stop, looking at me with those eyes, and see me for what I am." Isabeau cried. "I am a Beast, a human, conjoined in the most unfavorable fashion. My life gulled from me, leaving me forever, leaving me lost in some synchronous nightmare. Never to wake, never to regain the consciousness of before." She threw her face to the floor and cried.

"Don't cry," Emily said. "You just have to be brave."

Isabeau raised her eyes and smiled at Emily's sweet innocence; then the tears began to pool in her eyes again. Isabeau sat up, sank forward, elbows on knees, hands over her face, sitting on the edge of the hearth.

"Brave, huh? How am I supposed to be brave, when I am what I am, and the totality of my love and my fears sits mere inches from me?"

Emily smiled.

"You're not alone, in this," Emily said. Then outstretched her hand and gently stroked her hair. Isabeau opened her eyes and pulled back from Emily. She stopped for only an instant before noticing her hands had returned to normal. Free from herself she grabbed Emily and held her. Emily resisted for only a moment but then thought how she had just witnessed the nudity of her soul, and through the tears, Emily grabbed her, gripping her tighter than she had ever held her before.

13

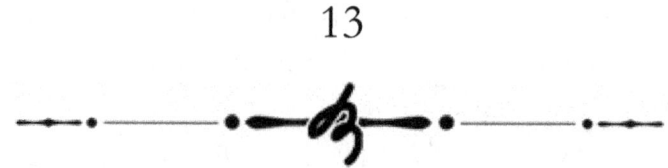

I must keep in mind that I am, or should I say, I have become, more of a hybrid persona—one part human, and one part whatever the hell else this is. But foremost I must do my best to remain human, to try with all that I am, to keep that part of me, even though I am to dwell in perpetual darkness, like some creature out of classical mythology. I am, I sometimes feel, though, losing this battle, losing myself. In this, it staggers my faith in regards to who, by what I can remember of the former me, for in those times they seem that I do not have one drop of humanity's blood left in my whole crasis. It is within those moments that I am the most frightened, for I know if I lose that, I lose me.

The next few hours, even though they seemed to have reconciled their differences and facts, were awkwardly complicated. Emily drew a bath for Isabeau, making the long trips back and forth from the well to the fire without a word. Isabeau sat within the room on an old caned chair, watching quietly and waiting. Once the tub was filled, Emily left. Isabeau undressed then climbed into the basin, slowly scrubbing, in a vain attempt to remove the night from her body. Then Isabeau just sat there submerged in the rose-colored water, dotted here and there with splashes of crimson that seemed to have a new life now in a liquid state once again. She sat there almost catatonic, barely moving, until the water chilled and her skin pruned. She sat there longer than she should have—teeth chattering, and afraid. She was afraid to emerge to the vulnerability that she now had exposed before Emily, and afraid to face the confrontation that was warranted, expected and still to come.

Maybe it would have been better is she had died aborning rather than to have grown, to have this as an indoctrination into womanhood. Emily had held her in such high regard, and she was to Isabeau like the light that shines on you, and sees you, even when you are quite all alone. She wondered now, would that light have dimmed and would the days to come, slowly turn sour. She wished she could have revealed herself to Emily unabashedly, carefree, open to exploring together, what she is without shame or restraint. But that was not how it was to be. No, she thought, but it just wasn't right. She was sure there were definite categories for people, such as decent, nice, evil and so on but she couldn't design herself to any of them, as far as she was concerned, there was no category for her, and she wondered if that made her soulless?

She arose from the cold liquid and stepped from the basin. Quickly she wrapped a sheet that Emily had placed there, around her wet body, then stared and sighed into the empty mirror hanging on the wall. Turning, she took a deep breath, then slowly opened the washroom door and walked up the stairs. Emily was lying on her back on the makeshift bed, arms up as they lay crossed upon her eyes. Isabeau, felt like the juvenile now, wandering aimlessly around the room, searching for the words that would have enough meaning to convey that she was truly sorry. She stopped, adjusted the cloth around her a bit tighter and sat down upon the edge of the bedding. Emily sighed loudly and turn slightly away from her. Isabeau dropped her head for a moment then spoke.

"Emily?"

Not a word was uttered.

"Emily, please. Talk to me."

Emily still didn't respond or even move.

Isabeau, stood, then looked back, to see Emily's eyes dart as she quickly covered her eyes again. Isabeau turned back and made her way downstairs. She went into the main room and sat down upon the hearth. Looking around, all of the former night's actions, replayed in her head and she put her head in her hands and prayed.

"I know you haven't heard much from me in a while, but I don't know what to do," she said in a whisper, tears running down her face into her hands. "The pain, agony, and unrest through all this abuse, I just don't want to leave as a hopeless child. Why am I here on this earth, doing the things that I do? Why am I tormented to think all these thoughts, quiet them, Lord? These spiritual battles of the conscious and subconscious self, who do I listen too? Tell me."

Isabeau took her hands away from her face, and as she did so, she found Emily was standing there facing her.

"I didn't hear you come in," Isabeau said quietly.

"We all have our gifts," Emily said as she walked forward and knelt in front of her. She touched Isabeau's hair then took a corner of the sheet and wiped her face. Emily turned her head to one side still stroking Isabeau's hair.

"You know, anyone who can pray, can't be completely bad," Emily said kind of half-smiling.

"You're talking to me, again?" Isabeau said cutting her tear-filled eyes up at Emily.

Emily nodded.

"It will be dark in a few more hours," Emily said. "Can we leave this place?"

Isabeau nodded wiping her eyes once again.

They made their way upstairs to the bed. It amazed Isabeau that Emily went to sleep almost immediately. If I knew what she now knew, I wouldn't want to be near me; I certainly wouldn't be so at ease as to sleep. Isabeau was so tired, she felt as though she could sleep standing up with her eyes open, but her mind was an assiduous blur of thoughts.

***

"It's getting dark Isabeau," Emily said in a vain attempt

to wake her. There was no response.

"We probably need to get going don't you think?" she said passing Isabeau a second time.

Isabeau moved this time, stretching on the floor, flailing her arms high above her head, and pointing her toes, moaning. She breathed deeply then let out a sigh as she sat up, stretched her shoulders a bit back and forth, then rubbed her eyes and face.

"Huh?" Isabeau said yawning. "What time did you say it was? I didn't sleep well at all."

Emily smiled and worked to help Isabeau up. She took the offered hand, raised shakily to her feet, then leaned on the edge of the cabinet frame, stretching once again and yawning.

They ate what little provisions they had left in the house and walked outside. Both of them were glad to be leaving, just to have this place and the memories it stirred, well behind them. That was the focus. Isabeau, had a renewed hope for the future, although she wasn't sure how Emily felt about all that they had recently been through. Isabeau thought that they seemed to have a lot in common, but they are also divergent in their personal mannerisms and in their emotional adjustments to life. Environment plays a much bigger role in our makeup than we would like to believe, and then poor Emily had Isabeau's affliction mired in there as well.

As they loaded the wagon with what little they had brought in, Isabeau stared skyward and watched as the lingering light was rapidly obliterated by the falling night and the stars lightly moving in, like drifting fields of glitter. The road was going to be long, Isabeau gazing out into the evening light, passing bleak landscapes, the withered sallow along dismally muddy roads, reminded her of the grayness of her life. They hadn't been underway long when they noticed the once salmon and purple light had transformed into a vast expanse of jet-black that engulfed the skies. The stygian sky—a universe of indigo, like the subtle sweep of a painter's brush, and the moon was like a glowing medallion pinned against a sheet of ebony paper. A canopy of now luminous stars materialized amongst the ocean of blackness. Some were dull, merely flickering into existence now and then, but others stood boldly against the velvety blackness, illuminating the path in front of them.

They both sat there, awkwardly quiet. Emily gripping her pack and leaning against the side of the buckboard lost in her own world and the one that was moving past. Isabeau sat staring forward, watching the path in front of her, manning the horse. The wheels bounced along the path beneath them, squeaking once every rotation, but otherwise not a sound disturbed the silence in the small wagon. Suddenly Emily yawned, which fortunately broke the silence, then took her arm down from the back of the buckboard and tucked her hands, as if to keep them warm, up under her thighs.

"Are you cold?" Isabeau asked.

"No, well not really."

`The silence returned. They had traveled roughly four hours, then Isabeau looked out, it was as if the night seemed to be trying to meld with them.

"Emily," Isabeau asked. "Reach in the back and get the front wagon lanterns and light them, will you?"

"Alright," Emily said still holding her pack as she was climbing up and over the buckboard into the back, giggling ever once in a while as the wagon tossed her gently from side to side. She looked around on hands and knees in the semi-darkness till she came up victorious. She returned smiling carrying two oil lanterns, her pack and settled in beside Isabeau once again. Then holding both lanterns at the same time, one between her legs and the other in her lap, she worked struggling to light them. Isabeau looked over, she started to say something, then thought, What the hell. It's keeping her busy.

Isabeau couldn't believe Emily was still there, still by her side, even after. She thought how they had spent sleepless hours in planning worlds they could never build. Maybe there was some possibility. The lanterns now lit hung on each side of the front of the wagon. Even though they were bright, it seemed even the shadows were swallowed by the encroaching darkness, as a galaxy of dragonflies and moths fizzed in through the beams of light, wings a blur in that magical space between darkness and illumination.

"Emily?" Isabeau asked. "What's in that pack of yours you seem so fond of?"

"Nothing," she replied, pulling the pack to her side, just opposite of Isabeau.

"Can I see it?"

"No!" Emily answered without hesitation.

"Okay, never mind."

Isabeau wanted to say that the wagon was hers and therefore what went in it was hers and that she didn't like secrets, but there was no sense in being pedantic. It was important for Emily to feel that she had a place and her own independence. Isabeau set the inquiry aside for now.

Emily watched as they passed an area of wetland moors where the water had moved in for the winter. It was womb quiet, and the water glistened, mirroring the dazzling assemblage of glimmering stars. The faint wind soughed through the branches of the trees and brushed against the water's surface, causing ripples to ruffle the stillness and shatter the reflection of the heavens.

Then the blackness came, scurrying like vermin from the darkness that surrounded them. It seemed to be crawling across the rail in front of them. No, it was coming from all sides, it moved to overtake them. Emily screamed as she watched as it seeped through the joints in the footboards and snaked out from dark corners and crevices within the wagon. Like an impenetrable fog, it soaked within their skin. This blackness had a sadness that emulated from it. It must have formed from some primeval hatred, or the collective despair of all those it's taken before. It closed in upon them bleeding into their shadows cast by their lanterns. Like Death, it began crawling up them as both Isabeau's and Emily's bodies almost inert, struggled to wipe it free. Isabeau whipped the horse, trying to move quicker through whatever hell this was. Death is a shadow that lurks within the dark. He crawls beneath children's beds and haunts the hallways and closets of our mind, and he is always there. In this was the horror for there was nothing they could do, Emily leaned back clutching her small bag in her arms and gazed up at the welkin, black only moments ago, now paled as if in terror. Isabeau struggled with the horse, now the fear growing within the animal as well. Isabeau pulled hard on the reins, and the horse came to an abrupt stop, throwing Emily forward and almost out of the wagon, and the shadow was gone.

"What, the hell was that? Why are we stopping?" Emily asked.

"Shhh!" Isabeau said throwing her finger to her lips, as she sat intently listening.

"What are you...?" Emily started.

"Be quiet," Isabeau whispered sternly.

Isabeau listened and gazed out into the night and found no other sign of activity. If anything, the night that lay before them seemed inimical to life, the blackness that had encroached upon them gone as quickly as it had appeared. Then suddenly a hundred feet or so in front of them, fire.

14

It is a dark root, with no name, in which grows nothing but horror and illness.

There were three of them. Well, at least, three from where Emily could see. They all appeared clean, well dressed with packs on their backs. But they were standing oddly, even across the path in front of them. It gave them the appearance as if they were almost waiting for Isabeau and Emily, each one standing in a blocking fashion, holding a torch to their side.

Isabeau slapped the reins, and the horse moved slowly forward, just a bit, maybe it too felt something was amiss. One of the men took a single advancing step forward, and the horse reared stamping its feet and throwing its head, panicked by the torches and the indecisiveness of Isabeau's guidance. Isabeau fought to control it against its reins then it stopped, and for a moment it was as if the poor animal was almost trying to back away, wagon and all. It was clear it was afraid. Then it was still, and it was as if the world had gone away as everything became deathly quiet. No frogs, no insect noises, nothing. Isabeau could hear nothing except her breath growing heavy and erratic.

"Get in the back" Isabeau whispered to Emily.

"But," Emily began.

"Get into the back Emily. Remember what we talked about?" Isabeau said slowly, quietly, yet sternly never taking her eyes off the three in front of them. Emily moved in around Isabeau and slid over into the back of the wagon's seat, her head popping back up, eyes just above the buckboard so she could see, and she watched intently.

"Isabeau Barnum," one called out. Isabeau sat there quietly not saying a word.

"You are Isabeau Barnum, are you not?" he repeated.

"I am," Isabeau said standing upon the footboard.

"And just who are you that is asking?"

"Just who we are is unimportant. You are to come with us," he said.

"And just why would I want to do that?"

"We were sent to bring you."

"By whom and where exactly would we be going?" Isabeau asked.

They closely looked at each other.

"We cannot say here. We just need for you to follow

us."

"What if we choose not to come with you?" Isabeau inquired.

"You need not fear us, my lady, for we are here to serve you, not harm you."

"Who said that I fear you?"

Who were these men and why her and why here? Her curiosity was getting the better of her as she looked back at Emily, wondering what troubles she was pulling her into.

"The child should stay here," one of the men called out.

"No! If I am to go with you, she will be accompanying me."

"This request is for her safety, for she is mortal is she not?"

"It doesn't matter, what she is, or I am, she goes, or I don't."

The three looked at each other and silently agreed.

"Very well, but we are not held accountable for her safety."

"You are not." Isabeau agreed.

"Isabeau, what do they want?" Emily whispered from behind the seat.

"I do not know yet, but for some odd reason, I feel I must follow."

The three travelers moved from the road and out through the forest. Isabeau and Emily still in the wagon holding on as it bucked and bounced through the rougher terrain as it followed slowly behind. The path they took had them working only through small trees maybe two to three feet in height which the horse and wagon could handle, but she wondered what was in store for them, and, just where they were heading. This isn't safe. They couldn't turn the wagon quickly here. This could be bad. Isabeau worried she had led them astray. Then, they came to a place where the trees grew strong, and one of the men turned and announced that they would have to abandon the wagon for now. Isabeau agreeing climbed down from the wagon and helped Emily, who still held firmly to the small bag in her arms, gripping it white knuckled like a security blanket.

They followed now on foot, as heavy underbrush choked the ground and thin mists clung to it, unwilling to disappear back into the void. It seemed to close in around them, confining their world to mere meters. The air was thick with moisture. Brambles pulled at Emily's dress as the wind whispered through the twirling leaves bringing a cold but woody smell. Oddly it gave Emily a feeling of security, a sense of familiarity and she embraced it. Never had Emily noticed the forest more, and never at night. The sheer opulence of it, to be surrounded by nature, was in a way, humbling and empowering all at the same time. She followed behind, eyes raised, walking through this city of giants, beneath the moss veiled trail and leafy canopy. Moonlight filtered through here and there in spots that seemed as bright as daylight and the shadows of the trees were blacker than the light between the stars, casting creepily down upon her. It was magnificent.

"Emily, keep up," Isabeau called from further ahead.

"I'm here, don't worry," Emily replied picking up her pace as she returned from her daydreaming.

Isabeau was starting to get impatient. Just how far was this, what was this, and where were they taking them? No more than this thought had crossed her mind, then they suddenly stopped.

"There." One of the men pointed out in front of them.

Isabeau looked and could just make out through the mist and trees the shadowy form of what appeared to be some sort of a structure—a house perhaps, with its prodigious cyclopean walls and the promise of a hungry fire with the push of a single chimney rising into the night skies. As it grew closer, they could see it was much smaller than it had appeared from the trail. It was maybe fifty by fifty, battle-worn and neglected. An old oak tree stood guard in the corner. Isabeau stopped, gazing out at the dilapidated house, the walls showed black decay from neglect, but still luscious roses lined the outer walls. Bright red buttery caramels formed a cornice on every window and like jellied gumdrops stick up in cone-shaped mounds along the roof. They even grew wildly in thick batches along its side, and for a single moment, she thought of Anthea.

The door stood dark and ominous, wet with rot and almost completely covered in vines and polypore mushrooms. One of the men attempted to open the door, but it did not give way easily, a forceful push was required, and it creaked as the clinging vines attempted to deny them entry. Once entered Isabeau noticed a jagged hole through the single window frame on the far wall, infested with vines and the tattered curtains surrounding it shook like they were laughing in the breeze. Isabeau noticed that the place was quite sparse, with the exception of a few chairs, one small table, and an old bedstead disassembled leaning off in one corner. She also noticed a fireplace on the far wall. As the others entered with candles, sharp shadows roamed around the room and cobwebs billowed in the draft. Shafts of light burst through gaps in the roof and black and grey-green mold dotted the ceiling in clusters, evidence of rain seeping through.

One of the men lit a fire and knelt stirring it until it blazed. The feeling of awkwardness yet security smothered Isabeau like the newly warm air. For some odd reason, she felt like she should be here and felt little to no fear. Emily moved in behind Isabeau in the old structure and noticed how the inside smelled of fresh cut grass and cedar, and she too felt oddly safe.

"Please," one of the three asked of them. "Sit."

They all took their places and sat there planted in the center of the room in silence while the smell of the old walls seeped in around them. He had that short hairstyle which is neither, laid-back, formal, or even attempted to be styled either way. Just short and choppy. The second had little to no distinguishing characteristics. He just blended, in a way that Isabeau almost envied. The taller of the three's gaze burns into her as he stares, and Isabeau realized that she was doing the same. He was beautiful, different from the others, perfectly put together. He had a thick studded belt looped around his trim waist, drawing her eyes back up to those striking hazel eyes. He lifted a hand to nervously run through his hair, ducking his head and letting the longer lengths of his hair fall forward. He was just too perfect, and Isabeau didn't trust this wolf in sheep's clothing.

Finally, the tallest man again spoke.

"I am Samuel, this is Joshua and Merritt," he said pointing each of the other two men out.

"Okay," Isabeau said. "Now we've met, maybe one of you, can tell me just exactly why we are here and more, why was this done with such celerity?"

The three men all looked at each other for a moment.

"We will come directly to the point." Samuel started as he sat down and pulled his pack off its iron buckles clanging as he lay it heavy on the table in front of him.

"We have traveled here from the Americas to find you."

"To find me?" she questioned.

"Yes, you are Isabeau Barnum, a vampire, daughter of Ressa, granddaughter of Kahil, and by right of bite you are our queen."

"Vampire, Queen? What the hell is that supposed to mean? " Isabeau said trailing it with a bit of a laughter. "My late mother's name was Jeanette. I've never met you or any of these people. I am not sure what you mean by Vampire and the whole right of bite thing. I really just don't understand. Now if you have brought us out here for some nonsense, I can assure you, that this is not the least bit funny".

"This is not a joke," Samuel began. The men begin

to explain each item as Isabeau and Emily sat and listened.

The man's words flowed from him like silk— sounding slick, refined, practiced and lacking any of the desperation Isabeau would be expecting after hearing their initial introduction. She listened but kept an open mind to the fact that all of this could be a ruse of some kind. Emily sat next to her nervously clutching at the bag in her arms. The room grew colder with each word. Emily shivered rubbed her nose on her sleeve all the time keeping her eyes glued to the men sitting before them. Everything they said, Emily observed that Isabeau just bobbed in agreement. The mood was uncanny, with strange perturbations in the atmosphere. The abstruse word choices seemed purposely jarring. What did they want? Was this real? To what purpose did all this hold? They continued to speak. Numinous – supernatural, mysterious, and awe-inspiring. Isabeau's life now unfolded in an atmosphere of mildly magical realism: a numinous shimmer at the edges of the everyday.

The travelers, with their pinched, ferocious expressions, tried to explain. All the while, they projected an aura of paranoia mixed with anxiety that permeated the area, and Isabeau was left not knowing what to believe. At odd intervals, each one would rise from the table and check the view out the window, and the door then would return without a word or motion to the others. What were they looking for? What were they waiting on? To be honest, she looked on all of this as pure folly, at first, believing it was just her perfervid imagination or that these men had recently escaped from some local asylum. But the more they spoke, the more the lines connected, and with each connection, whether she wanted to admit it or not, led closer and closer to her. When it was that they seemed to have finished, she sat for a few moments in silence before speaking, trying to let it all soak in, so to speak. Could this be true? It was frightening because it is inexplicable and also because man is an animal not far removed from the cave. The unreasoning fear of the dark and the unknown, remain lodged in the heart of modern man. No matter what common sense told her, the latter was still there.

Isabeau's eyebrows furrowed, and a scowl of confusion crossed her face, as she leaned back in her chair and drew in a deep breath.

"I don't know? I'm sorry I just don't know if I believe all of this. It's all just, just, all too magical and mythological to be real."

Deliberately languid, slow to rise to a dignified height, his handsomely graying wavy hair perfectly combed, Samuel sat most of the conversation with his long legs sprawled under the table. Suddenly he straightens and leans forward. His face mere inches from Isabeau's.

"Let me ask you this, my lady. Do you believe in God?" Samuel stated, slightly grinning, not blinking as he stared continuously at Isabeau. In all of Isabeau's years, she had never had the question so boldly laid before her? Instead of answering it she searched for safety for she knew what they were looking for, an answer, an answer to leave a foothold on a lyceum that they could preach from.

"Let me put it this way," Isabeau began. "I will be the first to concede, that both of the stories of Heaven and Hell and the stories of vampires, if I may consider them all separate and distinct genres, require an unusual leap of imagination, or hallucination. I mean, let's be honest. Vampires—why they're pure folklore."

"I don't understand your reservations or your confusion," Samuel asked. "Your way of thought my lady. I mean you can obviously prove what you are. God, on the other hand, seems a little less viable if I may say so. But it doesn't matter, for the serpent will still strike whether you believe in it or not."

Isabeau made a quick overview of the situation, attempting to colligate the loose ends of a somewhat fragmented book, but what they were saying, every damn word, actually made her think and as they spoke the history. It just continued to unfold. In the meanwhile, her hands were trembling. Her feet were cold, and she was filled with a mixture of excitement and dread. They explained that the fact that she was bitten and now born a vampire. They explained that the one who bit her, the one she had in-turn killed, was natural and, therefore, more a rite of passage, than a murder. In these facts, created cause and effect, therefore, she was then to assume the position of this less fortunate vampire, which made her queen. Isabeau wasn't exactly sure what that meant to her, but her curiosity had been piqued. They had just showed Isabeau the implacable facts of existence, illusions, deceptions, and the identity that the greatest mystery is found in the unsheathed reality of itself.

Their words were fluid and precise as they explained the order of succession that had ultimately begun with one they called, Kahil. He was, as far as they were concerned, the father of all vampires. They also explained that at a certain point in the lineage, things had changed. The fact that when males were bitten they were born sterile, but the birth did not change the females, for they remained fertile, and for this single fact alone, only the females now could rule. Females, unfortunately, were not able to breed with mortals and since male vampires were sterile, the only way to become one was to be bitten. Those within the faction called this being born.

The travelers took their turns, continuing to explain the history like each was given an individual script to read from. Their explanations were precise, informative and left little to no vagueness in their descriptions. Like the fact that if you are bitten then you were, therefore, the child of the one who chose you. They also explained that rarely was a vampire even created, and certainly not without choice. Isabeau's case being an exception, as she was the one who survived, even though they felt that was not the intention of her being what she was. The connection had still been made. Therefore the lineage was still hers to claim. The threads of stories grew stronger and stronger weaving together to form an exquisitely original fabric, bright, brilliant in color and tailored only her. Once her eyes were used to these shades, half the conclusions of fiction faded into thin air. Then they stopped and asked that Isabeau return with them to the Americas and assume the throne. They explained that there are many like her there and more could be explained there than could be here, this far from the faction.

"You have the right to choose your own name, be it that you wish to do so," Merritt added.

"Change my name. Why would I change my name? Isabeau asked.

"Don't know. Some do, some don't. I guess some just want to change completely, perhaps leave their former selves in the past and move on with their new life."

"I am proud of the former me," Isabeau stated firmly. "I have no desires to change who I am, even if what I am has."

"Very well," he said.

They spoke at great lengths, then like a committee they decided it was time to leave. The sun would be up in a few hours, and they needed to move to a more secure location. They gave Isabeau directions as where to go in the Americas. It seemed that there were two locations, the final location was an Island in the westernmost part of northern America. Isabeau explained that she and Emily would travel on their own. All the same, she succeeded in exacting from them the promise that they would depart the area forthwith. The group accepted this condition without demur and left Isabeau and Emily to make their way on their own.

Isabeau thought she had often accused herself of

being broken by the mistakes she'd made in her life, crippled to the point where she would rather cede power than wield it. If this was so, then why would she move forward with this power that is now being placed in her hands? In order to put into precise words in where exactly do their characteristic merits lie? She found herself in a strait, she found that the impression they made on her was powerful but indeterminate. They left her with the feeling that all is futility—all is frustration. That they are weak and foolish, hiding like she was and at the mercy of every untoward circumstance, often brutal and cruel, but something in her of vital energy protests that it is not the whole of it. She agreed to go to the Americas to see what there is there but made no promise as far as succession. She felt like the primitive female, having her entire world explained to her by these, harbingers of hers, and finding the fact that everything that she thought she had known, up this moment, was a lie. But, she thought, perhaps that there may be answers there, answers to a way out of this, maybe even a way back, if there was a back to return to.

***

As Isabeau and Emily made their way to abandoned wagon, Emily began to probe. She had apparently listened quite intently to everything that was said and had many questions for Isabeau. She sang like a magpie, with at least six questions a minute. Isabeau answered what she could but what she knew was little, limited to what was told to her and what she weighed to what was fact or fiction. Emily had been there through it all and Isabeau couldn't understand why she felt she knew anything more than Emily knew. Isabeau decided she just wanted to verify what she had heard.

"Emily, I don't know any more than you do."

"You're hiding something from me."

"Hide? Why would I hide anything from you?"

Then suddenly she looked at everything with distaste as if she had eaten too much of that mixture. She walked off murmuring wearily.

"We have absolutely nothing to discuss," trying to walk away more quickly but only making herself look foolish in a shortly way as the taller Isabeau easily kept pace. She watched Isabeau out of the corner of her eye, waiting for her impatient and irritated glance. But nothing came. This just infuriated her further for her attempt to suck Isabeau in had failed. The unique songs of the woods could only be heard in nature's quiet. Isabeau wanted to capture it, but you had to be able to hear it first, and Emily even though no longer talking, made her presence and her dissatisfaction known with odd grunts and groans and the occasional talking to herself out loud. She walked on her tiptoes trying to step on certain leaves, making a game of it in a vain attempt to remove the anger.

She had understood what Isabeau had been trying to tell her and Isabeau could have made an issue out of it, but Isabeau held back, which gave Emily precious time to mellow and maybe enjoy things. She went off nervously making a little braid in her hair, not saying another word for the remainder of the walk.

One of the things Isabeau found the most intriguing

about what she had learned from the travelers wasn't so much that there were others out there like her. She had assumed as much, knowing how she had contracted it herself. No, it was the unalienable fact that they were not so much tormented by this affliction, but were, in fact, embracing it.

Once back at the wagon, they decided to stake out a claim and stay in the back. They were far off the main road, and Isabeau felt they would be relatively safe waiting out the day there. She had decided years ago on the wagon as it gave her a place of semi-safety. If she were ever to find herself caught out in the daylight, she would have at least a fighting chance.

***

As night consumed the day, Emily moved the wagon back to the main path. Once there, Isabeau decided the fastest route was, unfortunately, going back the way they came and going on through to Maryport, on the edge of the Irish Sea. There they could catch a frigate or some other ship going to the Americas. They moved quickly, through the night. They returned to the Inn and made refuge there for the oncoming day. They could be at Maryport that evening as it was only an hour or two travel time from the Inn, but far too risky this early in the morning with nowhere to stay. Isabeau asked Emily to grab their bags and bring them in. Emily rolled her eyes at Isabeau as she went into the back of the wagon. The ride back had been awkward at best. Emily had wanted to talk about what they had learned with the travelers, and when Isabeau had not been able to answer the questions to Emily's liking, then she became almost angry. Isabeau tried to explain that she knew no more than Emily did, but this did not seem to quench Emily's desire for knowledge or tepid her anger.

15

"People don't understand that I do what I do out of need, not desire. If I could stop being what I am, I'd do it now. They have no love or compassion for me, and I don't blame them, I mean who sings a song for the spider."

Dawn had interrupted, and Isabeau slept, lying prone in the same bed, in the same room, she had paid for mere days earlier. So many things had changed in that short period. Mainly Emily. Emily still seemed to love Isabeau, but just in this brief time, it was... different. She loved her in the way certain dark things are to be loved—in secret and less forthcoming. Sadly, Isabeau could see in her negative way of thinking that the bloom was already fading and she feared it would not flower again. She had known from the beginning that there were no guarantees, for there never are. Time holds no guarantees—a month, a year, always, never.

Then there in Isabeau's sleep there came a whisper of something ghastly and beautiful. She opened her eyes. Still there was an eerie whisper, suspended, lucent, a greeting from Isabeau's mind that was like the touch of a feather against her ear, or from some disembodied spirit. There in her paralyzing half-sleep, she struggled to breathe...or even to move a finger. Because it, whatever this force was, continued to hold her in its suffocating grip. She closed her eyes as seconds ticked by, a feeling of dread settled over her. Suddenly her eyes flew open. It wasn't a sound, but the light —or lack of light – that had her attention now. She forced a breath into her lungs and tried to think. Staring into the void, trying to shake off her grogginess. Isabeau blinked into the darkness and listened. All her senses could discern was a slight chill against her skin. The curtains were thick enough to block out the moonlight, although its light seemed to seep in. It stretched over the floor boards in quivering dabs and strange shapes from where it managed to work its way through the fabric and forest's boughs. She wasn't afraid of the dark, in fact she never has been, but something was different. This darkness was all wrong. Awake now, she concluded the clicking of the closing of her door is what woke her. She was well attuned to sounds and knew instantly where a noise came from. It is a safety mechanism. But here was one she was unaware of. Her stomach was flopping with fear; she gets the sudden

strong feeling that she was not alone there in the dark...
A large shape partially consumed by the darkness of the
room, rocked excitedly where it perched on a rickety
chair over in the corner. Then there as her eyes
adjusted to the light, sitting, staring, rocking was Emily.
Slowly and methodically, back and forth, back and
forth, in an old rocking chair. Her knuckles white from
holding tightly to the wooden arms. But it was the
emptiness, the sheer emptiness of her almost chatoyant
eyes, and the cold blank expression on her face, that
left Isabeau unsettled. She lay there her shoulders
trembling as she stared, fixated on the vacancy of
Emily's eyes.

"Emily," Isabeau whispered.

"Emily," she called out again a little louder in
volume.

"What are you doing? Are you okay?" Emily didn't
say a word, she just kept rocking, back and forth, back
and forth.

Emily's creepy disposition spread like an aura of
heavy perfume that dispensed with the nostrils and
made straight for the spine. Isabeau slowly rose from
the bed and stood. Never taking her eyes off of Emily,
and at the same time too terrified to approach her.
Isabeau then leaned down a bit, bending to be closer to
her eye level. She looked so frail she could've floated
down from the sky.

"Emily," she called out again.

"Emily, sweetheart is something wrong?"

Emily's apathy reignited the tingle in Isabeau's spine.
She stood again and took a cautious step toward her.

This was driving her mad. Why wouldn't Emily answer her, and that rocking noise—that damned repetitive squeaking. The chair gliding back and forth, back and forth, squeak, squeak, over and over again. Isabeau thought she would scream. Then just as she took one more step, the chair suddenly stopped. There was no noise, no wind, no nothing. Never in all of her existence had the world seem so utterly void of life and sound. And still, Emily just sat there—not moving, staring off into oblivion.

Isabeau knelt down in front of her, examining her closely. Her eyes seemed to be transfixed on something, but following her gaze, Isabeau could find nothing to excite her curiosity.

"Emily."

Isabeau then reached out her hand and moved it slowly and cautiously toward Emily. Just to give her a little shake, a tap on her shoulder to wake her, if she were sleeping. Gently, she laid her hand on Emily's shoulder.

Emily's mouth slowly curved into a cruel smile as her eyes moved from nowhere to Isabeau. She then opened her mouth. Her lips peeled back, exposing long canine teeth. Then, she screamed.

Isabeau suddenly awoke and sat up in her bed.

Jesus Christ" it had only been a bad dream.

"Isabeau?" Emily said running into the room. "Are you okay? I thought I heard you call out."

"No. Yes. I am fine, I just woke up startled."

"Did you have a bad dream?"

"No, I'm fine. Isabeau felt awkward telling Emily

about seeing her in that setting and just tried to brush the whole incident aside.

***

Ellenborough tapered off behind them as they drove southwest toward the coast. Their plan was they would hit the Irish Sea coastline at the town of Maryport, taking the first ship they could find that would take them west toward the American shores. The war had just ended there, and ships were once again welcome. Even though it was a relatively short ride to the coast, Emily had very little to say. After sitting in silence for almost an hour, Isabeau could take no more and decided to break the proverbial ice, so to speak.

"Well, it won't be long now, a new country and a new adventure."

"Yes, I guess," Emily replied

"You don't seem too excited, and you are a bit quiet.

"Have I done something wrong?"

"Why do you think you've done something wrong?"

"Honestly, I don't know. I can't think of anything."

"Then just keep thinking that."

"Okay, I will then." Isabeau was getting a bit tired of these mood swings of Emily's. One minute helpful and loving, then in the very next breath she was, hateful, sarcastic, and even mean. Is this some teenage rebellion? Was she ever like that. She couldn't remember being that way. But she didn't actually have much of a childhood that she even wanted put to memory.

Emily sighed, and nothing else was said.

They moved smoothly, unfalteringly, passing

159

through the main part of town at a brisk pace. Their final destination was the rougher part, past the center of town, right on Munster-street and down near the waterfront. It was only a quarter of nine when they arrived in Maryport. They had made good time. The night scene of the quiet street was a collage of stark blue moonlight and bottomless shadows. Isabeau had wanted to get there as early as possible to try to find a place to stay, so they weren't subject to having to stay another night in the cramped wagon. Once they found a place that seemed somewhat secure to park the wagon, Isabeau stepped down, and Emily jumped down to join her.

"So," Emily said, climbing down from the wagon. "Just where do we start?"

Isabeau walked up to Emily and put her hand on her shoulder.

"Emily, I know you're not going to like this, but I need for you to stay here, with the wagon," Isabeau said.

"But I wanted to go with you," she replied in a whining voice.

"I know. I want you to go with me too. I want you with me always, but if we leave the wagon unguarded, everything might be stolen. I shouldn't be long, and then we can have our own place for a while." Isabeau explained.

"No one is going to take anything. What the hell is there to take anyway?"

"We can't take that chance. Everything we have is in that wagon."

"Oh, fine. All right then," Emily said, kicking a stone and climbing back into the seat of the wagon.

"Stay with it okay? I need you to protect it."

"I will. You just hurry back. I do have a life, you know," she said sitting down in her seat, arms crossed in defiance.

Emily's tone was a little more brass than it had been before. Was this just teenage rebellion that she had heard of or was there something else? Something more, something she was not owning up to?

Isabeau set off toward the harbor. She walked freely, for the hunger was not with her. She loved when she was around others, and she felt this way. Tonight was one of those times for the streets were busy. In fact, the streets are where Maryport happens. Life is lived here in all its chaotic glory. It's bustling, noisy and rather dirty. There is sometimes shocking poverty on display, but it presents the most striking example of a lively continuity. Isabeau went down to the pier to the shipping office first, to find out when the next ship left for the Americas. Once she found out that it was almost a fortnight she was off trying to find them shelter. She had only walked around the first corner from the shipping office when she saw it.

In the corner, barely visible within the windows light, there stood a sign "House for let." Isabeau turned, then walked up to the house and knocked just few timid taps. A dog inside immediately began barking at her, which set the other dogs in the neighborhood barking. There was movement inside. She could hear it. Suddenly she heard the bolt slide, and as it opened, a shadow lurched from the open doorway. An elderly woman emerged wearing a scowl beneath tired eyes. Her hair was dark and unkempt and had what appeared to be most or all of her teeth, a sign of at least once obvious means. She stood hunched looking up at Isabeau from the door frame.

"Yes, can I?" the woman said pausing, her high pitched voice screeching out the words, then just stood there staring at Isabeau as if she were looking into the face of death, then shakily she finished her thought. "Can I, help you?"

"Yes," Isabeau said. "I hope so. I am looking for lodging. I'd like a house, near or overlooking the harbor. I'm awaiting a boat, you see."

"Why would a young lady like you need a house? You don't need a house. I can rent you a room for much less."

"No," Isabeau said. "I am not on my own. There are two of us."

"What? Your husband?" The old woman asked as a part of her inquisition.

"No, a, a friend," Isabeau replied.

"A male friend?" she asked judgmentally.

"Certainly not. I'm talking about my, my daughter."

"Daughter, well, why didn't you say so? The woman said cheering up a bit in her tone. "Certainly. I only have the overlook up on the bluff. It's a bit of a trek, but it looks down on the harbor like you asked."

"Fine, I'll take it."

"Why my dear, I didn't even tell you how much it is. How can you be taking something when you don't even know how much it is?"

The old woman seemed now, even more, uncertain about the whole of the deal. She seemed guarded, cautious yet oddly helpful with Isabeau. Did she know something? What was she up to? There was some concealment. If only she could get a better reading of the figure in the dance of her words, then maybe she could understand what was being planned. There was a danger. Isabeau felt it. This was not the danger of the avenging justice of God that she so feared and knew was hers to face someday. No, this was manmade and near. Get a grip, Isabeau, she told herself, letting her imagination get the better of her again. The old woman reached for a key on the wall, her fingers curling around it one after the other, like a spider's legs enveloping its unlucky prey. Isabeau paid the woman but, unfortunately, the old woman tucked the key into her apron and insisted on showing her the house in person, and wouldn't relinquish the key until she did, even after all of Isabeau's urging of the futility of it.

The old woman talked ceaselessly, and she creaked as she walked like she needed to be oiled. And her cane, her damn cane it was driving Isabeau crazy. Click, click, click against the stone pavers. Isabeau was growing tired of her un-tented carnival act, and just as Isabeau thought she could stand no more, the woman stopped at the water's edge a mere two blocks from where they started and pointed out into the darkness toward the ghostly outline of the mountain that overlooked the bay.

"The house—it is up there, all on its own. You sure

you and yours will be okay up there, dear?" The old woman asked.

"Yes, it's only for a couple of days," Isabeau reassured her.

"Right, now you make sure you keep it clean and don't be going and getting on no boat before bringing my key back, you hear?"

"I won't forget," Isabeau said moving quickly off into the darkness, key in hand.

The air was crisp and cool as Isabeau made her way through the town back toward Emily. The light wind nested in each corner and prowled the sidewalks on invisible treads like unseen cats. The light breeze peppered her arms, carrying a chill warning of the weather to come. The warm temperature of the water against the cooler air created a drifting airy fog that whispered through the streets. Darkness had enveloped the sky above and only a slight curve of the moon shone as Isabeau rounded a corner, and the wagon came into view.

Emily who had been sitting in the wagon's seat when Isabeau had left was nowhere to be seen. She cautiously made her way forward and walked up to the wagon and looked around.

"Emily" she called out faintly toward the interior of the wagon. Nothing. Where was she? Isabeau had given her explicit instructions to stay there and to watch the wagon. Suddenly she heard some movement, toward the rear of the wagon. She made her way around, just as a puny rail of a man began to climb down from the back. Straddling the jockey box he worked to keep his

footing and balance while holding the few choice
burdens he had appropriated, from the wagon's bed.
Isabeau noticed the man didn't have the hands of a
thief. No, these were more the hands of a brick mason,
sturdy long fingers of calluses and muscle, all the white
and inconsequential scars that come from many years
working the hard limestone and granite. He must be on
hard times or just an opportunist, either way, Isabeau
wasn't going to have it. He suddenly paused, when he
saw Isabeau and gave a wincing smile, as his eyes
darted left and right. Isabeau moved forward, one step
and the man dropped his load and fell head over feet to
the ground. He quickly regained his footing and ran
limping off into the night. Isabeau shook her head and
began the task of picking up the packages he had
dropped and placing them back into the bed of the
wagon.

"Where is that girl?"

Once that was completed, Isabeau began looking
around, trying to search for Emily and at the same time
keep the wagon in some sort of view for safeties sake.
It was then she noticed the Alehouse, there at the end
of the street beneath a sign that read Grasslot. She
could hear the blending sounds of chatter, music, and
laughter all fermented by the alcohol that she was sure
poured forth like the fountains of the Crystal Palace.
The front door was open. A shaft of light made an
abstract geometric shape on the ground in front.
Isabeau made her way to the door and peered in.

The pub was heaving with patrons, this was a low in
lot, what one would consider the very dregs of the area.

But these were the workers of the town, and when they set their minds to off time, they went all out, as it seemed they were doing tonight. The alcohol flowed freely, and its effect merged with the dancing shadows on the ceiling from the raging log fire in that delightful plateau of consciousness that signals intoxication as Isabeau stared through the glass. Then she saw her, Emily. She was across the room dancing with a man no less. He was, at least, thirty years her senior. Isabeau stood and watched as Emily, slowly and what seemed affectionately intertwined her long slender fingers with the pudgy fingers of this stranger. What could she be up to? Isabeau closed her eyes and turned her back to the doorway, in an attempt to block out the image, and draw her mind elsewhere. But the sounds of the Alehouse and the scent of bitter – lingered in the air, that knowledge alone was enough to keep her firmly planted in the reality of the moment. Isabeau turned and as she watched the two seemed to move independently of the music as if they danced in silence, but to Isabeau, their silence spoke volumes about how intimate the moment between them was or at least appeared. Black fuzziness flooded her brain, and a lump was beginning to form inside of her throat, making it hard to breathe, in fact, she felt as though she might suffocate if she did not flee immediately. But her legs were frozen, and they wouldn't budge, leaving her with the faintest of hope that perhaps the rest of her would soon become just as numb. Emily then placed her arms around his neck and his around her waist, well sort of her waist. Isabeau watched as he worked to explore what Emily had to offer. Then the song stopped but this stranger didn't, he kept groping, trying to keep hold of her. She pulled back from him, and he pulled her roughly back against him, saying something Isabeau couldn't hear over the chatter of the busy Grasslot pub. He then tried to kiss her, his scruffy unwashed face, rubbing up against Emily's as she struggled to push him away again. Finally, she broke free and in attempts to perhaps calm the situation went to bow to her former dance partner. Emily bent from the hips like a lady, holding her waist straight. The man again moved forward. Isabeau then began to see, to Emily this was a game, a child's attempt to show she was grown up, but to the man she was merely something to possess, a means to an end, an end to a desire.

He grabbed her in another attempt to show he was not going to take no for an answer. Those around them laughed as Emily struggled beneath his grip. Isabeau rushed in. She cast a long shadow in the firelight, as it ran across Emily, she turned, her eyes leveled with Isabeau's. Her face ran flush seeing her fault and shame. Isabeau shoved the man back against the wall and grabbed Emily pulling her reluctantly from the building. Once outside, Isabeau began.

"Emily, what the hell were you thinking? Do you have any idea what might have happened to you if, if I hadn't come along when I did? Why were you not still at the...”?

Isabeau stopped, for there, coming from the building was the same stranger. It was that look on his face that was worrisome, and both Isabeau and Emily knew that look. He still had one thing on his mind and to him, in his state of drunken bravery, seeing two girls, only registered that his odds had just gotten better.

"Come on," Isabeau said, turning and pulling Emily down the street. The two started walking a little faster, arm in arm toward the wagon.

"Wait! Where you off to, there lassies? You can't be teasing a man like that, then leaving him in a fix," he called out, moving up quickly from behind them.

"I'm sorry, she didn't understand what she was doing," Isabeau explained, picking up her pace in a poor attempt at keeping him at bay.

"Don't give it another thought. We'll fix It," he said, swaying as he moved closer to the two.

"No, no, I don't think we will," Isabeau said.

"Oh, I know we will, they'll be no changing my mind," he said as he quickly grabbed Emily by the arm, pulling her free from Isabeau. Emily screamed, as he pulled out a long marlin spike from his shipman's belt and held it to her throat. Isabeau stood there, she had never felt so defenseless before.

"Let her go!"

"No, I don't be thinking I will. We got business—her and me," he said pulling her over toward the darkened area on the south side of the street.

"I said, let her go!"

"My, but you're a feisty one," he said, moving now up against a wall out of the view of the main part of the street. "I do think I like that."

"Oh, you have no idea," Isabeau answered.

"Isabeau, what do I do?" Emily cried.

"Just stay calm, nothing's going to happen. He is going to let you go." Isabeau said staring the man directly in the eyes.

"Oh, but you are the optimistic one. I do hate to disappoint you, you see, but I can't see that happening," he said, running his hand holding the spike down and across Emily's breasts back and forth. Emily squirmed beneath his touch, tears now running down her face, as the memories of her father overtook her head.

Isabeau could feel the anger growing inside her, and she worked to tame it. The sheer ignorance and brazen audacity of this man angered her all the more. Then suddenly like the unsuspecting chime of a clock, her entire disposition changed. And she smiled.

"Emily, maybe we should do what he wants," Isabeau said.

"What?" Emily said suddenly ceasing her squirming.

"There you go, that's a smart little lassie. Jakey, he knows what's best," he said the sternness slowly leaving his brow.

"Yes let's do what Jakey wants. Sounds like fun," Isabeau said again stroking his ego.

"What would Jakey want? Tell us Jakey, tell us what do you want? Maybe me, would you like me, Jakey?" Isabeau said easing forward with each word. "Maybe her. Oh, I know you want her. Hey, maybe both of us?"

"Now you're talking," Jakey said slowing lowering the marlin spike. Isabeau watched the spike, sweat flooding out of every pore of her body. She watched like in slow motion as it slowly drifted below Emily's breasts, then her midriff, until it rested at her side. The second she was sure Emily was out of danger, Isabeau lunged forward and grabbed him with one hand by the throat and in a single movement tore it free from his body leaving only his spine holding his head to his torso. Emily screamed! Isabeau grabbed hold of her and quickly ushered her back to the wagon. Leaving the body crumpled in the shadows of the street.

Only moments after, they had the wagon once again underway. Less than five minutes later they heard screams in the distance and assumed the body had been found.

"Emily, I am not going to lecture you."

"Lecture me? Lecture me? You tore his damn throat out, and you're thinking of lecturing me".

"Okay, enough about that. Let's move on. I am sure a lesson was learned."

"By who?"

"That's enough, just sit there. I have good news, We have a place to stay." Isabeau explained the ends and outs, and they went to find a place to put the wagon in storage and pick up a few provisions before the last places closed for the evening. It was that night that I realized that to save her I would murder the world. God help me.

***

As they made their way up toward the overlook the forest was heavy with rain and the trees were absolutely motionless. Beautiful flowers grew on the sides of the moldering cliffs, a strange vegetation of shiny puffed-up plants that looked to have no reason at all to be there. The late blueberry sprigs were yellowish-green, and there were cranberries as dark as blood. Hidden lichens and mosses grew like a big soft carpet leading them, higher up the hillside. Once they reached the pinnacle, the ground became rougher but even there, coming right out of the gravel there were primrose growing. They come up through the loose gray pebbles, their buds testing the air like snail's eyes, then swelling and opening, showcasing lovely radiant colored flowers. Looking out you could see out across the Irish Sea and to their left and right, the mountain pinnacles a thousand feet high protruding from immense timbered shoulders stretching toward the heavens.

Ahead of them standing like a shadow in the night was the overlook. They would be there soon. When the old woman had said it was a trek, Isabeau thought now that had been a bit of an understatement.

Emily moved about ahead of Isabeau, not talking or even like she was excited in any form or fashion. This whole off and on temperament was growing tiresome. What was going through her head? Emily at times seemed to lose her ebullient demeanor, but when Isabeau called her on it, she had a way of saying things. Her words were emollient and full of felicity but yet, there was still something furtive in her tone.

Isabeau questioned it all. The moment that they met it was something special. It had to be. There was something almost lilt like, about it. But now, now was different, she felt more like it possibly had been just an unhappy coincidence, a badly turned angle, some chance meeting of roof and sky. It was mere commonplace for at present, unfortunately, the magic was gone.

16

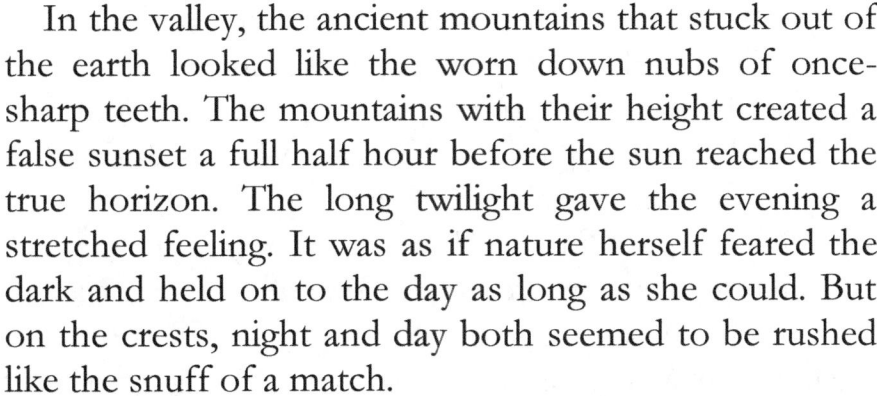

In the valley, the ancient mountains that stuck out of the earth looked like the worn down nubs of once-sharp teeth. The mountains with their height created a false sunset a full half hour before the sun reached the true horizon. The long twilight gave the evening a stretched feeling. It was as if nature herself feared the dark and held on to the day as long as she could. But on the crests, night and day both seemed to be rushed like the snuff of a match.

The house stood dark, like a shadow against the night skyline, looming high above. Its windows, like black empty glass eyes, stared down, as if daring Isabeau and Emily to move closer. It didn't make sense that this was merely a rental home. The ornate bronze and copper belfry gone green with verdigris atop its black steep-pitched roof stood more than thirty-five feet off the ground, with stone arches curling like serpents above fifteen-foot tall windows. It's scattering of other round and oval stain glassed windows suggested some absurd hybrid of house and cathedral. Its gabled roof dormers peeking out above the third-story eaves with blind-looking windows and striking the viewer most disturbingly, its massive, misplaced and somehow ominous size. It was surrounded by pleasant young saplings, the closer elms throwing shade on the lower half of the house. The shadows of their bare branches reaching across the yard like gnarled hands groping at the cornerstones.

Spectral clouds drifted within the night's sky, uncannily visible when no light is there. Eerie calls echoed through the cool night air. In the mountains, shrill calls were typical decoration. Wolves and other scavengers made their home among the shadows of stretching mountains and nearby pines and maples. Moonlight calls were expected. But still, Isabeau waited, shoulders decompressing. No one would find the baying near as disquieting as she did. She looked over at Emily and smiled, thankful for that.

They made their way up to the stone stairs gazing up at the covered porch. Suddenly there was a flash of movement as something rushed past them. Whatever it was, it was small and fast.

"What the hell was that?" Emily said.

"I'm not sure," Isabeau replied, stepping back a bit.

"Did you see it? Where did it go?"

Emily pointed quietly toward the bush near the stairway. She took a cautious step toward the brush to the right of the steps, then reaching out, slowly parted the foliage.

"Wait! There it is!" Emily said, jumping as it scurried up the stairs, now in front of them. It seemed intentionally attempting to block their passage into the house. Now, within the moonlight, they could finally see it. It was a cat. They almost laughed at the scene they had just made. This poor creature must have been feral for it seemed wilder than tame, mangy, skin and bones, its fur dingy, eyes weeping, and ears torn. It reeked of cruel abandonment—of things gone terribly wrong. The cat mewed and screeched, its voice ragged and pleading.

"Get out of here!" Emily shouted kicking at it. The cat screamed, hissed and ran down the steps and into the night.

"It was probably just hungry," Isabeau said moving past Emily in a position to open the door.

"It looked like it was covered in disease and wild to me."

Emily now stood cautiously behind Isabeau, like a child at its mother's apron, as Isabeau turned the brass key and gave a slight push at the door. It swung open creaking every inch. They both just stood for a moment looking through the black hole of the doorway before entering. This place had a fug all its own, a musty mineral tang, seasoned with rodent feces and time.

"What is that?" Emily asked, scrunching her face, waving a smell away.

"Ugh, something must be dead under the house or in one of the walls."

Emily found and lit a candle that was on a table just

inside the door. The candle illuminated the room in a flickering shadowy glow, revealing Isabeau's concerned face to Emily. The house was stale and smelled like mice—a sour stink came from the ceiling and walls, they were sure they were filled with nest and dampened with urine, but behind the mouse smell was something more sinister—the damp smell of decay. It seemed to be coming from the floorboards beneath them that lay shoulder to shoulder like the buried dead.

A quick examination told that the front room was much more compact than they both had expected from the outside. It was though well-dressed, adorned in beautiful but well-loved furniture, with its pale washed motifs. It was, though, oddly enough, even with the smell, relatively clean. There were carpets on the floors, made of colored tiles arranged in jagged patterns like a large quilt, dull dark curtains framed the windows and a large old ebonized clock sat as sentry at the base of the stairwell just to the right of the front door. It's bright face glowing against the inky wood.

The bedroom was on the upper level, Emily held the candle as the flame danced in the dark and they both slowly ascended the staircase. Suddenly there spewing forth from the brazen lungs of the clock there came a dull, heavy, monotonous clanging, tedious, lengthy and intense to listen to. The kind of noise you're not expected to have to attend in the scheme of things, a definite manmade noise, factitious, unappealing and synthetic. It startled them both in its brashness and tone and they laughed in embarrassment, again at their awkwardness. Once they reached the upper level, they found a lovely large room with an enticing formal bed, dressed in a down mattress and thick coverlets.

"Smells good up here," Emily stated.

Isabeau smiled and nodded as she moved beside the bed and lit the oil lamp seated upon the bedside table, and the room became bright and cheerful in an instant. It was done in a whitewash, pressed flowers in frames hung along the walls and beautiful gay curtains bordered the French doors.

"Oh look," Emily squealed, "French doors" as she quickly opened them and stepped out onto the balcony.

The cool evening air pleasantly invaded the room as Isabeau followed and they stood leaning against the banister, gazing out into the night. The view was wonderful. The sky seemed so large from up here, the stars stretching the length of her vision reflecting faintly on the tranquil harbor far below. It was as if the heavens were never ending. Their boat would be there in a couple of days, and their new adventure would be underway.

Isabeau returned to the bedroom and collapsed back onto the bed as Emily remained mesmerized by the view. Isabeau wondered if she were really up for this, she wasn't sure what to expect. She might feel better about the whole of it if it weren't for Emily. Her demeanor had changed lately. She couldn't just put her finger on it, but something had definitely altered her. But what? Oddly she seemed fine with knowing what Isabeau was and even where they were heading.

Isabeau remembered when she was a child, how she had once attempted to follow her father into the mine shafts one day secretly, but when she found herself lost, she remembered how the shadows had danced on the carved walls of stone, forming creatures she dared not look in the face. Her imagination had and would always get the best of her. She had never been brave, no, not, even now, when she was, and is the dominant species. Oh, she could put on a front, but most of the time, if challenged, she would have faltered. Perhaps she was just reading more into Emily's disposition than there was, again, letting her imagination run wild.

Although there was no doubt that Emily's moods would change, sometimes moment to moment. Unfortunately, there were no apparent igniters to avoid, no phrases, no comments, or words that provoked her moods. In fact, there were times, no words at all were even spoken between her abrupt changes in demeanor. It was just that her words didn't wear so well anymore. Her eyes were always wide and her tongue always quick to retort, a painful fact which showed no tendencies in the nearby future to break down or peter out. Isabeau wasn't sure what had changed, or why it changed, but something had.

Emily came back in and together they went throughout the house blacking out windows and any void where light might penetrate. Then Isabeau slept as Emily wondered around the old structure looking for any cracks in their strategy before she, too bedded down for the day.

***

By only the second day they felt the effects of cabin fever. Isabeau herself couldn't spend another day just roaming around this old house, waiting, especially with the silence between them both. The silence didn't sit well with her as she stood surrounded by sofas and tables and things that weren't hers. She had never been one to stay put for very long and being this far from the village below made going into town during the early evening more trouble than it was worth. Besides, it would only cause them to draw unwanted attention to themselves.

Isabeau walked aimlessly through the house. It was large, comparatively, and it felt grand, and though it didn't provide many clues, she imagined it had been designed with only luxury in mind at one time. There were a few of the finer things in life still here, like the piano against the far wall. This had once been an object of refinement, but now? Isabeau didn't know anything about pianos, but she knew this one even though the exterior was clean its insides were unloved and so it failed to work. She imagined that the only reason it was still in the house was that it was heavy and if removed it would have made the room appear vacant. Its presence seemed almost engineered into the architecture, and it gave the appearance of elegance in its facade. It was also nice to see something from maybe the origin of the house, even if it was broken. Isabeau pressed her finger to one of the old keys, cold beneath her touch. It let out a puff of dust. Isabeau pressed it again and imagined the effort inside as the mechanics attempted to conjure sound. A second exhalation was all she got.

"Isabeau," Emily called out from behind her.

"Oh. Yes, Emily," Isabeau said with a jump. "I'm sorry. You startled me. Are you okay?"

Emily was young and felt suffocated in the house, craving life, being seduced by the world. "I'm bored. Can't we go to town tonight or something?"

"We only have a couple of more days here, and besides, it looks like it's going to storm."

Emily walked over to the window and gazed out into the night skies. "It's dark. You can't see a damn thing. How do you know if it's going to rain or not?"

"I just know."

"Oh, you just know? I want to do something. I want to get out of this damn house. It stinks in here."

"Emily, look it is only for a few days."

"Well, It seems like a lifetime."

"You will survive."

"Oh, I know I will. You can stay cooped up in here if you want to. Not me. I am not staying in this house another minute. I'm going to town," she said, putting her face in Isabeau's.

"Emily you're going to stay her. You know that. We must remain invisible until the boat arrives."

"You're not my mother! Why you're not even my friend! Is this the way you were going to treat your daughter? If so, it's no wonder your God took your child from you."

Isabeau slapped Emily hard, and she fell against the wall.

"What a horrible and unforgivable thing to say."

"Unforgivable is what you just did," Emily said slowly standing, rubbing her face with tears in her eyes.

"You'll be sorry. You'll be sorry you ever did that! You hear me? You'll be sorry!" Emily screamed, turning and stomping up the stairs. Isabeau could hear the upstairs door slam as Emily further announced her rebellion.

Isabeau turned toward the window and gazed out into the night. "What the hell was that? Where did that come from?" Isabeau didn't understand any of it.

Isabeau's bones spoke of the storm, often hours before it came. It was always that way with her. Her body, her instinct told her things before they happened. She had grown used to it, even to rely on it, though sometimes she listened and other times she didn't. Tonight though it wasn't just the storm, no, there was something else coming—something different permeated the air, and she gave it her full attention. She wasn't one to frighten easily, but something about this did, and she braced herself as best she could against the unknown. The darkness crept silently over the sky as she walked outside and drew in the crisp night air. The rich earthiness laced with the aroma of an approaching storm was intoxicating, and one that was normally soothing did little to distract her caution. A lightning bolt tore across the night sky, but there was no sound that followed the flashes in the dark. Then minutes later a slow rumble grew in the distance, growing and growing in sound and strength then suddenly climaxing into an explosion of bright luminosity and thunderous roars as the storm ripped apart the heavens.

She sat on the steps watching the night as the rain poured down on her, blending with her tears. She was really worried about Emily. She knew that she had roped her into this by dragging her along. But, the way Emily was acting now, it just didn't make any sense. It came on her like a sickness. This sickness was growing inside of Emily. It was a sickness of the mind and heart, and wherever sickness thrives only evil can follow. Isabeau watched the lightning feeling the kinship between them, wriggling and writhing with the pain of its existence. It flashed once again, like liquid steel, silver streaks forged into forks above her and she never felt so alone.

17

Madness itself can be endearing, for in the moment of complete release from the world and everything you're supposed to be, there is a euphoria, and in this, a person can find the ultimate freedom. But sometimes, they can awaken in hell.

Isabeau opened her eyes; she stretched, then breathed in deeply and lay there in the silence for a moment, her eyes searching blindly for... wait...something felt wrong. She felt something, something warm and wet against her back. She sat up in the bed and pulled the sheets and blankets back, and "Oh God" they were red with blood. She rose and threw the remaining covers back from the bed and looked over at Emily.

"Oh my dear God!" The sheets around her and even her neck and face were covered in blood.

"I've killed her."

She threw herself crying onto Emily, pleading, begging.

"I'm sorry, please forgive me. I'm so very sorry."

Then she thought she felt something, movement. She rose and quickly stood, clinging to a pillow, as she looked down at Emily's body. She inched closer and wrapped her arms around herself squeezing the pillow tight as she tried to keep her wits about her. Blood spread out from her body, blending with the pink damask roses and seeping into the ivory background of the bedding. The candle light illuminated the side of Emily's face, casting long shadows from her sharp profile. Her eyes were open, as well as her mouth. Isabeau stood in horror, unable to move, mesmerized and terrorized by the sight. Time stood still. The ticking of the clock in the corner couldn't keep up with the metronome of her racing heart. Then it was there.

"Yes, yes" there was movement. Isabeau watched as Emily's chest slowly rose and fell with each breath. Her eyes and mouth then closed and she slept, her full lips parting just ever so slightly, to allow her breath to escape. Isabeau finally breathed again, taking each breath in slowly and deeply, her heart quieted just a little. Isabeau reached out and tucked a stray wet strand of hair behind Emily's ear with a shaky hand, and in looking closer, she could see two small blebs on Emily's neck. The full reality of it all washed over her now. "Dear God in heaven, No!" She had bitten her, somehow, sometime in their night. She bit her, and she lives.

"God."

Forever poised at the edge of adulthood. It would have been better if she had just killed her. There was a flash in her eyes, a moment where she was teetering between life and death, the pillow the fulcrum between finishing something very bad or starting something new. But, no, there she lay. Isabeau thought this child once glowing like albedo but now only through no fault of her own, now only visible as a dark scar, slicing across Isabeau's world. Isabeau looked upon her face, her words once filled with felicity and expression, but no longer and now with this. What would they hold?

My poor ethereal Emily, my little chastity, how my urging prayers lay apparently cast aside and unheard for I had no longing for this to fall upon you. Oh, is she made to suffer for my greed? Is this some temporal punishment exacted by God? She could see no other reason.

She worried her. It was amazing how quickly the days had soured. Emily's entire disposition had changed in just a few days. No longer the beautiful bashful child she had first found and was so drawn to. The fear had grown within her that Emily now wades across the gene pool of that bastard of a father of hers. Isabeau tore her gaze from Emily, turned and made her way down to the main floor, wringing her hands, intensely deep in thought. The foul stench still permeated from the walls and floor, and only added to the atmosphere and made what she had done to Emily that much more vivid. Isabeau took a deep breath and smoothed a hand over her stomach.

"I feel like I am going to throw up."

She stood there in thought. Emily had changed and not for the better. No, and now with this evil settled upon her world, what would... wait! Would it, did the bite mean that? No, maybe, could it be that she didn't have that ability to force that upon another? Oh, if it were only true, but still, guilt whined around her head like a nagging, persistent mosquito.

What have I done?

"Oh God please let it be so that I do not have this power," Isabeau said, expelling the words in a shaky breath as she paced the floor. She was, what? Nervous? Yes, nervous and a little shaky. This breakup was already inevitable as even just the past few days alone with Emily had not been pleasant ones, to say the least, but now? How could she abandon her now?

Last evening's conversation and Emily's crass display of anger had been the final straw. Something inherently had changed within her. Isabeau repeated this over and over in her head, reaching, searching for cause or reason. The real fight was now with this, and her personality changes, that perhaps she should be more than a little worried and possibly even scared. Isabeau had replayed Emily's words over and over again in her mind, and she knew she had to get out of the relationship. She had planned just to walk away, but now there was this looming over her, this guilt of what she had possibly mothered.

"How in God's name can I leave her now, after what I have done?" The question of how they had ended up in bed together last night was still playing heavy in her mind. She had no memory past the rain of the evening. Isabeau slowly paced, waiting for a theory she had not even thought of until now, a theory now being tested.

Then there she stood, Emily, a penumbra of the girl Isabeau thought she knew. Isabeau's mind labored, furcating as it will between the love that she felt but still frantically angling for the unseen truth and motivation behind Emily's recent actions, and the unknown possibility of the change that might have just taken place. Isabeau would never admit it openly, but the fear that now grew in her was ineffable.

There Emily stood, blood-soaked, arms at her side, head tilted, staring down at her from the top of the stairwell. Isabeau bit back the shriek, which swelled at the back of her throat, but it stuck, a lump which was harder to breathe past than she would have liked. She brought her hands up to her neck, attempting to work it down, but she couldn't steady her hands long enough to help. A tear track of sweat slid behind her ear though she was sure it was the caress of death, assuring her certain damnation to hell. Isabeau's was tight, toneless yet tremulous, as she spoke in an undertone and a ghastly whiteness spread over her face. She could feel her lungs expanding against the walls of her chest. Emily just stared at her with a grim and shuddering fascination. What was she going to say?

"Hello, Emily. My, but you do move quietly," Isabeau said as confusion herd her voice.

Emily smiled slowly, shrugging her shoulders.

"We all have our gifts, lover."

Isabeau watched as she slowly descended the stairs,

covered with nothing but a sheer blood-soaked nightshirt which hung only a quarter of the way down her thighs. Blood ran down her pale legs. Her small breasts translucent in the wet garment and the portion of her long hair not matted in blood bounced as she conquered each tread, looking down and smiling as she moved closer to Isabeau. Even at this moment, she was, beautiful. Her smile though, was more of a smirk, blood-soaked beneath those emerald eyes as if she had done the biting. Isabeau had seen this smile before. The night Emily's father died, and it shot through her like a scream in the night. Emily had some other game in mind, and Isabeau must find out where and how she was going to play it. She walked right past Isabeau still holding that damn smile on her face, licking the blood from her fingertips.

"Emily. Are you okay?"

Emily tilted her head, and her mouth lifted higher into a mocking half-smile.

"Am I okay? Well, I should say so," she said while running her fingers through her hair. Then stared at the blood on her hands, and giggled. Isabeau noticed the flaming rose that once blossomed within her hair had darkened to a deep crimson, which in this light at times seemed to become lost within the brunet.

"Why, I've never felt better in all my life. Why do you ask?" Emily continued turning and tilting her head, moving in uncomfortably close, well within Isabeau's bubble, her voice sounding oddly more mature.

"Because sweetie, you're, you're covered in blood," gesturing to her attire.

"I know," she said looking down. "It's mine, it's my blood," she said pulling on the night dress and pushing it down between her legs with both her bloody hands, moaning coyly. "Mmmmm, isn't it wonderful?"

"Did, did I?"

"Did you do this to me?" she interrupted smiling. "Oh, yes my love, most certainly. You dragged me into your world, the same world that has forsaken you."

"I, I didn't mean to. I didn't know, I."

"Oh, I know that you didn't mean to. But you did it anyway, and now, I am, what you never wanted for me. What you felt you had to protect me from, what you intended to deny me."

"Deny you, deny you? Emily, what in the hell are you talking about, deny you? I wouldn't have wished this on anyone, and most certainly not you."

"Well, how fucking noble," she said walking around Isabeau, sizing her up with each and every contemptuous step. "Aren't we the good one, how fucking precious can one get, I ask?"

"Emily, what's wrong with you?" Isabeau asked backing up a bit, as Emily just smiled and inched toward her.

Isabeau watched with mounting premonition and tension, for something was about to take place.

"What are you, what are you up to Emily, and what exactly are you planning?" Isabeau said tilting her head in thought. There was something there, like a black cat running from shadow to shadow, it remained unseen.

"Ha, ha, ha!" she laughed, Are we actually nervous? Well now, isn't that just amazing, her majesty, nervous?"

"What are you talking about?" Isabeau said backing up, now actually beginning to fear Emily.

"You just don't understand do you?" Emily said reaching out to touch Isabeau, almost with compassion in her voice.

Isabeau backed away. Images and conversations played through her head. Like seeds within sand, germinating, growing into thoughts that seemed impossible and unreal. It was inconceivable, but were they all lies? Had Emily stood before her each and every night and lied? All with that bedeviled smile on her face. All for the sake of a crust of bread, for the sake of a warm nook, for love, or, no, had she known what Isabeau was all along and worked her, manipulated her, played with her emotions, to achieve what she now held within her breast? No, no, it couldn't be, could it?

Isabeau looked at Emily, and the words ran from her eyes.

"It wasn't always. No, not in the beginning, in the beginning, it was just you and me, but once I found out just what you were. I then knew what I could be, and I thought never again, never again would I be the victim."

"Why didn't you talk to me about it?"

"Because all you ever do is complain about what you are, and what you've done. You would never have just gifted it to me."

"Gifted? No, you are right there, this is not a gift, it is eternal damnation. The hell you will cause, the human wreckage you will leave within your path, and Emily, Emily, you will never, ever, grow up. Never. And whether you want it or not, you will always, be its victim."

"You see?" Emily said slowing circling, encompassing Isabeau in her movements. "That's what I'm talking about. I will be just fine, especially now that I found out you're going to become the queen. Because as you well know, whomever you bite, well they," she said pointing at herself. "Will be your heir, and my darling Isabeau, to the victor, belongs the spoils."

"I knew there was something different, about you, but I had no idea to the evil that was within you."

"Oh don't play the innocent victim here. It doesn't suit you."

"I'm not saying I'm innocent. I've never said I was innocent. But I never worked to become what it is that I am.

"I know I never understood that. All that power and you don't even play with it."

"What has happened to you? You were so sweet, so innocent, and now…?

"Now? Now is now. Now is the fact that I am just like you, just better at it."

Emily crossed the room and turned to sit on the piano seat, and Isabeau ran out the front door, down the steps and out into the night.

Emily walked out onto the front porch.

"Isabeau, you'll be back. There are only two hours till sunrise. It takes longer than that just to get to town."

She turned toward the door, then turned her head. "I'll see you in the morning," she said as she closed the door behind her.

Isabeau sat, her face moon freckled within the trees, trying to decide what to do. Then there within the hollow of the night, Isabeau saw a single light, like a beacon calling out. She could see it, there in the distance coming from the overlook. Isabeau moved closer where she could see. It was a rear window that sat gleaming brightly through the foliage. Where Isabeau was she could see inside, every once in a while Emily would pass by the glass. Isabeau couldn't make out what she was doing, but she was afraid. She hadn't been afraid in a long time, and it wasn't a feeling that she wanted to replay. Isabeau had to admit that Emily was much smarter than she had originally given her credit for. Especially if she was outside hiding in a bunch of shrubbery while Emily walked around seemingly without friction or fear. She had to find a way to end this and resolved to break a yoke that had grown intolerable. She just wasn't sure how yet.

Isabeau remained a long time gazing through the window which now and again became obscured as the breeze swayed the branches of the trees. With no effort at all the un-faded image of Emily first setting foot in her life played before her eyes, the tiny girl walking up to help her with her horse and her room, the tiny girl who caught and held her eye.

Isabeau heard something, a single movement within the obscurity and quickly pursued security within the trees beyond the house's edging. She stole through the crowded timber, planting every footstep silently in the soft pine-needled ground. Isabeau now stood beside the stalking Willow, staring through the verdant strands as they churn within the gentle winds of the eventide. There she stood, Emily, hard against the sky—her thin, childlike frame now visible within Isabeau's own. Fear seemed to dominate her view perversely. She dared not move, for Emily had changed, and now even merely speaking with her had become a bit weighty and cumbersome. No longer illustrating the honeyed innocence that once had radiated so freely from her and that had so originally entranced Isabeau. Even through the horror and tragedy, her beauty still radiated, but there was no love left in her eyes. No, now she was much rawer, no longer eagerly inclined to conform but more to reject, oppose and fight, and Isabeau believed, even kill.

Isabeau, although she loved Emily, had to accept the inevitability of it all and find a way to distance herself from her. She knew this, and it had become a daily routine to curse herself for her weakness of another day and now if she had only left her yesterday. Slowly and cautiously Isabeau backed into the ever expanding shadows of the twilight until her view was consumed by the darkness. At one point she thought how freeing it was that she didn't have to hide what she was when she was with Emily, but now with things the way they were, she found that hiding from Emily was just as bad, if not much worse.

Isabeau hid as Emily called out to her, sometimes angrily, other times like a child, pleading for her mother, any ruse to entice her from her hiding spot. Morning was almost upon them, and Emily walked from the house, searching once again. The harsh dark blue sky hurt her eyes, bright like a child's drawing daubed in crude, unblended colors squeezed directly from the tube. She could hear the forest birds as they claimed their territories high in the canopy as the night slowly faded into the morning light. It was beautiful, and she was fine. She was the chosen one. She knew it. Then just as quickly she became warm, no, hot, something was burning. She looked at her arms, blazing in the early dawn light, and then she looked skyward just in time to see a great shadow move across the slither of sunlight and pull her into the darkness of the house. Emily looked down at her body still bubbling from the sunlight, and she screamed.

"What the hell were you thinking?" Isabeau screamed.

Slowly Emily rose and stood above Isabeau still crouched on the floor. Emily stared down in amazement as she watched her wounds heal before her very eyes.

"What was I thinking? I was thinking you would save me."

"Of course, I would try to save you. I love you."

"You're pathetic."

Isabeau dropped her head. Emily's words seemed to throw Isabeau off stride with her opening swipe. She was sharp, straight and spang on target with every gesture, every word. A bottle obviously corked for far too long. She didn't quibble, about getting to the point and Isabeau realized for the first time the horrible fact of what she had done. She had created a monster.

***

"Poor, poor Isabeau," Emily said, smiling. "You've never known this feeling before, have you?"

"I don't know. I'm not sure what it is that I'm feeling," Isabeau said her voice trailing off to a whisper, as she dropped her eyes.

Emily moved slowly forward, then grabbed Isabeau by the face and kissed her deeply. Then feeling Isabeau slowly start to wane, her arms inching up her body, moving to caress her. Emily suddenly pulled back, only inches from her and stared into Isabeau's eyes.

"It's called, rejection," she said, then dropped her hands and turned her back on Isabeau.

Isabeau collapsed against the back wall.

"Why, what, what has happened to you, Emily? What is it that have I done to you that you could be so unfeeling and cold to me?" Isabeau pleaded beseechingly, her pale eyes swimming with tears.

"What have you done? What have you done?" Emily screamed, running up to Isabeau.

"Until only a little while ago," she said pressing her body up against Isabeau's, her face in hers, "I had been nothing more than chattel to you, a piece of property as much my own as your fucking parasol."

"But that's not true Emily," Isabeau started.

"Shut up!" Emily said, smacking Isabeau across the face.

"It hurts, doesn't it?"

Isabeau recoiled and sat back against the wall,

watching in horror as Emily's eyes glowed, a glow that imbued a feeling of both hatred and satisfaction.

"No more, never again." Emily went on as she marched about the room, arms flailing like she was a conductor of some large orchestra. "That was the past. No one shall own me. No one shall rule me. The future, my dear Isabeau is mine. Do you hear me? Mine!"

She grabbed Isabeau by the face "Mmmmm," she cooed, breathing in deeply, licking the new blood from Isabeau's lips.

"And I'm afraid that there is not a damn thing you can do about it," Emily said, touching Isabeau on the nose. Then suddenly she kissed Isabeau. She kissed her hard, then flung her back against the wall again. Isabeau fell to the floor, broken in spirit and mired in heartache. She just didn't have it in her to fight Emily back. It wasn't fear this time. It was love and guilt that held her to the floor.

"You weak, pitiful thing," Emily spouted, shaking her head in disapproval. "You disgust me, and to think I once admired you."

"Admired me? Admired me? You loved me, and I loved you."

"Love," she said then laughed. "You? I never loved you!"

And with those four words her happiness died. Isabeau backed up slowly, tighter against the wall.

"What are you going to do?" Isabeau asked again.

"Let's just say what I am about to do is something, something not befitting a lady."

"But Emily, what about us? What about, always?"

"Sweet, sweet, innocent, naive, Isabeau, there was no us, and there is no such thing as always."

Isabeau felt the glaring eyes of Emily on her and smiled bitterly at her fate. But even at this daunting moment of peripeteia, she was still in love with her and felt pity for what she now held the reins to. Isabeau looked up into Emily's eyes. They were disdainfully proud, staring with an exalted arrogance that curled her very soul.

There Emily stood purposefully, boldly, beside the window, then reaching out with her left hand grabbed the curtain's edging, holding it tightly within her fingers. She stopped at one point and shut her eyes, mustering up that final bit of strength. Then she faced Isabeau directly, stretching her body like it had just formed a new skin, her glowing faceted eyes glared at her, and her mouth opened, and she spat out a goblet of blood hitting Isabeau directly in the face.

"I am sorry Emily," Isabeau said, "but there is no cure for your new hunger, you know. You will never be free. You will, at the very least, always be its servant."

"I am a servant to no one. And you, you tried to save me from what would become your nightmare," she said, then laughed as she pulled the curtain open to one side, cursing Isabeau as faceless, as light tore through the window, and the devil could be seen in her mind outwardly as he rubs his hands together.

From that point forward, it was like everything painfully moved in slow motion.

The sunlight bathed the inner flank and spilled out

onto the floor, pushing the shadows from the room as it ran quickly along the floor and wall until it covered Isabeau, carrying her back against the brick form. Isabeau screamed as her body, face, legs, arms and hands became instantly red and steaming, blisters began to form from deep beneath her skin as she burst into flames. Her body shook, and breathing became immediately difficult as her skin began to crack, and lesions ran like webbing, violently the length of her body. Her hair crinkled, vaporizing down to her scalp, steam and smoke rose through her blouse, flames licking at the walls, flames from her body burning. Her fluids began to evaporate, and she could feel her muscles and bones as they began to boil.

Emily stood there within the shade looming over Isabeau's burning, screaming and writhing body. She stood there caressing a burn she had sustained herself on her hand from the window and breathing deeply with the tremulous quaver and cackle of an old woman's utterance. They came strutting out of her lungs, like the crow of a cock, or the blast of a clarion.

"Now I am the Queen."

Once she had said it, it was amazing to watch. Her entire disposition completely changed, she seemed to burst into bloom, like the flower's buds in the spring with effervesces that seemed to erupt pouring forth a new life. Emily gazed down sending a simpering smile into the sounds of Isabeau's screams as her eyes fed upon her deed. Even through the hellish pain, Isabeau's mind still furcated as it does, wondering was this the conception of her death or were these the birth pangs of her soul? Isabeau had always feared death to the extent it prevented her from living. Yet she found as her existence came to an end that it was never death she feared, but life itself. Suddenly, Isabeau's body stretched within the iniquity, eyes wide with horror, mouth rigid and open as she screamed for the final time. She rode on the curve of the white light, no longer the dark nights and the surge of horrors unabated, just the ebb of the deep sleep till her life's deeds drowned her in a deluge of flames and fire, that boil her blood and blister her flesh. Her only tragedy was that she couldn't perceive in life what was so clear to her in death, but perhaps now, finally she would receive, the restful rapture of an inviolate grave.

Then everything was silent; the room bore little evidence of the events that had just taken place. Emily listened to a beam settling one more fraction of an inch toward the center of the earth as she stood proudly above where Isabeau had just been. Although she should have been in disgrace, for she had just killed the one person in this world who cared for her, the one person who loved her. But Emily felt that it was worth every gram of it, for she had immortalized herself, starting with her being queen and now, never again to be the meek, and abject one. No, the world will know her and the world will bow to her and her alone.

Her hand was raw. The flesh at the back of her palm had peeled back in a sheet. She placed the web of her hand in her mouth and used her teeth to sever the flap of skin and spat it to the floor.

Finally, she feared nothing—Nothing but the

ordinary sunlight. That same sunlight, she had walked in all of her life.

18

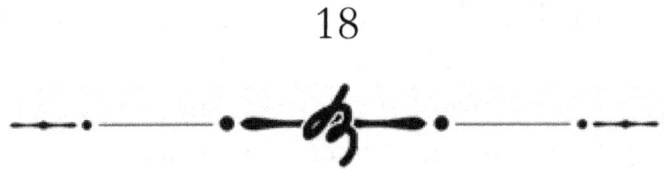

The bit of timber that had burned so very brightly in the world had gone out. Now, the new seed germinated and formed something anew, something it had never created before, something repugnant and horrible, and she was about to set fire to the world.

When Emily arose the evening she was to depart, winter had settled upon the world. Emily moved out of the Overlook and looked out. The snow had settled onto the heather fields. The purple hues glistening through the snow were always one of her favorite things. Snow lay heavy on the land. The black lines of trees, the small footprints of birds, the whitewashed sky, even at night bleached of all tone; everything had been pared to its essence. Emily wished she could see it in the daylight. There were scrubby bushes in the lea of the hill, and there was the winding pathway that meandered through them and down into the valley. She remembered this even with the snow camouflage. She pulled her cloak around her and began to work her way toward nearby Maryport's Ellen Bay, the forest floor crunching beneath her. There she could catch their ship. Her ship, she thought, correcting herself and smiling inwardly. She would be glad to be away from here, for this place held too many damn memories.

An angry wind howled over freezing snow, ruthlessly sculpting it into a subservient knoll as it passed. The snow below undulated to the gale's beckoning, like a cobra swaying to the lute of its personal charmer. Etching its imprint, the wind forayed on. It was in its everyday choreography, snow, and wind in a grotesque ballet, under the limelight of night's frigid gaze. Emily stood there and felt the scar upon her hand. It ached, and it wasn't a pleasing thing to look at. Now it was almost like a curl of wood with a flappy loose edge, but you could not pull it off, and it itched, it always itched. Why the hell did it not heal? It was like this little underlying annoyance, a callous reminder of the immorality that she had done. She wanted to say it hurt, but she couldn't qualify it as pain, but she couldn't get away from it either. It became the sole survivor of her conscience. She rubbed it annoyingly against her thigh then moved deeper within the woods that took her down.

Emily stood at the edge of the cliff that jutted out into the usually vicious, black, churning sea. She stared at the strangely still horizon as the last of the dying sun's light dipped beneath the waves. High above, moisture-laden clouds spanned out over the sea and mountain tops, resembling a magenta-colored quilt standing against the sky. The fractured light that danced gracefully upon the shimmering water was broken with the appearance of an oncoming storm in the distance. In front of her, a broadening division in the clouds crests in a final effort to avoid succumbing to the enveloping shroud of night. The snow swaddled the earth like a mother would her infant child and made even the night bright and clean.

She could see from where she now stood the port far down the hillside. She smirked, grabbed hold of her traveling bag, hitched up her skirt and dashed for the piers of Ellen Bay. The trail zigzagged downward to the foot of the mountain, winding through aspen trees whose leaves were the deep orange-gold of autumn. Light breezes produced cascades of rustling surround-sound that commingled with the crunching of each step as she walked downward in the cold fresh, clean air. Clambering off the crumbling cliff's edge, her boots met the deeper snow resting on the soft grass of the spit before it met the icy pebbles and ballast stones of the streets. The area here was beautifully softened by an abundance of trees, creating the impression of a city tucked into a forest. The coastline, in particular, was lined with towering bird cherry trees, many of them with limbs extending thirty-five or forty feet, creating more than a half mile of elegant shade. Their finger-like branches delicately reach down toward the sea, trying to touch their reflections. Emily could imagine even in the dimming light what it looked like in the spring filled with flowers and birds of all sorts. It must be glorious.

The sun continued setting against powerful dark

weather rolling in from the west. Clouds formed then broke as she made her way onto the pier and across the icy, briny boards. Emily was amazed at just how quickly the weather had turned. She pulled at the heavy bag she drug behind her filled with the elegant clothes of Isabeau. Gulls screamed across the sky, pulling her eyes with them until they came to rest on it. There it was, it stood rising bold against the skyline, triumphal at the end of the pier, yet quite ominous against the stormy backdrop. Boxes of every shape and size along with barrels, lined the pier standing guard along her path as she made her way toward the gangplank. Men moved about her in the evening air, pushing and pulling about at the many items. One man walked uncomfortably close beside her, and she became nervous until she saw he was lighting the posts down the length of the pier. All of this and yet none took notice of the young maiden alone on the board way. As she moved closer, she saw in boldly-painted letters across the back of the ship it read: "City of Adelaide." The name, she wondered where or who it was named after and imagined great stories of the crew and this sailing ship in her head.

She saw ahead of her a heavyset man holding a sheet and talking with a couple who seemed to be bargaining to gain access to the ship. She watched for a moment, then jostled her way through the throng until she reached the quarter-deck. She moved up and stood behind the couple. Once they had made their way on board she advanced two steps forward. The man looked down at her with angry eyes, tapping his unkempt callused fingers on his passenger sheet, chewing roughly on his pencil. She hadn't even spoken; her appearance alone must have produced the impression of something unseemly. She felt ashamed of the unruliness of her hair, the scar on her lip and the fringe on her forehead – and it seemed that if she had only chosen her dress better than she could have disguised the fact that she was not "respectable" and would not have felt so frightened to face the unknown.

"Aye, and just what can I do for you lass?" he leaned forward, inquiring.

She paused for far too long, unsure of herself for a moment, thinking how this man didn't sound like he carried himself, with his guttural seemingly uneducated Irish accent. Then the words fled out of her mouth as if in fear, but none the less, well-rehearsed.

"Yes, sir, I am here to book passage to the Americas, North America, to be exact," she said in one breath.

He examined her even closer, removing the pencil from his mouth and moving uncomfortably within her bubble.

"Where'd be your mother?" he inquired, anxiety and strain bringing oaths to his lips as he tapped on the proof with his pencil.

"My mother? Just why would you require my mother, sir?"

"Well, to be honest, we don't be letting no lassies, unescorted on board this ere ship. So be off with you," he said, brushing the air with his hand. She furrowed her brow at the briskness of his tone. She wanted to spin on her heels and retreat so he would regret speaking to her so curtly. She had to remind herself that she needed this ship and she was to play a part to get what she required.

"Listen here, my good man," the words flowed from her. "I may not look as old as I am but I am twenty years of age, and I want, no, I demand passage on board this ship."

"Well, I am sorry lass, I didn't mean to imply anything, but you must admit you do look a bit younger."

"That, sir, is from fine breeding," she spouted again in a cracked voice from working to stifle a slight giggle from deep within her.

"Ah, right, well then that'll be twelve pounds," he said.

"Twelve pounds?" she said in an unbridled astonishment.

"Right, that's for your own shared cabin. That is unless you want to sleep on the deck? That's only four," he said, leaning forward, smiling, showing not only the decay of his teeth but his trust in her performance.

"No, I'll pay the twelve," she said, giving the man the evil eye while opening her bag. She then handed the coins to the man, counting them out one by one as she placed them in his large hand. After this expenditure, she only had fourteen pounds and twenty pence left. She sighed and shook her head. It would just have to do, she thought.

She received her voucher, and he spared her a non-prudent nod, waving for her to move past, then up the steep angle of the gangplank to the main deck of the ship. She stared at him as she passed, wondering why he didn't help a lady with her bag. She dropped her rucksack and stood there for a moment, breathing in deeply, taking in the salty air that imbued with the sweet scent of anticipation, and she smiled to herself. As she looked about, she realized she was receiving some attention as it seemed eyes were everywhere staring at her young frame. In any other circumstance she might take it as a compliment, but here it made her feel more than a bit uncomfortable. They spoke of her in hushed gossip-ridden tones. She loathed the way they hungrily leered at her, as though they had never looked on a woman before. Suddenly, a large man ran beside Emily pushing her to one side announcing to all within a whispering range that Captain Oglethorpe was outside on the quarterdeck. Men scattered into fragments across the deck working hard to look like they were working hard. Emily turned and stared, the lantern's light was just right, shining brightly from one side as Captain Oglethorpe, vibrant and handsome, stood on the top step at the entrance to the quarter deck. Emily watched from her spot upon the deck moving to hide a bit between two barrels. He intrigued her, this man, for some reason, with his gruff and chiseled face. His well-kept beard and cap formed a powerful profile, but she dared not approach him. But she did watch him for longer than she should have before she moved toward the foc'sle, her shoes clicking against the hard wooden deck as she crept.

**

Emily walked out, then sat down toward the end of the bowsprit just above the figurehead. She gazed out for a moment, just letting all this new soak in. She thought she would enjoy being this new thing, neither animal nor human but somehow both. An amalgamation, a composite, a being apart.

The ship was moored facing outward toward the Irish Sea, and she hoped that the night air might wash away the memories of the previous evening. She couldn't believe it, but somewhere deep down in that blackened heart of hers, she missed Isabeau. She hated that human side of her, it was nothing more than a damn weakness. She stood up for a moment, wriggling her arms in front, attempting to shake the feeling out of her before deciding to see the accommodations she had just paid handsomely for. The ship was not as wide as it appeared to be from the pier, in fact, it was quite narrow. She moved down a series of steps into the very bowels of the vessel and after a short search found her cabin. If that is what you want to call it, it was no more than a glorified box-maybe twelve feet by nine. It was a cramped space, beset by the pungent aroma of damp wood and the tangy flavor of salt, both of which mislaid their initially agreeable virtues after the first week at sea. Fold-down cots hung from the walls, one on the left and one on the right, with a small alcove behind the right one. A long crate rested beneath each one, she assumed these were for her belongings. She closed the thick door and pulled the left cot down. It hung from long fiber ropes tied on the two ends, and the entire back was strung with runners and mounted to the inner wall. She climbed up and lay back, listening to the creaking hull and the wind that whispered lonely sounds as it blew beneath her closed door.

Thoughts began to plague her as she began to wonder just how she was going to keep the others on board unaware of what she was. She obviously could not go out in the day and a passenger who stays in her cabin all day every day is a curious one and may start talk. Obscurity. That is what she needed at this point, as it was the only weapon she had. If she were found out and pulled into the daylight it would be all over and, unfortunately, the crew was already painfully aware of her presence. The lascivious stares from earlier made that clear. A young girl aboard a ship with nothing for the most part but men certainly called attention to her, and they would start to question her absence in no time. She needed a plan, she needed... Then she sat up quickly.

"The man who sold me the ticket-he said shared. Shared?"

Just then the door came open, and a muscular man in his early to mid-twenties entered her cabin.

"Oh, I am sorry miss," he said stepping backward rechecking the number on the door. "They told me I am to share a cabin."

"With me?" Emily said with anger and astonishment in her voice as she quickly stood up beside her cot.

"I am sorry, I am sure there is a mistake, I will go and speak with the captain."

"You certainly will."

Then she thought, no, this is it, this is the distraction

she needed. He needed to stay.

"Wait!" she called out.

"Miss?" the man said, turning within the doorway.

"Are you a gentleman, sir?"

"Me?"

"Yes, you."

"I like to think I am," he said with a smile.

"Very well then, you may stay," she said, brushing the hair from her eyes and turning to make it seem like it was a gift she had just bestowed upon him.

"Miss, are you sure? I do not wish to put myself in the way of your reputation!"

"My reputation is my own to forge, and not yours to worry with. But yes. I am sure. It will be nice to have a man around. To be honest, I do not feel the safety that I would like, with all of these derelicts and ruffians around."

"I am honored. I will stay then," he said, smiling and setting his bag upon the crate to the right. He then closed the door behind them, turned and lowered his cot on the wall. Once his cot was down the cabin instantly grew quite compact. He turned, and they both found themselves breast to breast. Pressed between the cots new inside dimension.

"Hello there. My name is Conor," he said, smiling as he slid sideways and backed up so she could climb into her bedding.

"Emily," was her only reply as she turned her face from his, then sat and pulled her feet onto the cot. It was unfortunate, she thought, that she needed to use him. He was handsome.

Conor climbed into his bed and lay back, his head facing the door, the opposite direction than hers, and they both lay there staring skyward in an uncomfortable silence.

***

Once the ship was underway, Emily went up onto the main deck and walked around mapping out the ship, learning where things were and trying to make sure she knew exactly how many people were on board. She must be aware of her surroundings. She had learned that from Isabeau. She looked out back at Maryport, and suddenly she had the strange feeling she would never see it again. She thought she was alright with that. At one point in the evening, she met the couple she had seen earlier bargaining their way onto the ship. She found out that besides this lady she was the only other female on board. She also learned that the couple was actually from North America, somewhere north of the port of Savannah where they were headed. A place or town called Tennessee. They explained that they had only come to England to close on her family's estate after the passing of her mother and they were now returning home. As Emily walked the length of this long, narrow wooden vessel with its loft sails and many shadows she felt uneasy. She could feel the stares from the men that were on deck, their piercing eyes clawing at her clothes, desperate to remove them from her body. She stayed well within view of the officer who was on duty and in the security of the ambient glow of the moonlight.

Emily looked out at the ever-present Isle of Man,

even in the failing light it balanced upon the waters, reflecting a perfect vision of its unblemished counterpart. It was a mirrored understatement of nature's true beauty.

19

The sea was aglow in front of her with a hesitant violet light that luminesced along its breaking waves.

It was only Emily's second evening aboard the "City of Adelaide." She and Conor sat on the deck together. She found that she enjoyed his companionship and the fact that he hadn't even questioned her yet about her staying in the cabin during the day. Looking around, Emily came to realize that many of the men looked the same out here whether working or on watch in the dark, with their layers of flannel and wool covering with heavy waterproof greatcoats, bulbous mittens protruding from voluminous sleeves, and heavy caps with floppy ears pulled tightly. Some wore scarves wrapped around their heads until only the tips of their noses were visible. She gazed skyward as darkness enveloped the world around her, only a slight curve of the moon shone in the night; consequently, making the perfect stage for viewing the shimmering stars. She noticed that the stars overhead burned cold and steady, but those near the horizon not only flicked but shifted when stared at, moving in short spurts to the left, then to the right, then jiggling up and down. They had power and gave her peace, a bit of solace if only for a moment. The massive shoulders of the mountains reared above them. She was awestruck by their sheer massiveness. The air was clear, so clear that even miles away, she could see snow-clad peaks sloping sharply down to clusters of trees. She had the sudden impression of insignificance, this massive wooden ship was now just a speck in comparison. Crags of rock thrust through snowbanks and occasional firs bowed under their loads of snow. They sailed on, and even the sound of the wind in the sails and the men working seemed muted by the overwhelming structures. Emily looked out and realized they were leaving the Irish Sea.

She gestured toward the mountains behind them, vast, towering, fading even in the dimming light a sharp green to pale gray-blue in the immense distance, with snow visible on the rocky crags.

"They are amazing aren't they?"

"What is amazing?" Conor said, staring only at her.

"The mountains, they're amazing."

"Oh, yes, yes they are," he said, still only admiring the girl before him.

She sat there with Conor watching the mist of his breath as he now nervously paced in front of her, thinking how cold it appeared and yet, somehow it didn't seem to bother her much. She thought it was strange for she had always been one not to deal with the cold very well. She passed it off as either it wasn't as cold as she thought or it was Conor's presence that made her feel a little warm on the inside. She had grown almost fond of him in the short time they had spent together. They sat there most of the evening watching the mountains in the distance gradually becoming hills then flattened until they bled against the sea as they sailed off into the infinite offing.

"Aren't you cold?" he turned to her and asked as if he had just read her thoughts.

"No, not really. Funny you should ask, though. I was just asking myself, that same question."

"Are you sure? Do I need to get you a blanket or a jacket or something?"

"No, really I'm fine. Thank you."

Conor came over and sat uncomfortably close to Emily.

"Are you cold?" she asked.

"Unimaginably," he said with a smile. "Why? Does it show?"

"Well, to be honest," she said with a smile looking down at the absence of a gap between them. "Yes."

He leaned daringly closer.

"Sorry, I was just borrowing some of your warmth."

"It's okay," Emily said smiling again.

The rind of a moon had moved halfway across the sky when Conor announced that he was going back to the cabin to get some rest. Emily thanked him for his

company and stated that she had decided to stay on
deck a little longer. It was only minutes after he left that
it began.

"Uhhh!" She groaned. She hurt, yes physical pain.
What the hell was this? She questioned herself. Almost
immediately she knew, as only one who is, would
know. It was the hunger. Two days in and already she
had needs. Needs she had not accounted for, at least
certainly not at this early stage in the voyage? It hadn't
even entered into her thoughts or plans. How could I
have known? She thought. I didn't know; I didn't know
what torment Isabeau had fought as a part of her daily
routine. She had been brave and hid this part of herself
from me. I have a new admiration for Isabeau even
now only minutes into it. It hurts, Jesus it hurts.

She fought to control the pain and the urges as they
advanced upon her. She held her stomach and lay back
as the pain progressed.

Then there maybe thirty feet above her she noticed a
lone sailor working the main-mast boom rigging. He
stood balanced there in the dark among the many lines
and apparati that were the formula that made up the
masts. He had very long hair which hung over his
forehead. His face was sunbaked and spotty and even
in the moonlight shined of oil. His appearance shown
more of vagrancy rather than those running important
duties on a ship. His long thin but muscular arms
pulled and pushed at the rigging cables as he restrung
eyelets in the canvas, and she found it odd that this
man was dressed like the temperature was more mild
than cold. He hadn't seen her yet, and she watched him

closely. A bitter smile twisted Emily's lips. As she watched, that side of her she didn't know well, pulled at her. She backed away watching, taking in calming breaths, inhaling the amniotic salinity of the ocean. Slowly she slid down onto the deck, sinking herself back into the shadows, trying to hide in this moment of weakness.

It started in her gut, like nausea or the feeling that she might vomit. Then it burned and spread out from her stomach, hot pains erupting racing up and down her body, into her chest and throat. The pain was a claw roughly scratching its way up her windpipe. A gurgling sound escaped from her mouth as her larynx convulsed. Then it was in her head, a hailstorm of nails being slowly driven into her skull. A roar hammered against her eardrums. Her hands squeezed the sides of her head, trying to block it out, but it just wouldn't go away. Her eyes bulged outward from the agony inflicted on every part of her body. She clawed at her ears, willing to tear them from her head if it would stop the pain. She felt like she would go insane if it didn't stop, and it seemed as if she were going in and out of consciousness. She bit her lip hard trying to muffle the sounds that longed to come from her as she fought the changes that were happening to her body. She felt like she might falter lying there writhing in the darkness. The fear of what she was and of being caught both plaguing her mind, yet through all of this her eyes never straying from her intended target, it was like some animalistic trance. Her head ached. Thoughts churned too fast for her to hold on to anything coherent. Her muscles pulled and tightened, and she felt like her bones were being broken from their own will of force. She pulled at her hands in an attempt to stop the pain in them, the flesh drawing taut against the bones it felt as if it were tearing her fingers apart. Hell, it felt as if her whole body was breaching. Then suddenly: it was over.

She lay there within the shadows breathing hard. She could taste the blood she had caused from biting her lip and as she ran her tongue around she felt the sharp teeth that she now bore. Slowly, cautiously, she raised her left hand up in front of her and saw the long boney fingers, thick muscular knuckles, and razor like nails. But she didn't scream, no, there was no fear in this. In fact, she felt the corners of her mouth slowly rise into a devious smile. In her at this moment was a feeling of contained force, ready to burst forth in violence, a longing to apply it with her eyes wide open, all of it, with the rash confidence of a wild beast. It was in evil alone that she could breathe fearlessly, accepting the air deep into her lungs. Nothing gave her as much pleasure as evil. The thought of embracing this surprised her, yet, she embraced it. She felt the perfect animal inside her, full of contradictions, of selfishness and vitality.

She stood then steadied herself on the ship's rail and peered out making sure she was not seen, all the while keeping a steady eye on her man aloft. Every nerve steeled in preparation. She began to shake and even salivate with anticipation as she slithered beneath him. Waiting for her opportunity, looking out across the deck then back at this man working away. Back and forth, back and forth, waiting, waiting for just the right moment. Then a trace grin played along her face and like a huge wave, she swept the sailor off the boom, pulled him in behind and under the cockboat, claws deep in his head and shoulder and sunk her teeth into his fleshy neck. His cry sounded like the dry bark of a dog, then it was silenced.

She held the sailor's body close to hers feeling his warmth, squeezing it, kneading it back and forth with her claws, like a kitten milking its mother's breast. It is not at all what she imagined. The taste is gray, slightly reddish, a bit bluish in odd parts, and it moved like gelatin, sluggishly. Yet there was a euphoria that was unsurpassed. She held him for a long time savoring the warm liquid and the new strength and vitality that it seemed to award her. Once she had her fill, she stood crouched beneath the cockboat, feeling a warm stickiness seep between her fingers while still gripping his lifeless form in her hands. She for a moment stood admiring her work. The huge slit throat looked like some horrible grin across his neck like some demented cartoon villain. She glanced left then right making sure once again that she had not been seen while she had been lost in her blood orgy. Then as quick as she had taken him she thrust him overboard abandoning his body to the sea. Shafts of moonlight illuminated the dereliction, like purity and ruin, and for only a moment, the world rippled then closed over the hole it created and he was gone. She stood waiting, listening for a call out from someone, anyone who might have seen him go overboard, but there in the darkness there was nothing.

Her life now was a kind of madness that death creates. She looked down and saw that without any pain or knowledge she had regained her feminine qualities. No longer the creature she had been, she wondered, but, had bigger problems at the moment. She was saturated in the sailor's blood. Searching she found not a few feet away a deck-hands bucket filled with seawater and she reached out grabbing hold of the handle and slid it beneath the boat with her. She disrobed completely and looked at her blood soaked clothing, shrugged and threw her garments overboard. She washed thoroughly, then through the entire bucket overboard as well. The bucket made more noise going over the side than the sailor had and she cursed herself for being so careless. She huddled beneath the boat a while longer until she felt for sure no one had heard it bounce against the side of the boat. Now came the tricky part, how exactly was she to gain access to her cabin completely naked. A shiver ran down her spine, for everything was cold and intense, like a tub full of ice. The stairwell was a least thirty feet diagonally across an open area and there were people still on deck and possibly even within the riggings above, she just wasn't sure.

Slowly she moved to the backside of the cockboat to get a better view. Taking each step cautiously and quietly making sure not to bring attention to her movements all the time clinging to the ties of the upturned boat. The edge of the deck mere inches behind her she could hear the black water coursing violently below. The salty spray had a knife-edge sting on her naked form. She peered over the edge of the boat and along its shape scanning the deck. She coursed out a path, then when it looked favorable she made her move. In and out from under the cockboat across and around the mainmast to just beneath the gun deck and into the stairwell below. Once inside she closed the door quietly she could hear the men laughing and carrying on within the corridors and cabins ahead. Hers was in the first hallway to the right. She stepped forward and heard someone approaching, she turned into the first hall and stood there silent against the wall, her naked breast heaving with the stress. There were two men moving down the hall and once they arrived beside her they paused for a moment before continuing on and out onto the main deck. Like an apparition she moved from the hall to the cabin sliding up the hallway. She closed the door behind her and turned her back against the wall and closed her eyes, thankful she had made it.

"Is this a new game," Conor asked, then smiled.

Oh, my god!" Emily exclaimed, opening her eyes pressing her back to the door and attempting to cover herself. She had in all her hurly-burly forgotten the existence of Conor.

"Are you okay?"

"Yes, yes. I am fine."

He stood there looking at her confused. His scowl soon softened as he contemplated what might have left her in the predicament. Conor quickly took a blanket off his cot and moved to give it to her, then he stopped.

His dark brows drew together, and an endearing furrow appeared momentarily between them. His big blue eyes fastened again and again on Emily's then moved up and down her form. She cleared her throat and his eyes flicked up to hers and his expression changed to one of deliberate innocence. The heat of his body radiated through the small space between them warming her bare skin. He slanted a look up toward her, his blue eyes flashing beneath dark lashes as he grinned his wonderful white teeth against his dark stubble. No one's eyes had ever held hers like that. The blanket fell to the floor as he stepped forward and reached over and caught her hand. Drawing it slowly up his neck and rubbed it against the skin of his jaw as though he was a big cat claiming territory. Emily felt the pulse pounding in his throat, then the bristly rasp of his beard as her fingers slid higher. His hand held her prisoner. He turned his face a few degrees as his lips slid over her palm. Warm firm lips. Warm soft breath. Such an intimate and unexpected sensation that her small whimper of want and appreciation escaped into the shivering air between them. His hair was dark, crisp, newly cut, the line at his neck precise where it met his skin. Olive skin. His body heavy and strong moved, pressing her firmly against the cabin door. She swallowed hard. Emily loved the toughness of his face and wished she didn't. He continued to kiss her hand. His lips on her neck would be nicer. His lips settling at the join of her shoulders and neck, and then nibbling higher to that tender spot, just below her ear, and down the sensitive edge of her jaw until they met with hers. He touched the side of her face with his hand, then staring into her eyes raised her chin to match his advancement and before she could withdraw her mind from the events of only moments ago, his arms were around her. She felt the rush of helplessness, the sinking acceding, the surging tide of warmth that left her limp. It was as if all the other sounds of the world went silent. And suddenly she drew close to him. Emily compressed her lips, then licked them. Her full lips puckered – almost to a kiss. She tipped her head to one side and regarded him with her sapphire eyes as his lips pressed against hers. He tasted like champagne and smelled like heaven. Hot little ripples of pleasure pulsed between her thighs. When his lips broke with hers, her pulse was beating fast, her heart throbbed, it was as if she were about to suffocate, yet she wanted another.

20

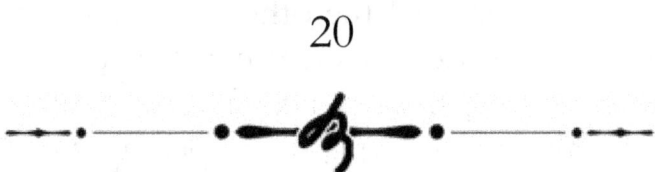

The City of Adelaide drove on, obscured by sheets of heavy rain that blurred the outlines of the world.

She lay below.

Amazing though it was, it wasn't until mid-afternoon two days later that they even realized they were missing a crew member. Once his berthing area had been checked the captain along with the rest of the remaining crew began a full ship-wide search even coming to Emily and Conor's cabin to inquire. Conor had answered the cabin door allowing Emily to sleep. Finally, after only an hour or so of searching they surmised the man had fallen overboard since he was last known to be working aloft. So was the life of a sailor.

***

"What did they want?" she inquired raising her head from her bunk wide-eyed with wonder even though she had heard them clearly.

"They were checking our room.

"Checking for what?

"They said one of their men is missing, they think he probably fell overboard and drowned, but they had to check, I guess."

"How horrible!"

"Yeah, suppose so. Hey, let's do something."

"Let's not, I told you I don't feel well."

Worry filled his eyes. He suddenly sat up straighter then swiveled his head to look at her raising his dark eyebrows.

"Sunshine, Em, what you need is some good old-fashioned sunshine. Hell, I can't even remember the last time we were out on the deck in the sun."

"I don't want to go out right now."

He jumped down from his bunk.

"Night walks, that's it, that's what you like, moonlit strolls along the deck. You cannot get the vitamins you need Emily from the moon."

"Believe me, Conor, if there is one thing that I know for sure, it is that I do not need sunshine."

"But you have said twice already today that you didn't feel well, and you haven't been out of the cabin in days. You need to get up and move around, it isn't healthy staying cooped up like this. What do you say? Come on let's go up on deck together and get a little sun?"

Her eyes flew up and she leaned forward, gripping the side of the bunk.

"No, I don't want to."

"Well, fine then. I'm going up on deck."

"Good, have a lovely stroll, enjoy the sun."

"Fine," he said, marching angrily out the door.

Emily lay there on her back, one arm draped over her head, gazing at the water stained ceiling. She turned, sucked in her lower lip and snuggled deeper into the bedding. She couldn't go up on deck not just because of the man she knew they were still searching for but the sun was still burning black in the sky. She lay there, eyes sparkling. She had to find a way to control this, this strength and this weakness, jumbled within her heartbeats. She scrunched her eyes, trying to think of a way. Each idea she conceived seemed to have wings but they never seemed to land anywhere.

***

Work continued on board the "City of Adelaide" after the loss of the sailor. The captain, using the excuse that it would bring the men's morale down, and, of course without an actual body to send to the depths he passed on a funeral service altogether. The men for the first day or so spent the majority of their conversations on the missing man. But life as it does eventually returned to normal again and the crewman for the most part just faded into a faint memory. Lite storms and bright nights came and went until the days and nights begin to meld.

***

By the twenty-third night, Emily was an orgy of

emotions. Moods back and forth. At moments she was crying from the pain. At others, she was calm and collected, almost giddy with the hopes it had passed. Her insides though burned. She had the thirst. She had worked so hard trying to control this and at times, she had almost convinced herself that she could. After all, she had not fed in weeks. A much longer timespan than she thought Isabeau had ever gone without and praised herself for being so strong. Conor had gone up on deck, leaving her without his knowledge to writhe within this agony alone. She was glad though that she was alone.

This thirst, this need crept across her, smothering her senses in a cocoon of darkness and without her permission took her and hid her completely in only seconds.

Then suddenly without warning the door opened and shut as Conor entered.

"Oh, you should have seen the sunset Em, you would have…

"Jesus Christ" he screamed as his eyes leveled with hers backing up into the door, again and again, blindly attempting to get out without turning away from her. One arm up waving madly in a protective manner the other behind him reaching, searching for the knob. Then she moved. He just froze in fear as she slithered down off the bunk and stood straight now more than a head taller than Conor. Her gaze lifted suddenly, the glint of predatory eyes glaring at him through the red tresses of hair that had spilled over her face. She looked down at him her face ash-grey, eyes as black as pitch.

Conor searched his mind and when he came to a conclusion, he looked like he might throw up. "It was Emily."

Her dark lips made her eyes look empty and vulnerable. A sly smile spread across her face. Her long gravid arms well past her waist with clawed hands larger than a human head. He winced in revulsion as she cracked her fingers and drummed them against her thighs. A silence crept across the empty space between them. She eyed him as if he were a cockroach about the scurry across the room. His large eyes unblinking as he watched as she moved closer.

She moved in turning her face toward his, moving this moment between two elements: one, excitement; the other, fear. Slowly she moved closer. He didn't move. He didn't scream. He struggled just to draw in a long quaking breath, then another. He focused centering his mind on each and every breath that followed trying to pull himself from the moment, so the moment passed not in minutes but in breaths. Need ripped through her like a wildfire, burning a hole in her will. Her hair smelled like salt and sand. Her gaping maw dripped with dark saliva and her voice was wincingly raspy, almost masculine as if she had screamed too many times.

"Conor."

Something flashed red.

***

At approximately 7:22 on the thirty-second night, the sky grew dark, like a curtain pulled across the heavens.

"She's moving in from the northwest, sir!" comes an

alarm down from the masthead.

Captain Oglethorpe stood tall upon the deck, pulling his glass from his jacket, stretching the brass, before placing it against his eye.

"Aye. Storm, ana she's gonna be a bastard," he shouted back.

"Battened err down lads." The boatswain screamed.

"Keep her on course, Mr. Rogers."

"Aye, Captain, was the response.

The distant sound of thunder rang out, like a pack of hounds, hunting in the next valley. Pig-tailed seamen, scattered checking, ropes, lines, and deadeyes ensuring that everything was running correctly and was secured. The ocean waves began to lash out at the boat as the storm, gray and leaden moved closer crawling across the sea and grumbling like an old man. The wind sang through the sails and masts as the caps formed across the sea and slowly but steadily the ship began to rock. Hours past and the storm moved ever closer. A party moved below deck for a foulness on board had been found. Otherwise, nothing changed less the devil lying in repose below the deck. Darkness enveloped the world around the "City of Adelaide" and now within her very bowels, she stirred.

***

At 9:15 that evening they banged, and banged, again and again, against the cabin door. Demanding entrance. Emily fidgeted against the navy velour, heart thumping a bit louder as a faint trace of nerves overtook the hunger pains to settle in the back of her throat. She sat in the corner as deep in the small alcove that she could press her birdy fine figure. She couldn't let them in. The hunger was upon her but at the moment she felt like a tethered goat and Conor, well Conor was well past ripe. He had laid there for almost ten days. She had wanted to take him and throw him overboard the first night but couldn't find the nerve-too worried she would get caught. Now she was paying for it. The smell had overtaken the entire ship and now they had found its source. Such a stupid mistake, she had played her part so well, the perfect monster, blinding and numbing her victims with her feminine innocence and stately gait. Convincing them that nothing was wrong and that there was no need to flee, only then consuming them at her leisure. With this façade, it had allowed her to pick them off whenever the need arose, never having to confront them face to face but from a direction they weren't prepared to defend. But the ruse was up, and she now found herself wrapped in a blanket in attempts to veil her panic, like some vermin that flees from the light.

It hurt. The pain now pulling at her. She couldn't let them find her like this. Rational thinking fought for clarity through the blood lust fog of Emily's mind. Emily drew in a heavy breath, filling her lungs in an attempt at calming the tidal wave within. She began to shake, her legs keeping time to an inaudible melody, the devil's music, of pure, uncontained violence. The ferocity, the richness of her color, reddish around the lips and at the base of her nose, pale and bluish under her fixed eyes. Her hands began to ache and bleed at her nails as she began to change. She whipped her head back toward the door as suddenly a long crack slid down her only exit. "They were coming through, they were coming through and there was no way to stop them." She tried to calm the epileptic-like twitches that invaded her and lifted the navy blanket up and over herself trying in a last vain attempt to conceal herself from the reality that was soon to stand before her.

After much persuasion and an axe, the door finally came creaking open. The cloying, nose-clogging, overwhelming stench of Conor boiled out of the berthing cabin like a fog rolling in off the ocean.

"Jesus Christ. What a stench."

The Captain and a few of the crew backed up for a moment then stood frozen outside the door in amazement and horror. The walls were a study in atrial spray-painting, with arcs of blood droplets reaching to within a few feet of the ceiling. The bedding was soaked, with dried blood and it had dripped from the mattress onto the floor causing dark pooling all over. Bare footprints could be seen within the patterns on the floor. Someone had walked back and forth through the blood numerous times. The body, or what was left of it, lay open on the right bunk.

"If that's the lad Conor, he's not new to what he is. This one's been here a while."

The bunk to the left lay blood spattered open and empty. They followed the wall along into to the small alcove, dressed by a large blue blood-soaked blanket covering something.

"God lord. It must be the girl, God bless her heart."

"She was a pretty little thing. What could have killed

them both? What the hell happened here Captain?"

All eyes turned toward Captain Oglethorpe. But his strange, expressionless, almost waxen face was not lined by experience at this moment. Rather, this experience seemed to have washed it perfectly smooth, pale white like a stone on a beach whose fissures have been eroded by successive tides. His was a face without answers, without hope.

"Get both the bodies and bring them up on deck. Hell, I can't look at this any longer," Oglethorpe commanded resisting a shudder.

He walked out. Footsteps echoed along corridors and up stairwells, from the curious, but the sound seemed muted and out of sync with any motion amidst the shadows. He pushed his way through, moving higher. He just needed to get outside, he just needed some air.

***

The ship was really rocking now. Not a gentle two and fro rock, no, a twisting, in and out, up and down and around. Her figurehead drowning on every dive. Threatening clouds raced across the heavens, swirling and colliding in vast bursts of fire. The "City of Adelaide", swam headlong into the blinding sea. The sea with its foaming mouth and curling currents pushing hard, as she battled to reach warmer, calmer waters. She sat heavy in the water as the sea crashed hard across her decks and she began taking on water. Lightning flashed across the masts lighting up the sky. Even now when the boatswain calls all hands to lighten her; when bales, boxes, and jars are clattering overboard; when the wind is shrieking, tearing at the sails and the men are yelling, and every plank thunders with trampling feet right over Emily's head; in all this raging tumult. Emily sleeps her hideous sleep.

21

When I was a child, I was always afraid of monsters. I never knew that when I grew up, I would become one of them.

At 10:21 that night, lightning zigzagged across the stygian skies, followed by a thunder that caused the ship to tremble along with her helpless crew. Great waves the size of houses rose up and burst across the deck. Captain Oglethorpe was well seasoned but never had he faced a storm such as this. Unfortunately, the one that was hailing down from the heavens was nothing in comparison to the hell that seemed to be lurking in the shadows of his very own craft. He was fighting to regain control of his ship but every order he yelled, every command the wind raged its mighty objection and was quickly carried away never reaching a sympathetic ear. He felt helpless and lost.

Then somewhere whispering within the winds that

howled past him, Captain Oglethorpe thought he could hear the sounds of screams, horrible pleading, heart-wrenching human screams, one right after the other. His eyes searched through the wind and rain there in the dark, but he could see nothing. Great waves crashed across the bow and torn sails and lines danced around the deck like some perverted snake charmer's production, making every movement slow and perilous. Oglethorpe's vision was impaired greatly within the heavy winds and rain and with the dramatic lists of the great ship, he found the only progress he was making was just maintaining his footing and balance. The hair bristled on his arm each time the sky flashed. The ship moaned and groaned as the angry storm pounded it from all sides. A long reverberating inhuman howl-like scream echoed through the dark ship as if to reinforce his fear. Moving along the captain now became aware that he could no longer locate any of his crew. He turned to look back at the cockboats checking they had not abandoned ship but even through the tempest he could see the lashings were firm against the deck. His head whipped around when again a sudden high pitched scream echoed across the ship.

There he stood, the sky growing ever darker. Blinding flashes glazed the deck as lightning snaked through the air above, followed by instantaneous deafening thunder, roaring through the night like some terrible Leviathan bent on destruction. In another flash of lightning, he saw a shadow dart across the deck from one side of the ship around behind the main mast. But this shadow had a shape, animated and beast-like, as it crawled, quivering, moving along the deck toward the shadows while any light it crossed seemed to sink into its blackness as if it were a breach torn in space. He drew back for a moment. Whatever it was, it was close, he then pulled his knife from its sheath, feeling the cold ivory handle smooth within his hand, the blade flashing white beneath each brilliant fulmination. Captain Oglethorpe planted himself upon the deck, widening his stance, arms out in preparation for whatever this might be and wiping the rain from his face in a vain attempt to see this villain. Where was it? Seconds past in what seemed an eternity. The silence, it seemed, was worse than the sounds. The silence was, in fact, deafening. This thing was coming. Then he saw it again, strange and disfigured within the rain. This time, it moved away, back and around behind him and the gun house and out of view. He longed to make it up to the forecastle, where he could get a clear view of the entire ship, but that was a long way off.

Thunder clapped and the sails above her chilled and shivered in the wind as Emily clung to the sides of the gun house. Slowly she moved digging her claws into the wood, moving up, off the deck crawling along the wall, working ever closer to her target dragging the shadows along with her. From where she was, the back of the shadowy, darkly timbered cabin it was difficult to see most of the ship, but she could see him, and she could see him well. Her eyes flashed as his movements brought him to within mere feet from her hiding place, his back almost to the edge of her lair. The knife glared at her from his hand as she watched him continue to move closer. He moved with his back to the wall keeping a vigilant watch for whatever was loose aboard. It was pitch dark, but then a sudden barrage of constant lightning flashes like some celebratory fireworks show from heaven exposed a world of slow-motion horror as Captain Oglethorpe gazed out. The deck was littered with the dead. The deck, the masts, the riggings, everywhere he looked, the dead and dismembered bodies of his crew, lay or hung, their half-naked white bodies with brick red hands and faces waving limply to and fro along with the ship's movements. He thought he might falter, feeling his body forcing the food to rise within him. Backing away slowly he turned, looking out his eyes leveled with hers. This shapeless, nameless form clinging to the side of the gun deck. The wind screamed as it ran the length of the ship, then within Emily, there was a great still moment with nothing inside it. She dilated her eyes, waited, then within a brilliant flash of lightning she leapt from the shadows. Her denticulate claws tearing the clothing from his form and digging deep into his flesh like some monstrous cat. The winds howled, muting the Captain's screams. They fell hard, the boards beneath them moaned as they danced upon the deck.

Lightning screamed down from the heavens lashing out in anger tendering sail and mast together. Sparks illuminated the air as large flaming pieces of timber and canvas fell and swirled around them within the wind as the ship rose and fell tearing white gashes into the sea. Emily's blissfully jittery hands of corruption had orchestrated the evening's bloodshed, and it filled her with a rapture she had never experienced or imagined. Oglethorpe pulled with all his might trying to tear the long claws from within his chest. Emily grabbed him and flung him hard against the mast dislodging the knife from his hand, and it skittered away into the dark. His broken body lay crumpled on the boards. He looked over. He could see it there in the shadows. The knife. It lay spent upon the deck far too far for him to reach. The lines from the mast ran loose in the wind weaving their fingers together to form a braid whipping around him. Oglethorpe grabbed at the lines trying to pull himself up, but his strength was faltered. Great waves washed over him, shoving him about at the same time cooling the burning from his wounds as she sat crouched in front of him. The whites of his eyes wide, he could see her clearly now, this horrible blood-soaked misshapen form, its unfeeling eyes, its long, dark, amber hair reaching down in wet strands sparkling beneath each fire-bolt, both haloing and obscuring its face.

"Www-what are you?" he screamed.

Emily tilted her head further, and her mouth lifted into a mocking smile. She raised a clawed hand and fingered her lips and mouth, the gore pulsated from within, and long tendrils of bloody saliva ran from her mouth and danced in the wind, breaking this way and that. She then placed a clawed hand on the deck, and it was as if the whole world went silent and he could hear clearly as each nail clicked against the deck. The distance between them appeared to shrink simultaneously with each labored gasp he took. She then adjusted her footing once again moving a little closer, her foul breath now gagging his thoughts, her face only inches from his. Her eyes wide and emotionless as they examined him closely.

Her voice was reedy and phlegmy, genderless.

"I am death!"

Then she lunged.

***

On the thirty-fourth day, at 11:47pm. September 3, 1865, the USS Crisp happened upon the flounder vessel.

The water gently lapped at the "City of Adelaide's" hull as her sharp bow slid through the calm sea night. The tattered sails fluttered softly plump with the mild wind that urged the ship forward. Something was definitely awry, the entire crew of the "Crisp" could see that plainly even in the dark as they pulled up alongside the "City of Adelaide." Her sails were war-torn, her broken and burnt main mast lay gimbaled across her deck, and there was no movement aboard.

"She appears to be derelict sir, it's like there is no one on board." someone announced.

"Moor her up Mr. Davenport, make it fast, have her searched," the captain ordered.

It was as if the ocean was moving slowly away from the ship as they grew closer. Once the two ships were berthed alongside one another. A small group of men, torches, and swords in hand boarded the "City of Adelaide" and began examining what was left of her crew. Horrors they could not have even imagined lay before them. Dead crewmen sprawled about the deck and hung within the mast lines, torn apart, chests ripped to the spinal column. The deck was dry now, deeply stained with their blood. Flies circled the churned mess, buzzing in near perfect spheres. One sailor swatted fiercely at them, his eyes gleaming with defiance. A sickly-sweet aroma wafted from the ghastly scene.

"Everyone aboard is dead!" he screamed.

"It's cursed!" cried another.

"It's a death ship. It's a damned death ship!"

"Easy men, there may still be someone aboard, check below."

Several men moved cautiously toward the front of the ship.

Then they saw her, the only one left alive aboard. They froze in fear and surprise at the form before them, her hair burning crimson in the moonlight, face eclipsed in darkness. She appeared an emaciated figure in the flickering torch light. She wore nothing but a torn petticoat and a bodice that accentuated her pale breasts nicely, the striking mane of red hair curled naturally about her head and spilled down to her waist, forging an illusion of beauty, but cloaked in brown blood from head to toe. Her long hair glowing in the torchlight was lifted by the icy breeze and haloed her delicate face, beautiful in her pretend sadness. She seemed so lost, so out of place there on the bloody ship. She took one wobbly step toward them, then suddenly she screamed and collapsed to the deck.

***

The next evening Emily waited as the daylight waned and night came on. They had carried her somewhere the night before-she wasn't sure exactly where but, at least, it was away from the sunlight. She had pretended to faint in the beginning but as the night, then the day ran on, she found herself sleeping.

Now and then a starburst of lights spattered the drawn curtains. Stealthily she sat up, pulled the curtain aside a little and huddled against the cold milky glass of the porthole that misted over with the warmth of her breathing, gazing out at the dark. Where am I? There is no movement beneath me. I must not be on the ship.

Shimmering folds of light lunged but then quickly withdraw like the colorful arms of aggressive specters. They were men moving about in the dark carrying torches. Then she realized what they were doing. They were moving bodies from the deck. She was still on the ship or, at least, a ship, but it was apparently moored. She lay back sprawled atop the tangled sheets, her hair spread out on the pillow. An arm here, another there, crucified by lassitude. It had been a long trip for the young girl. She realized she must be in America. Her wonder started as a feeling and grew into hope. The candle flickered overhead, casting a sickly pallor over the room. She realized after a few moments that this could be the only time in the nearby future that she would be alone, so she decided it was time to leave.

She cracked the cabin door and peered out. It seemed the passage was clear. Then looking to the left, she saw wooden steps leading upwards disappearing into shadow after about the first meter, teasing her with possibilities. Emily went to the cabin down the hall, knocked and then entered. It was empty. In searching, she found some men's clothing and donned as many layers as she could to help hide her frame. She looked down at her long red hair. If she could only change it somehow. Suddenly before her eyes, it faded to black. Then she thought red, and it returned to her natural fiery color. A devious smile formed in the corners of her mouth. She could change things about herself. She had no idea of this new found talent or if there were other things she could change. Now was not the time. She focused again on black, and she watched her strands fade into a beautiful raven. She went to tucking it beneath her hood and focused on blue eyes, hoping this worked as well, then returned to the corridor.

Once outside the safety of the room, she realized voices were all around her, and from below where she was, there could be heard the tremor of feet pummeling the deck above. Slowly she made her way up the stairwell and out onto the deck. She was still on the "City of Adelaide." They had brought her in. She looked out as the horror of what she had done. Carnage stared at her from every corner of the ship. Quickly and quietly trying not to draw attention to herself, she made her way across the busy main deck. As she moved, she attempted to observe her surroundings looking for the fastest route to break free of the crowd.

"You?" a voice suddenly rang out from across the deck. "You, give that man a hand."

She suddenly realized this person was speaking to her; she nodded keeping her head down and moved to where a man was busy trying to lift the dismembered body of one of the crew from the "City of Adelaide."

"You, take what's left of that end," the man laughed.

Emily didn't say a word she looked down at the body before her. There were no words to describe what had been done to this man. She found it odd, but she actually felt a little sick.

"Come on now. He won't bite you, lad. Give us a hand."

Emily remained quiet, she bent in her middle, pushed some loose strands back into her hood and reached out to lift the man by his arms. As she began to lift, she realized one arm had been snapped above the elbow and flexed like a rubber hose. His head dangled from the torn neck and shoulder and scraped against the deck as she followed the man's lead across, then down the gangplank and off the ship. Emily squinted her eyes as the dead man's head bounced up and down, twisting and turning as it bumped across each skid cross board on the gangplank. They moved over to a wagon already inundated with the dead. Together they swung the body, back and forth building the momentum, then flipped it head-over-feet into the back of the wagon. Emily quickly turned to move away from the boat.

"This way, lad, we got more to move."

Emily suddenly placed her hand over her mouth and bent like she was going to be sick, then ran to the other side of the wagon.

"Oh, alright then, little man," the man screamed out, "Come on back when you're through then." Then he turned and climbed the gangplank moving slowly out of sight.

Once on the other side, Emily saw that she was not being followed and quickly made her way into the shadows of the shipyard. Moving through the boxes and crates then out onto the ballast stoned streets disappearing into the dark undercurrent of the city.

22

Once what was considered the New World now works to pull itself from the shadows of war, unknowing that upon its quiet sandy shores, she, now brought new, darker shadows.

Emily, tired, frayed and tattered spent hours moving in and out of the shadows that crawled beneath the buildings and large trees that bled with Spanish moss which drooped pendulously from their branches, like gray smoke hanging over the battlefield. Moving about this city she found hiding was much more difficult. First, the terrain was alien to her, and there were many, many more people moving about than she was accustomed. She sat crouched in the shadows watching as they moved along the ballast stone streets. She lifted her hands and smelled them, crinkling her nose. God, they stunk of the dead man she had moved earlier. Emily, working along the back streets, found her way into the back of a closed clothing store by the route that rats might enter if they were born for stealth as she was. After discarding her manly attire, she confiscated two dresses, one costume jewelry necklace, one pair of shoes, a hat and a few undergarments to cover her now nude figure. Once dressed, she made her way back out, bundle under one arm into the streets. Now with her new found flair she was able to move once again more freely. A small boy ran past her selling newspapers screaming out "Extra, Extra." She watched as a man and his wife quickly flipped through the evening paper they had purchased, then almost angrily tossed it into a bin not far from Emily. Once it was clear, she moved over to the receptacle and cautiously pulled the periodical from its casket and retreated to her shadows.

The Savannah Daily Herald

"July 7, 1865 – Abraham Lincoln's conspirators on trial today."

Then there at the bottom right-hand column, in small text.

Sailing ship "The City of Adelaide" found adrift with only one survivor.

See Page 2. Why it wasn't even front page news?

It seemed, after reading, that the people of the city of Savannah, Georgia ascribed the ship's misfortune to scurvy. Scurvy? The bloodbath of dismembered bodies, bodies tore limb from limb, throats ripped completely off the spine, claw marks, across their chests and backs and all of this because of scurvy? She felt the result was by choice; the alternative was too much for them to embrace and instead of causing panic they opted for this tale for the sad little ship, keeping the facts from the public at large. Either way, there was no mention of her disappearance. The good thing about the fear of these people was with Scurvy taking the front seat as the main culprit, it allowed her, she felt, the ability to move about with little to no fear.

Walking along the roadside beside the river, the sky suddenly opened up. Rain came down in torrents, like a soggy afterbirth of winter. Emily moved down by the river to see if there was a place of refuge under a bridge. What she did find maybe eighty feet from the bridge, built in the embankment was a tunnel bored into dryness. Its moss covered handmade brick arches once bowing gracefully now stood crumbling with time. There were actually two separate tunnels each side by side. Both almost filled to the crown and keystone from neglect with earth and debris. The night was waning, and she looked up. The full moon shone in the cloudless sky, its timeless face as cold and crisp as the waters around her it illuminated. Emily looked about as the still waters shivered in the wind. She was alone. She then disrobed, carefully folding her garments to keep them clean then waded through the brisk water and squeezed beneath the haunch pulling, digging herself deeper into its shadows. She moved deeper into its cavernous underbelly, the subsurface passageway that dead-ended into a large stump. An oversized bit of timber had found its way in many years earlier she guessed in some torrential flood. It was wet and stunk of mildew in the tunnel. Emily puckered up like she'd just sucked on a lemon and her face turned a mottled red. She found a dry shelf like area and placed her clothes there for safety and pushed the dirt in behind her to seal the light from penetrating, even though she was a good twenty to thirty feet inside the tunnel. Now she just lay there waiting. In the sliver of time that followed, nothing happened.

***

Night.

Emily awoke discovering she was sleeping next to some of the biggest rats she'd ever seen. She backed up as far as she could as they chittered about in the darkness. Emily gathered up her clothes as their long thin bodies covered in matted hair writhed around in the obscurity. Emily swatted at them sending them fleeing from her movements, some scampering across her bare feet.

"Bloody hell, I hate rats," Emily said pushing and kicking at the cold earth moving her way back through the tight opening of the tunnel and into the early night air. She slid from the opening and into the river. The water was cold, but it seemed to swaddle her like a mother would her infant child. She breathed in savoring the twilight silence in that fragile interval before the night came nocturnally alive to break the perfection. She gazed out as golden moonlight touched the heavy limbs of willows by the stream, a patch of white daisies beyond blooming in a vain attempt at survival this time of year. She bathed and stood in the shallows as the cool gentle wind slowly dried her skin. Once she had gotten herself clothed, she folded and placed the dress she had worn the previous day under her arm and made her way back up onto the road. She was only a couple of miles from the city of Savannah and was amazed to see very little activity. Port towns are usually busy even at night, so she expected to see more people and wagons on the move. Walking, it seemed to the eye the road went on forever and went nowhere. The trees on the side of the road were towers reaching up into the sky, keeping her boxed in, keeping her from choosing another direction. She walked for hours and hours along the dirt road. Every so often a wagon or rider would pass her but no one stopped, and no one inquired about the girl alone on the road.

She walked for several hours when she heard it. Its unmistakable cry, screaming out into the night. It was far off but still it was a way. Then horror struck her, and for the first time in a long while, fear. For there ahead of her, above the trees, above the mountains, bleeding into the horizon, was color. SUNRISE. She picked up her pace. Then she saw it, through the trees. The great beast lumbering across the land, spouting smoke. It's one bright eye stretching out in front of it as if were searching, maybe for her. It was moving toward her. She ran as fast as she could trying to find a place where they could meet. Finally, she found it crossing the very path she was on and stood centered on the rails watching it move toward her. She was in luck-it wasn't moving very quickly. On the other hand though, it might not be moving quick enough. The

horizon was growing green, and red. Emily crouched in
the brush beside the track and waited for the great iron
beast's engine to pass. Finally, the engine came clanging
and whistling past her, snorting at her as she quickly
ran toward the cars as they moved past, looking for a
place to grab hold and a car to gain access. There was
one with its door open wide like a welcome mat and
quickly she ran alongside the train trying to match the
speed of the great beast. She ran with a great gait, and
felt the sweat flooding out of every pore of her body,
but it was the crunch of gravel under her feet that
seemed to soothe her growing paranoia. She watched
the sun rising in the distance like a sparkle on the
horizon, and she watched as it ran piercing through the
trees like knives from heaven. Then she reached out to
grab at a railing and in the wash of daybreak a hand
from within the car seized her, hoisting her up into its
interior and the darkness took her into its cold and
empty embrace.

The stranger's hands were rough and calloused. He
had used them his whole life. Emily landed hard on the
wooden floor of the shaking clamorous train-car. Still
breathing hard she raised her head and saw him for the
first time. He had a white-gray beard and one of those
tough exteriors where all the skin looks baked, cracked
and hard-almost like he had his own tortoise shell. In
turning, she found herself lying in amongst large bags
of corn grain and wheat grain. She rolled over onto her
back still gripping the second dress tightly and gazed up
at her new mixed company. There were three of them-
all men and all three were standing directly over her;

nasty, hairy, unkempt and even from this distance smelly; the stench of living life without purpose or direction; of living a lifetime in an unwashed body. Emily was about to thank them when she saw it. All of them, each and every one, eyes wide filled with desire and lustful lechery. A woman, that was all they saw before them-that's all they were thinking. These were men who had nothing to lose, after all, they had nothing. Emily pulled the spare dress to her chest and attempted to backup and sit up at the same time.

"Thank you, gentlemen, for pulling me on board. I didn't think I was going to make it."

"Carl done that," one said.

"Yeah, Carl, and we's awfully glad too."

"Been a long time since we's had a woman."

"Well, that is nice. I am glad, so it's been awhile since you have had a woman to travel with."

He raised a silver eyebrow.

"No, you misunderstand Miss. It's been awhile since we had, a woman."

That trauma of what seemed so long ago in time but in reality wasn't, covered her memory like a fog. Never again, never again.

She looked past one of the men between his legs and saw another had moved back from the shadows over to the boxcar door, standing in the morning glow he was working feverishly to close her in. If they only knew what the sun, now sliding its way inside the car, crawling slowly across the floor meant to her. How if they dragged her into it for only a moment, that moment might be enough to destroy her. But luckily they were thinking with a different part of their body. Two of the men began moving forward, eyes still wide, black rotting teeth grinning, closer and closer to her. Emily jumped to her feet backing away until she found herself pressed against the opposite wall between tall stacks of grain bags. One reached out for her-his fat claw-like tobacco stained fingers sprawled toward her. She pushed him back against the grain towers and kicked the other toward the still open doorway. She then grabbed the first one and lifted him high above her head as he screamed, then pitched the man across, slamming his head into the door before the rest of him flipped around it and out into the daylight. One down.

She turned and faced her foe. They didn't even seemed fazed. Her apparent display had not intimidated these two as she had hoped.

"Bitch you might as well understand. This is gonna happen."

"Yeah, you may a tossed Charlie, but I gonna get mine."

Emily looked, and both men were moving toward her. The doorman had apparently abandoned his post, so the door now remained open approximately two feet. Both men were now focused and appeared to be working more as a team. One on each side of her even though she remained between the towers of grain. Each time the train changed the slightest in direction, the sunlight moved across the floor. One of the men took out a knife and struggled to open the blade. Then once he had accomplished this he began brandishing it. Emily looked at the blade and took her eye off the second man for only a moment. He pulled her down hard onto a short stack of grain. He pushed her skirt up, her bare legs and buttocks see-sawed back with him, leaving her feet with nothing to purchase on. Suddenly the other man was at her throat with the knife.

"Wait," she said.

"There will be no more waiting." He said as he shoved his trousers down to his ankles, smiling.

She dug the fingers of her left hand into the bag beneath her. Digging deeper and deeper feeling the smooth grain running between her fingers. Digging, trying to get to a solid point, digging until she was sure she had a decent grip. Then she flung herself up, and the two men jumped on top of her, and all three came crashing back down upon the bags. The man sliced her arm wide open with the knife. Then slapped her across the face. She turned and looked back at him. Anger in her eyes.

"See that? You do as told. Lesson to be learned here Miss."

The cut was deep almost to the bone. Then his eyes suddenly widened, and he began nervously slapping the other man on the shoulder.

"Arnie, Arnie, would you look at that?"

Both men stopped and stared as the blood soaked cut on Emily's arm before them slowly sealed itself, and then just disappeared. The one man dropped the knife and Arnie let go of Emily's legs and began backing up, pants still swaddled around his ankles. If he had been ready, he wasn't any longer.

The two men turned, and moved quickly to the other side near the open door, desperate to get away from her. The lust in their eyes now replaced with fear-pure unbridled fear. She was no longer the woman of desire. No, they now saw her as an ominous, dark figure now rising and following them across the car's interior. They clung to the edge of the doorway white within the sunlight, and on their faces, fear-numbing, agonizing-both barely able to breathe as she slowly moved toward them. The train was moving much faster now, and they looked down, and out the door at their only option and then at each before they both leapt from the moving train. She never even heard them hit. Emily walked over to the back of the sliding door away from the sunlight and slid it shut. She scrapped her hands together in an attempt to clean them, then bent over and picked up the dress that lay fanned upon the floor.

***

Emily lay there in the shadows in her makeshift bed staring at the door. Wondering if it would open before the daylight waned. She curled away from a glare of light pouring in through a crack in the poorly constructed car. There was a large painted logo; Pullman Palace, done quite professionally, all in blue and white on the inside of the door. Someone else at a later date had taken white paint and drawn a large cartoon angry face beneath it. They had also taken some, of what looked like large rusted steel saw blades and fashioned them as its eyes. It was a rather gruesome figure and even to Emily, almost unnerving, as it continually watched her with its metal eyes.

She slept in the middle of a makeshift fort vainly seeking warmth between the bags of seed and pressing her back against the wooden mortises of the side panel behind her. When Emily awoke, she was in pain. Her hands clenched. She woke with her bloody nails deep in her palms-she had transformed or at least somewhat in her sleep. Normal now, she realized, she had to get off the train. She didn't know what would happen if she were to change and there was nothing to feed on. She felt ashamed and immature that she had not just fed on one of the drifters that she had thrown from the train the night before, but she was still learning. It was already night, again, but unfortunately, there were only a few hours left. She slid the door open a bit and looked out. The full moon shone in the cloudless sky, its timeless face as cold and crisp as the snowscape. It illuminated. A pure undulating blanket of white stretched out in every direction as far as the eye could see.

Snow. No, cotton. They were cotton fields. She had never before seen it growing. It was beautiful the way it glowed beneath the night sky. Cotton meant farms-farms most likely miles apart, secluded, perfect for her. She had teethed on the horrors of poverty so she felt she could fit in here at least until she had fed.

The train slowed as it rolled into a station, and Emily jumped from the car.

Calhoun, the sign said Calhoun. Emily assumed that must be where she was. It must be the name of the village or town. She moved quickly off the main road and away from any contact with a crowd. She worked her way through a field looking-searching-for a place away from, well away from everything, so she could feed and figure herself out.

23

She lay there and watched the blood escape from her and spread out across the hewn wood floor, too bright and theatrical to be real. She couldn't move; she couldn't scream, then nothing.

The wind was starting to pick up outside, so much so that the limbs of an adjacent tree scrubbed and scratched at the outer walls of the small house. At first they were pinprick taps and scratches, just enough to crawl into the sleeping mind. Now though there was an unmistakable, rhythmic thudding, Kathy Fowler awoke and lay there and listened, there in the dark, not wanting to move. The whole house was in darkness save for a bit of light penetrating through the front windows in the house that filtered down the hall to her open bedroom door. Finally, after some thought convinced herself that getting up now would entail less work, so even feeling disgruntled she flung back the quilt and got out of bed. Stretched and yawned, then she took the lamp in her hands and shook it; a slosh of fuel. She bent over pulling a match from its box, and scratched it against the striker. It sparked then blazed into life. The gentle flame licked away at the darkness of the room as she held it over the lamp until the flame jumped to the wick and she adjusted the knob and the contours of her room flashed to life. She blew out the match, shook it then dropped it in the metal tin on the bedside. Lifting the glass dome she angled it as it slid into place onto the lamp. Kathy then picked up the lamp. The shadows followed her as she crept down the hallway and through the house. She walked out onto the front porch, the cold night's brutal edge shocked her awake as she gazed out into the night. The air was heavy with the smell of rain. She sighed and opted to remain barefoot. She retrieved her basket from within the front door and walked out across the dark side yard near the looming barn. There it hung, the laundry grey in the night sky blowing wild in the wind as she made her way over to the wires.

A cold breeze swept across the pasture, tilting the browning wheatgrass. Emily looked up at the moon, drawing in the scent of earth and the sweet odor of manure, realizing that she didn't have much time until it would fade with the morning sunrise. There across the field, silhouette against the sky, was a small farmhouse. It's yard was flat and wide and framed by heavy towering oaks. A barn stood off to its left with more fields in the rear. She worked her way across figuring maybe she could hide in the barn or one of the buildings until the new nightfall. Standing out by the barn, there she found a young woman. She appeared to be taking the laundry down from the lines and placing them in a basket. Emily knelt, watching her from the tall grass at the edge of the kept lawn. She was pretty, with long blonde hair and wearing only a white corset cover and petticoat; that clung to her as the wind blew. The pale cloth danced around her young frame like a beautiful ballet. The same wind blew across the young girl and settled on Emily. Immediately Emily felt it, the need, it was on her again. She disrobed. Knowing now more of what to expect. She sat there, naked and still, waiting for this twisted creation to paint itself upon her own canvas. Emily closed her eyes there in the darkness where no one else could see as she felt the pain of birth cascade over her.

The lamp on the ground flickered, dimmed to a low glow before returning to normal. Kathy stopped what she was doing and looked around then shrugged it off. She then placed her hands on her hips and bent back a bit, feeling the stretch of her spine. Then she slid a hand up her body and placed it on the back of her neck twisting her head back and around, lifting her hair letting the breeze reach in beneath and soothe. Then she dropped her hand and paused looking out toward Emily. She then brushed the hair off her ear and turned it away from the wind and listened.

Kathy thought maybe she heard something. Something close, the grass swayed in the wind glittering grimly in bilious lamplight. The depth of darkness made the warning signs difficult to see. She took a tentative step toward where she assumed the noise was emanating. It was to her right, somewhere behind the clumps of chest-high grass. They swayed back and forth. Something skulked within them, moving closer. Even though her eyes had acclimated to the night, she was finding it harder to make out shapes. The grass parted as it rose into view, a large, menacing shadow against the storm covered moonlight. Her heart skipped a beat. The fight or flight instinct was battling for control. She took a step back. She couldn't make out any details in the dark, but she could see it was huge. Suddenly she turned and ran, screaming. The shadow edged closer, snarling. What the hell is it?

"Run Kathy, run" she hissed through her teeth, trying to motivate her feet to do more than they were. She tripped over the lantern tipping it over, and it went out. Around the edge of the barn and back toward the house she ran. She was not even sure what it was she was running from, but there were teeth, and there were claws. Running was all she could think of doing. It followed behind her, crossing the yard in great hitching strides. Kathy ran as fast as she could her long blonde hair dancing back and forth across her face in the wind. Her long, rangy legs, making great strides through the grass as she pulled her petticoat high up on her thighs. Her screaming cries of terror barely masked the other unearthly sounds that ghosted her every move. She was almost there, almost home. Kathy could hear it behind her, it's heavy breathing, the animalist galloping sound. Upon reaching the house, she was up the three steps, across the porch, and through the door in seconds. Kathy flung the door shut with all of her might, locked it and collapsed against its base.

She placed her back hard against the door pulling her knees to her chest, squeezing her eyes shut, trying to get her breath back and trying to force the fear from her mind, trying, but still she was listening-listening for she knew it was out there. She knew whatever it was, had not gone away, and it wasn't going away. Sweat clotted on her skin. A deep thrumming emanated from beyond the door, a sonorous hum which was not so much heard as felt. Kathy felt it vibrate her chest walls, disrupting the hammering rhythm of her heart. Fear slithered into her guts as she knelt craning her neck peering out the small window into the moon-bathed road and woods beyond. Where the hell was it? She had never felt so far from town until now. Why did Tommy have to work tonight, of all nights? Why tonight? Kathy slid back down to the floor. Then suddenly the sound grew louder and louder, Wham! Something hit the door, knocking her off her feet. She landed hard on the wood floor. She raised herself up on her knees and braced her hands against the door, crying when it hit, again and again, cracking the door jam on the locked side. She looked up at the door, A couple more hits like that, and it will be in. Then it suddenly stopped. Everything grew quiet as she knelt sobbing, her muscles tense as she still was pressing with all of her might against the base of the door, tears running down her face and dripping onto her arms, her knees aching with the pressure. The house was once again silent, and the darkness only seemed to intensify her fear. Her breathing was hard and labored as Kathy cautiously dropped her hands from the door to the floor. She closed her eyes and listened again, but everything was still. She slowly moved toward the door, lifting her eyes higher toward the small window centered on the door. She jumped then realized the glass had reflected her own image. She took in a deep breath. Then Wham! Something hit the door and the lock and jam shattered. The door came flying open, half on its hinges and half off, sending the poor girl head over feet into the main room. Kathy quickly regained her footing and saw the strange, malformed figure that now crouched at the edge of the shadow of the doorway. Then it came gliding from the blackness. Kathy turned and ran down the hallway. The creature lunged in pursuit. The floorboards creaked behind her. A slight groan of wood protesting the weight of every single, heavy footstep.

Kathy tried to stop at the first doorway but slid down onto the floor and past it, just as the creature's claw connected with the wall just above her head tearing a gash across the framing. She ran into the next room and slammed the door shut. She looked around the bedroom, searching for the perfect item to brace against the door. The room was pitch dark, and the only items were large pieces of furniture, much too large for her to move. She felt around and found a chair and braced it up under the doors knob. She crouched listening for the telltale sound of breathing. Would there be breathing? Or would it come in silence, without warning? But there was no breathing but her own, no sound at all but the desperate thrum of her heart. Then she could hear it moving in the hallway, its large body scraping against the sides. The creature had a musky smell like river, earth, and the willows and it clawed its way into her nostrils. There was a sound of scratching, scratching on the walls, like a large determined cat, trapped between the rafters, which echoed through the house. Then it became more pronounced, more centralized. She yanked open dresser drawers and rifled through them, searching for anything to defend herself with. The walls suddenly shook from the force of, Dear God it's coming through the walls. Kathy searched the familiar room there were no windows, and it was coming through. A quick breeze whispered along her back in the sealed up room. She stopped abruptly, slowly closing her eyes and lifting her head, it's in here; it's in the room. She spun around and opened her eyes and faced the empty darkness behind her, almost collapsing with fear. Then a heavy rumble shook the floor beneath her feet, as the beast caromed against the outer wall. In that instant, there was a great explosion as the wall failed. Kathy screamed while shielding her eyes as flying debris rained down on her. A clawing blasted from a fresh portal as the wall shook from its repeated efforts to widen the gap. The creature slashed at the wooden wall, and light shone through as it worked to climb through the jagged edges of the hole. Kathy screamed as she tried desperately to get closer to the door as the beast squirmed within the void. Then it growled and without warning it shook its head wriggling hard, pulling, clawing, trying to get its head and shoulders through the gap. Snarling and snapping almost moaning as it writhed within the divide. The wall shook in defiance and chunks of wood and rubble hailed down from within the break and ceiling. Then it stopped. It slowly set its giant claws on either side of the window it had created, fingering the hole, then lowering its head until its huge eyes and teeth filled the frame, holding Kathy with its glare.

Slowly, this time, the beast worked, gouging her fingers into the gap, drawing herself onto all fours. Her mouth a bear trap of blood lined teeth, was open wide. She pulled at the sides of the hole with her claws, timber, and plaster cracking as she moved her head angling it left then right gradually further and further in and through the passage.

Suddenly a noise tore Emily's gaze from Kathy. It was a cry from the first room, a cry like no other forcing its way through the thick wooden walls. Emily stopped and tilted her head listening. Her mouth, salivating at the sound.

"No!" Kathy screamed.

Emily almost purred.

"No, not my baby, please dear God." Kathy shook her head, tears filling her eyes as she dropped her guard and flung the door open taking a single step outside of the room into the hall, now facing this massive beast head-on. Kathy watched in horror as Emily pulled her head and shoulders from the hole and turned away to pursue the noise.

"No," she screamed again. Running toward Emily, vaulting herself onto the back of this massive misshapen form. Emily roared spinning in the hallway clawing at her back in an attempt to reach this woman clinging to her. Kathy held on like a stubborn snake latched to a meal beyond its means. Emily finally grabbed her with her left claw. She was quick. Her large clawed hand wrapped around Kathy's throat before she had any foresight to move. The great beast held her up, its face crowded down on hers, its thin lips rolling back to bare its long yellow sharp teeth as the gossamer threads of saliva dripped from its open mouth. Kathy could feel the creature's hot rancid breath on her as she struggled to move. It stood there perched on her soul. The beasts other hand grabbed at Kathy's crotch and its fingers curved to hold her painfully in place. The thing just held her there breathing pure heat down upon her. Kathy's hands uselessly tried to push and beat at its chest, but its grip was like iron. It squeezed at her crotch, and an involuntary noise escaped her. It sounded like a whimper, and the beast smiled. Then turned and tossed her, flinging Kathy backward against the end of the corridor, concussing the wall with a bone-jarring bang where she fell and slumped against the wall, helpless.

Emily then turned her large malformed body around focusing on Kathy's eyes, hot, slow rivulets of saliva dripping down like warm syrup from her fangs. Kathy lay their eyes wide, trained on the beast, shaking uncontrollably yet frozen in terror at this horror and its proximity to her and her infant. The low guttural growl in its voice echoed like the empty cry of a man stranded at the bottom of some remote and abandoned canyon. Its head dropped down as it stared out at her through burning eyes that glinted from beneath a jutting brow. Kathy looked up at the teeth, serrated and curved, that awful knowing smile glaring at her as the beast turned and crept into the child's room. Kathy screamed.

At the far end, centered on the back wall, Emily found a white crib standing alone. Whatever was making that noise was still screaming, even more so now. Emily edged over even closer. Oddly as soon as her massive shadow bled across the bedding, its cries were instantly muffled. Kathy screamed from the hallway hearing the end of his cries, imagining the worst and knowing full well that this thing had just devoured her child.

Emily stood there towering above the crib, gazing down at the tiny body quietly cooing beneath her. Her long fingers curling, gripping the edge of the crib as she cocked her imposing head left then right, eyeing this little thing in its sterile surroundings. She took in a deep breath, her chest rising as she inhaled the sweet smell of this sweet young flesh. Her claws tightened on the crib as the intoxication and anticipation overwhelmed her, and she moved closer.

***

The sky was darkening quickly, and rain hung heavy in the air as a young husband on horseback moved over the ridge. Eyes squinted half shut as if they had a secret too valuable to share, looked out. Tree branches thrashed in the gusting wind as if angry giants shook the trees by their trunks and yet through it Tommy saw trouble. Looking down from the ridge he could see his house and barn, and the front door was sitting wide open? Just a gaping black hole. Kathy would never leave the door open when he was gone and certainly not without a candle or with the oncoming storm. The sky growled and flashed in the upturned face of Tommy. "Come on girl," Tommy said kicking his heels into the side of his prize Appaloosa. Faster and faster he rode down the trail toward home. Blasts of lightning forked the sky, freezing the scene in his eyes, followed by an earsplitting clap. Trees lining the trail snapped back and forth in the wind, and the air was filled with leaves and twigs that had been torn off and sent spinning. The moon dipped in and out of the clouds causing the land to fade in and out, then streaks of pure silver and fire ran the length of the sky and thunder clapped angrily. The closer he got the more Tommy worried. Even with the motion, the doorway to the house seemed wrong.

Kathy crawled down the hallway, her body beat and broken she didn't even dare to look into the baby's room as she passed for fear of seeing what she already knew. She almost slipped on the hardwood floor wet with her tears. Tommy came through the busted doorway holding an axe and knelt lifting Kathy from the floor.

"Jesus Christ Kath. Are you okay? What the hell happened?"

Emily suddenly turned hearing the strange voice, moving, tearing the door from it frame as she traveled through and out the bedroom doorway around and into the main living room. There were two of them now. Tommy, almost screamed, yet he jumped in front of the beast. He threw his arm out and pulled Kathy in behind him as she clung to him and they both slowly backed away from the creature, further and further into a corner. Its long human-like torso moving eerily in the moonlight that speckled through the curtains. It moved closer, cracking its long saber-like claws, its eyes never leaving Tommy. The tension of building agitation made Tommy's jaw flex and expand like a reptile. Tommy left Kathy against the wall where she slowly slid to the floor unable to support herself. He then moved forward swinging the axe out in front of him.

"Where's the baby, Kathy?"

Kathy didn't say a word.

"Where's the baby," he screamed.

He glanced back quickly at her. Never had an expression without words struck him as so full of meaning. So in came Tommy, axe in hand. Standing just under six feet with a slender but sturdy build. His pallid complexion was in contrast to the charcoal eyes fixed beneath a full head of dark brown, messy hair. Tommy in anger raised the axe high, but the beast pounced with such a dizzying speed. Tommy's arm was torn free from the shoulder before he could even swing. The axe remained in his hand, fingertips still white with pressure, as the limb dropped to the floor. Another slash and Tommy's throat disappeared in a flash of gore. He flopped forward, then rolled backward his severed arteries showered a paralyzed Kathy until she was crimson. Kathy screamed as the beast's shadow stretched from the walls like a sentient ink spill and engulfed her.

24

The house was eerily hushed, silent, dark and empty, with the exception of a gentle coo that rose from a motherless crib.

Emily lay there. Alone in the windowless room. Her body felt loose, disorganized, drained. She shifted disconsolately. There was pain and the memory of pain. The blanket gently swayed from a breeze running down the hall from the front door that she had used to cover the hole in the wall. She lay there, stealing time beneath Kathy's bed. She awoke, green eyes peering out from the darkness. She could sense it was still daylight, but, something woke her. Something was, different. There was movement, voices. Emily's heartbeat raced as the first jolt of adrenaline coursed through her system. Emily felt trapped. Perspiration beaded on her face; she licked her lips to taste the salt. A crawling claustrophobia moved in. The darkness would give way to shades and sounds leaking through the cracks. Soon her eyes would find the narrow boundaries of the space beneath the bed. Soon she would hear her racing heart, faster, and faster, a wretched drum that would drown out that perfect clock in her head. She was panicking and had to force herself to inhale slowly from her mouth to dampen the noise of her own breathing in her head. There was nothing worse than being alone in that infinite, unforgiving shade, knowing that right outside that door, right outside was certain death.

***

The sheriff walked across the wet porch and stepped through the torn threshold into the darkened den and stared mouth agape through the umbrella of flies.

She lay there on her side, her head resting in a pool of coagulated blood. Her long blonde hair partially obscured her face, and her arm was bent behind her at an impossible angle. He was at her side or at least parts of him were.

"Oh, Jesus Christ, Jeb? What the, what the hell happened in here?"

She was face-down, her long blond hair splayed out around her, and she lay in what looked like a lake of blood. The man was in parts, just everywhere. The grizzly site brought bile to his throat. He coughed a few times to hold it back, turning away he reversed from the room and planted his back limply against the wall, closing his eyes and placing a hand on his heart, panting while the lingering images of the woman and the man's dismembered body laying just inside the door dissipated. His breath came in shallow gasps, and he felt infinitely small and isolated. The sheer horror of it circled the logic reality of his subconscious. He had never seen anything like this before and just wanted it out of his head. But the image wouldn't go away.

"Well, I was riding by Sheriff and noticed the door was busted in. I could see it from the main road and so I came over, thinking maybe it was the storm and, well, this is what I found. Once I looked in the front, I jumped back on my horse and rode out to get you."

"I appreciate it, Jeb. But what in the hell did this? What do you think? Bear? Cougar?"

"I don't rightly know Sheriff. I ain't never seen nothing like this before in all my days. Doesn't even look like neither one was eaten on, just kind of, torn up. The young girl, there she just had the one bite on the throat as far as I can tell and don't look like no bear or cougar bite to me."

The sheriff closed his eyes, trying to gather himself again. A bubble of spit popped at the corner of his lips. He took in a long deep lungful of air feeling his chest rise as the tight muscles of his neck unwound like bands. Then he breathed it out slowly. He then opened his eyes and stood up straight regaining his posture.

" Jeb, I'm gonna, I'm gonna need your help. Can you run out to docs and get him to bring the wagon? It will be dark in less than an hour, and I don't want no animals to wander in here, and, well, you know."

"Yeah, I know Sheriff. Shore will. I'll go now."

"Thanks, Jeb, I'll stay here with the bodies."

"Better you than me, Sheriff."

"Back as quick as I can."

***

The Sheriff stood alone outside the broken door-frame of the small farmhouse, examining the damage, trying to formulate just how this happened and making damn sure he didn't look inside again. He was a brave man, but that in there was downright unnerving, and he wasn't going back in, no, not without someone else being there. That he was damn sure of. He watched Jeb move out of view, then he turned back toward the house, that's when he heard it. Noise, a movement? His eyes went wide, and his jaw went taut. There was something alive in the house. He fumbled with the snap on his holster, shaking uncontrollably finally pulling the pistol from its cradle. He then backed up against the wall and slid himself slowly toward the doorway. He then slid his body sideways cautiously peeking around the molding and past the unhinged door.

Then he heard it again. Like the muffled wail of an injured animal. He moved a little closer, and a little closer until he was standing firmly within the threshold of the crippled doorway. Then its cry was heard again. His eyes widened even further. It was a baby's cry that he heard.

"Dear God, there is a baby in there."

Emily heard it too. It was that damn child. But there was something else. Something else moving in the house.

The sheriff slowly stepped beyond the entrance of the doorway. Something he had sworn, he wouldn't do. But there was a baby somewhere in this house. He walked in little steps, eyes forward, trying with all of his might, with all of his being not to look to his left, not to look at the horror he knew was lying there. A sharp intake of breath lodged like a nut in his thorax-swelling, chocking. His lungs gasped for air, feeling the room tilting around him. He tried to stay focused and he soon found himself at the beginning of a short hallway. There were two doors on his left and a huge hole between the two covered from the inside in what appeared to be a large blanket or coverlet. He walked to the first door. He didn't hear anything. The blanket rustled in the light breeze. He took another couple of steps looking at the deep furrows spread out across the wall all leading to this large hole in the center. Emily's wary green eyes stared from beneath the bed as the figures shadow danced against the fabric wall. Cautiously he reached a shaking hand out toward the hole, toward the blanket. If he could just grab it, then he could see inside the room without having actually to go inside the room. His hand moved across the wall and slid slowly across the groove and around into the opening, his fingertips almost gripping the fabric when there suddenly came a cry from the first room. He nearly jumped out of his skin, pulling his arm back like he had be shocked by a thunderbolt. He turned back toward the first door and paused, staring at the door's knob afraid to even touch it. Then he heard the mournful cry again and grabbed the knob, turned and entered. The room was empty with the main items being a rocking chair and the a cradle against the back wall. He quickly looked behind the door and ran to the bassinette. He looked down at the infant and scooped him up, blanket and all and retreated from the room and house altogether.

The sheriff stood there on the front porch, cradling the child in the crook of his arm, pressing his tiny cheek up against his, squeezing him a little harder than he probably should be, just feeding off its aura and basking in the glow of the child's innocence. But he was still alone. Where was Doc and Jeb? He stood there looking out and watched as the sun disappeared as though forever, leaving only a scarlet smudge across the horizon – like the last remaining evidence of a violent crime. A scattering of stars poked holes in the darkness and the shadows crept in, gathering confidence beneath the towering black canopy.

Emily lay there, her sanctuary now in danger. Her breathing was becoming heavy, labored, still panicking. Her head pounded in rhythm with her heart and her tongue tasted like something had curled up and died on it. Soon they would find her. Soon she would find herself struggling against the shadows, the invisible boundaries of that personal universe, the extent of her existence in that cold darkness, that tomb. Soon the air would curdle, a mixture of sweat and pine, and her tongue would swell, and her throat would tighten. Then the door would open, and the sun would come in, and she would burn alive. Then she felt it. Darkness, sweet darkness. Suddenly she burst from beneath the bed, shattering the framing sending splinters against the walls.

The Sheriff turned cradling the infant and peered

through the broken doorway, he heard what sounded like a low growl. His skin prickled. Un-holstering his gun, he stepped through the threshold.

Emily pulled the blanket from the wall and crawled like an animal through the hole. Slowly she crept down the hallway and to the edge of the main room, where the bodies of Tommy and Kathy lay rotting in the eventide.

The Sheriff stood there as a shadow lurched in the hallway, watching in horror the materialization of this young girl from the shadows within-naked, thin and drawn, crescents of darkness like fading bruises around her eyes, blood matted curls of finely spun copper haloed her face. But more she was covered in blood from head to toe. A prolonged silence filled the void, rising like the sea from the bottom till it engulfed the whole house. Then he alone, still holding the baby, knuckles white, slowly raised his hand still gripping the gun. His hands shook uncontrollably.

"Miss, are you, alright."

Emily stood there and bestowed a cold smile on the sheriff. She just stood there in the twilight's shadow, stark and ominous. Then suddenly she leaned forward, arms out, arching her back, she screeched with a loud animal intensity, that it shook the sheriff's very confidence. He shook firing a single shot just missing Emily. The baby screamed. A feral savagery possessed Emily as she bounced toward him, swiping him with her bloody arm as she passed through the threshold across the porch and disappeared around the side of the house. She ran into the field and began crossing through the short growth. She ran westward, past the flicker and hum of fireflies slowly turning into a silhouette backlit by the amaranthine glow of the Georgia sunset.

The cold gave an air of lonesomeness to the empty roads and windswept fields. Emily found a bosky woodland in crossing the meadow they encircled. The wood was stark and open, the twisted trunks and gnarled branches standing out black against the dark wall of the sky. She could see the steam rising from each breath; she had to clean up and find clothing, but she had to stay hidden as well. The woods were foreboding and defiant. Brambles and bristles and thorns gather to hinder her progress, scratching her skin as though guarding some secret. Never again would she put herself in such a precarious position. She ran and ran, trying to put as much space between the house and herself. She fell against a dead tree and paused, sliding down against its base in attempts to catch her breath. She lay there against the tree, inhaling the sweet rot and dankness, the bark rough against her skin.

There buried in the woods, she found what appeared to be a flooded area of land next to a river. First looking around she waded into the green water holding her arms above her head. It was so cold. She stopped when it was just below her breasts as a wrenching juxtaposition of warm and cool shocked her causing a shiver to run the length of her. Then holding her breath pulled herself beneath its surface, running her hands up and down and across her naked body.

Scrubbing in the cracks working to remove the evidence of the former evening. Then she rose to the surface steaming as she ran her fingers through her russet hair and listened. Then disappearing once more beneath the waters green algal murk, as ripples called wide silent echoes over the surface.

25

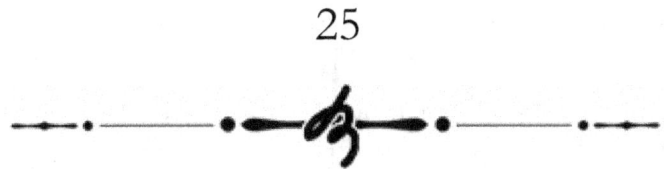

That night was penetrating deep into the heart of the South.

Emily sat there in the forest, a strange stillness settled in around her, as though the whole world was holding its breath. The clouds above shifted and the moonlight trickled down through the treetops sparkling across the water's surface. A single chill sashayed up her spine. She was still a long way off from where she needed to be, or at least that was how Emily saw it in these waning days of September as a soupy fog descended upon the swampy land. Barefoot and naked she began making her way back toward the town. As the fog thickened, branches of obscured trees poked through the haze as if out on their own. She was in need of clothing, and she needed to get back on the train before sunrise if she were going to make progress northward and now she only had the waning light of the shadowed moon to guide her.

She wove a jagged path through the forest, shoving through spare, scratchy branches and scrub which seemed intent upon hindering her progress. Then finally as she emerged from the forest, the fog began to dissipate in milky strands, and the town slowly appeared in front of her. The center of the small town glowed in the nearby distance, its lights stabbing at the night. It had a strange vitality to it that was opposed to Emily's preconception of the area, seeing the rural countryside that surrounded it. It was adversely vibrant, brightly lit and full of life. Wagons in constant motion, people transferring boxes and crates and passengers readying themselves for travel in and out around the train depot, the epicenter of it all. Her eyes normally only green, glowed with an orange hue. Like twin coals in the amber light of the town.

Emily crept as close as she could, still naked and cold in the night air, weaving in and around bushes and parked wagons. Silently she surveyed the activity until a young man and a woman pulled up in a wagon on the shaded side of the depot. She minded as they went up onto the platform, leaving the wagon, and their luggage momentarily unattended. Quickly she made her way across the street and crawled up under the wagon, then she crept into the back and opened up a large camelback chest. Rifling through its contents, she located some of the woman's clothing and quickly pulled them free and closed the trunk, stealing away into the night. She had all she needed now, except money and shoes.

The sky was a grim vault of sorrow as she stood

chewing on her lip in the shadows, pushing and pulling in attempts to make the clothing fit and look appropriate. There were no undergarments in the luggage she had checked, and the dress was large yet tight in those areas that were sure to showcase everything. A tug here, a pull there, she just didn't want to look like she came from the carnival's girly revue. The dress was black and ran the full length of her to the ground. This was about the most beneficial thing as it would help camouflage the fact that she wasn't able to locate shoes in the luggage.

Boldly she walked up the steps to the long loading platform the boards now stretched out in front of her. Normally she would want to blend, but she had no money and needed to board this train. She kept her strides simple in a vain attempt to hide her lack of shoes. But no one was watching her feet. Her hips swayed as she walked and exuded an oblivious sexuality that could only be achieved by the young and naïve. She walked up to the ticket clerks glass and peered in. A slender young man fidgeted behind a narrow wooden desk shoved underneath his office's solitary window.

"Excuse me," Emily said.

His eyebrows furrowed then arched as he looked up as if suddenly aflame, as she came into view. Emily stood there outside the ticket window, abruptly adjusting the bust of her oversized dress.

"Yes," he said stuttering, his knee musically cracking as he attempted to rise from his chair. "Can I help you miss?" he added attempting a smile, his eyes wide behind round glasses, wisps of brown graying hair mussed, dress shirt wrinkled and askew.

His face was a nice face, but it appeared tired and grim, but Emily could tell it could be a pleasant face too, warm and open. He had a smile that perhaps once had enchanted women, but not anymore.

"Oh, I do hope so young man. I seemed to have misplaced my ticket somewhere." She said as she dove into her small cleavage searching for the non-existent ticket.

"Lost ticket huh?" he nodded, staring unabashedly. He brought his fingers to his mouth and stroked his lips.

"Yes."

"Where were you headed?"

"Why, New York," she said leaning in the opening pressing her breasts against the shelf that mantled the window. Making sure to keep his mind away from the obvious. "Can you help me?"

"Do you have a name the ticket is under maybe I can find the copy of the receipt and get you another one made?"

"No, I'm sorry my mother bought it for me. She'd been saving so I could go and see my dying father in New York. As you can see, I was running to get here on time, and I lost it. Can't you please help me?" she said cutting her eyes at him, pressing a little harder, letting the cut top of the dress blouse a little more than she should.

He sighed audibly, "Well, I'm not supposed to do this."

"Oh, I knew as soon as I saw your handsome face

that you would help me. I could just kiss you."

He smiled, and his face turned a shade of crimson.

***

Emily stood there alone, ticket in hand, at the end of the train platform staring aimlessly out into the night. The mist was rising, reaching, billowing up into the sky, slowly putting out the stars. Her eyes are drawn to the empty track and followed it out as it disappeared into the blackness. Suddenly she had that special childish sense of adventure that one gets at a train station, of new places about to appear in your life. She turned, leaning back against the railing. There were a large number of people here, their voices commingling along with the squeaks of shoes on the wooden platform and screams of quarrelsome children. Her nerves were on edge and her senses high. Across from her, a woman was sitting on a bench on the other side of the platform maybe thirty feet away, reading, and it was as if Emily could actually hear her turn each page.

Suddenly a rumpled old man dressed all in black stood up across the loading platform and began speaking loudly. Everything else went silent, and all eyes were upon him as he slowly shuffled toward Emily. He had a bible clutched tightly against his chest in his spotted arthritic hands. He looked like an old preacher without a pulpit as he walked stooped over and spouting out scripture, getting closer and closer and none of what he said made any sense. All frightening metaphors about sin and salvation. But his milky white eyes spoke, and it felt as if he said each word directly to her.

"And they shall no more offer their sacrifices to devils, after whom they have gone a whoring. This shall be a statute for ever to them throughout generations."

"I give you everything. But you shall not eat flesh with its life, that is, its blood. And for your lifeblood, I will require a reckoning, from every beast."

Suddenly a woman came running and grabbed him by the shoulders, turning, carefully coaching him back to where they had been sitting.

Rain began to fall, and it hummed on the station roof overhead as a plump little man came out onto the platform announcing that the train was about to arrive. People immediately began moving from their sitting position, gathering up their items and making their way closer to the tracks.

The train chuffed into the station with whistles and sharp hisses from the steam, casting a shadow over the platform and the many waiting passengers. Emily waited as the crowds hastily boarded and un-boarded then she rose and strutted toward the train, into the light and disappeared inside. The train was dirty and utilitarian, and it seemed even louder inside, as the engine kicked into motion. Spinning wheels, steam spewing, whistleblowing, grumblingly and laboriously the train began to haul itself out of the station.

The sound of the pulsing locomotives pounded through the night until the deep booms of its powerful thrusts quietened down to gentle beats in the heart of the night and its steel wheels blindly followed its predetermined path.

***

The berthing car was configured different than the others. The bunks stood stacked one on top of each other three high and lined both outer walls of the train with a passageway down the center. They stood bolted both to the floor and the ceiling, and there were no windows or skylight in this car. Searching Emily finally found her bed, number 213. Situated on the bottom, she quickly knelt down and climbed inside pulling the curtains shut behind her. The realization that this was all the privacy she would have on this trip did not sit well with Emily. She thought though maybe she could just stay here the entire time. She pulled the dress off and smoothed and folded the fabric so she could wear it again, dapping the tail that had somehow gotten wet with the sheet from her bunk.

She found quickly that having the lower bunk was going to be a problem. It seemed that everyone that traveled down and through the passage pushed her curtain a little each time and eventually she was left exposed. She tore a bit of the bedding fabric and tied the edges securing the curtain. She was tired and immense pain shot through her temples, settling to a dull throb at the base of her skull. She fought to keep her eyes open needing to remember where the hell she was. Slowly she gave into the heavy, drifting sensation listening to the rumble of the engine until she drifted off.

***

Emily rose from her bed in the berthing car just as a

woman and man were walking toward her. The woman stared at her like she knew her, either that or she knew something about Emily.

"What? Can, I help you?" Emily said toward the woman with a definite tone to her voice.

"No, I am sorry for staring, it is just, I know you will find this odd but I have a dress just like that."

"Do you, now?"

"Why yes, and I was informed it was a one of a kind when I purchased it."

"It was," Emily said making her way passed the woman and her stunned husband. They stood staring at her as she made her way down the narrow corridor toward the dining car.

***

The temperature in the train had dropped dramatically, in fact, it was freezing now that they had moved further north. Emily finding very little to satisfy her appetite in the dining car returned to the berthing compartment with the intentions to cover up and seal herself away for the remainder of the trip. As she knelt to gain access to her bunk, she noticed a note pinned to her privacy curtain. She reached down and pulled it free stood, looked around and unfolded it. The message she found was written with the bold, jagged lines of an angry child, the tip of the pencil all but perforating the page. It was from the woman that had accosted her in the passage earlier inquiring about the dress that Emily had poached from her baggage before boarding. The woman was calling her out. Written was the demand that it be returned to her at once. She had given her private cabin number which was located in the richer section of the train. She couldn't believe this was happening the whole thing was a surprise, but more it was gruesome and a complication. Cursing, she leaned against the beds, warily scanning the passageway and started weighing her options. She could ignore it, but then the woman could make a fuss and bring the authorities to her during daylight hours and cause real problems. She had no choice. She sighed audibly as she crept down the hallway and made her way toward the cabin

26

I have a body, and everything that I do is a
continuation of my beginning.

Emily stood nervously outside the couple's cabin
wrenching her hands. Shaking them as the sweat built
up in her palms in a vain attempt to dry them. She
needed to get through this and remain calm while
doing it. She didn't need the unwanted attention. Then
without even knocking she walked in, closing the door
behind her and stood inside the cabin's enclosure. She
needed to make sure she always had the upper hand or
at least gave the appearance as such. Looking she found
it wasn't as elegant as she expected and taller than it
was wide. They both sat there before her. The man off
to her left holding the daily paper, her only
acknowledgement a quick glance and rough adjustment
of his paper as she entered. The woman was seated to
her right and glared at her as she entered. A deep
furrow immediately dug its way into the woman's brow.

"Well you have some nerve, have you not heard of knocking young lady when entering a person's residence?" the woman announced.

Emily just stood there, staring at the woman, not uttering a sound.

The woman looked her up and down and began to protest immediately. She had fat pink cheeks that made her look like a talking porcelain doll. She began by announcing that the dress Emily was wearing was stolen from her. Explaining that she was not going to stand for this and had full intentions of bringing the law into this situation as soon as they arrived if it was not returned to her immediately.

Emily's face hardened, her eyes narrowed.

The stilted woman sat there sipping her coffee, wearing her precious white gloves, ranting and raving. She shifted her gaze to her lap and picked at a loose thread at the hem of her skirt, peering up now and again at Emily with condescending disgust. The kind only the rich can dish-out. Emily looked down at her husband, who avoided eye contact but whose eyes she now noticed were quite attached to her figure. He was an unassuming man slight in stature with wiry red hair, and his face was so splattered with freckles that they grouped together in blotches.

Emily turned toward the woman and cleared her throat.

"The dress is mine. It was mine before we left and it is mine now."

"That dress is most certainly not yours. You took it from my bag. I paid good money for it, and it is mine."

She then bent in the middle leaning forward, her face only inches from the woman's. Emily licked her lips and considered her words as blood thrummed at her temples. Then in just a mere whisper she spoke. Her voice reedy and phlegmy, genderless as it floated across the small cabin.

"Listen, you pretentious little bitch. I'm trying to be nice about this. But the dress, if you want it, take it from me. I dare you. Show me your claws."

The woman suddenly dropped her cup as if stung by a wasp and stood up. Then grabbed Emily's arm and pulled her toward her.

"Sit down, what the hell are you going to do?" Emily said shoving the woman by her head immediately back into her seat.

The woman sat there shivering. Emily could tell by her trembling look she was seeing way too much in her. She seemed hesitant to answer. She kept licking her lips like it was a compulsion while she repeatedly nudged her husband with her foot. It was apparent that this entire confrontation was his wife's doing, and he wanted nothing to do with it. In fact he wasn't even aware of what was going on, with his libido distracted the blood never moved any higher than his waist. The woman sat there and she just kept on stubbornly plugging along, chastising and degrading Emily, calling her everything from a vagabond to a thief. On and on, ranting on, something about not respecting her, and she wasn't a fool, and just never shutting up. Visions flashed in front of Emily, horrible visions and she squeezed her eyes shut and shook her head to rid them from her, digging her nails into her hand so the pain would be a distraction. Little sparks lingered atop the waves of her mind like a swarm of electric spiders as she tightened her eyes in another attempt to block the woman's presence. But nothing helped. She just wanted her to stop talking. Emily breathed deeply through her nose, trying to quash the anger that threatened to spill out-trying to, but it was no use. It had begun.

The woman looked up into Emily's eyes and mid-sentence her heart seized. A tiny little shrill, an escape of air rose from the back of her throat, past the pale lips of the woman like air leaking from a balloon's pinched neck.

She needed to get out. Now.

Some deep animalistic instinct told her this. Get out of the cabin. Now. Run.

But she just sat there passive and inert as a toad. Lost in the grip of fear and panic. Emily's eyes aglow, her face and body starting to undulate and disfigure. The woman's husband sat salivating next Emily completely oblivious to the reality of it all. Then he looked up at Emily, seeing he had just been caught staring started to laugh, but the laugh died in the back of his throat, gagged on a sharp bone of sudden, inexplicable dread. His eyes went wide and his complexion faded from his face as he worked to cobble together the horror standing before them. They sat there these two at the center of the lantern's pathetic yellow stain, as Emily's mouth twisted and contorted. Her angular figure, unstable, modifying before them. A horrible deafening silence followed, punctuated only by the nearly imperceptible sounds of confusion and fear coming from the two.

Emily's legs ached and vibrated. When her vision wavered, she closed her eyes, welcoming the darkness overtaking her. Then her stomach gave to a severe jolt of pain. Her back arched so violently that it threw her down onto her knees. Her arms shook and waved of their own volition. The couple backed away in their seats with staring eyes and outspread hands. The sensation grew stronger, digging its claws into her chest and gnawing at her stomach. Her jaw ratcheting out, her gums tearing, bleeding as new elongated teeth pushed and forced their way into her mouth, shearing flesh, digging rents into her face. The dress ripped and tore as the body beneath expanded and flourished. Her hands burned as the skin was stretched, and pulled taut as claws sprout and swell from her fingertips. Her features seemed to writhe and knot and assume in many moments a dozen different aspects.

Then there was silence. As if the whole world were gone, nothing, not a sound, then Emily took in a deep breath and she rose, ominous, like a great wave before two tiny craft. Her henna like hair cascading down her naked body. Her hoarse, guttural breathing floating across the small room. Emily heard what sounded like water dripping and turned back toward the woman. Water ran down her leg and the cushion and dripped to the floor beneath the woman. The warm acrid smell of urine wafted up as the woman wet herself. The ultimate admission of fear. Emily smiled, saliva and blood ran in slavering strands from her open maw. Trailing her arms out to the side, her nails splintering the wood, tearing deep furrows into the decorative wainscoting on both sides of the room. Her massive form dwarfing its interior. She looked over at the man his dull blue eyes flared like a trapped fox, wild and feral as she lunged. He writhed within her claws and steam rose and curled from her bite. Gurgles emerged, and when he tried to breathe his throat whistled. The seating groaned beneath her weight.

The woman screamed. She slid farther away, pushing herself up against the window side of the small enclosure, fetal, shaking, too shocked to defend herself. His vision ebbed away and the world went dark. Emily stood, covered in blood, her shoulders pressed hard against the ceiling emanating a wet guttural, breathing like that of an animal. His head slumped forward onto his chest, and blood ran blending and puddling on the maroon cushion beneath him. Emily now turned her attention toward the woman. Emily's entire neck was vibrating, her artery jolting beneath the skin like a heavy metal drum. The woman shook, the whites of her eyes so wide and full of questions and fear. Emily attacked. Her copper hair swirled around her as blood filled her mouth and the woman's small frame fought and bucked beneath her struggling to say something, her weak voice too small to hear. She clutched at her throat, feeling a warm stickiness seep between her fingers, then her eyes rolled back and she was gone. Emily stopped dead still and sighed audibly as a cool draft rose slowly to surround her, and she shivered, turning her attention back to the door. She listened as death lingered in the cold air. Nothing. No one moving outside the door.

Emily stood-her feeding calmed her although her heart pounded heavily in her chest. She closed her eyes, her lips quivering through the pain as she returned to her normal state. She looked down at the reality of what she had done, the room peppered with blood and her body glistened crimson. She threw some clothes down on the floor and found the water pitcher almost full. She wiped as much as she could off her then washed herself over the basin to clean the rest. She patted herself dry and looked around the room. Searching she found some of the woman's clothing. There was little left, a white long dress and a black jacket, gloves and a bonnet hood. She put on the dress and the rest she placed into a cloth satchel. She listened at the door, nothing, and quickly left the room stealing away as quickly and quietly as possible

She lay there resting her head on her palm rather than the pillow. She just lay there without moving, straining her ears to listen but hearing little beyond the beating of her own heart. Emily sighed audibly. A crawling claustrophobia moved in. She had to get a hold of herself, but she felt trapped, cornered, like an animal. She closed her eyes and just listened. Then a long reverting scream echoed through the dark corridors of the train as if reinforcing her concerns. She tried to raise up and bumped her head on the bed above her. Would they find her, she wondered rubbing her head. But her mind was a mix of movement her curiosity aflame. Why were there not people running up and down the passageways, why were there not crowds gathering to see what happened. There was nothing. Just ordinary movement along the passageways. Had they indeed found the bodies? If not what was that scream? Was the railroad keeping it a secret? She just didn't know. She was tired and an immense pain shot through her temples, settling to a dull throb at the base of her skull. She fought to keep her eyes open-needing to remember where the hell she was. Slowly listening to the rumble of the engine and the track beneath, she gave into the heavy, drifting sensation.

27

"So long as you are in pain, you aren't dead."

Emily awoke to the taste of blood on the wind. She opened her eyes, unsure of just how much time had passed. She attempted to sit up, banging her head on the bunk above her. This is getting ridiculous, she thought. She lay still for a moment feeling the person above her stir in their sleep. She wanted to get out and find out what had happened and where she was, and she needed to find a way to stay on the train at least until Boston and beyond, if she could. She pushed aside the rumpled bedroll and musty blanket and slipped through the curtain rolling out of the bunk, into the passageway then standing.

She brushed the wrinkles from her dress as she slowly made her way down the passageway. Now dressed more appropriately she felt she could move about without advertising her difference. But still, it seemed everyone was aware of her. Heads seemed to shift and twist in her direction, or was it just her self-conscious mind that made it seem so.

A man, and his wife with a little girl on her lap sat off to her right—their eyes never leaving her. In fact as Emily looked down the aisle the only one not staring in her direction was a lone man in what appeared to be a dark uniform, his head lolled forward in sleep. A thatch of blonde hair hung over his forehead as he slept, covering his eyes. Everyone seemed to chatter and joke as she walked past. Was she just paranoid or was it her? Ahead a man working for the railroad came through the opposite door and moved down the aisle toward her. Emily tried hard to keep from making eye contact and just before they met, another man rose to her left startling her as he stood blocking the aisle. He immediately apologized as he placed both hands on the railings above and across her allowing her passage beneath him. Emily ducked as she passed. It was obvious this man hadn't showered. Whether he forgot or has sacrificed his social life for some elbowroom, was puzzling.

Emily's head popped up and she found herself face to face with the train conductor. He raised his red shaggy head, and two piercing blue eyes widened. He was fairly attractive but she could tell the war of freckles across his nose and cheeks had forever relegated him to the role of the friend when it came to the ladies. He smiled and asked if he could be of any assistance. Emily shook her head and awkwardly made her way quickly past him. Glancing back, she noticed he was carrying a piece of luggage. She had an idea and turned to follow the conductor back down the aisle. He traveled through several cars methodically moving at a slow pace, occasionally stopping long enough to ask each passenger the same question he had asked her. She stuck to him like a limpet, keeping her movements as slow and deliberate as possible, again trying not to draw attention to herself. Finally he came to a car—one you could not pass through. This one was locked. Emily stood chewing on her lip as the conductor sat the bag down and pulled a ring of jangling keys from his belt and unlocked the car. Once he was inside she moved closer and peered inside. She watched as the conductor moved deep within the darkened space which appeared to be the baggage car. She watched as he moved in behind some large crates. With birdlike quickness she slid past the doorway moving quickly to the left and hid inside the luggage storage car moving not far in but finding a place behind a large chest. She waited, crouching there until he closed and locked the door once again.

Trapped! She hadn't thought about it till now but yes, she was trapped, but also and more importantly, she was well hidden. The things Emily didn't know could fill a book, but she was fast, and filled with perseverance.

"What a mess," Emily said as she looked around in the half light and wrinkled her nose. The organization in this car had a lot to be desired, but she thought she could make it work to her advantage. The car she was in was an older one, made almost entirely out of wood with large wooden rafter beams in the ceiling. Thin shards of light shot through the dark reaching across some of the boxes like fingers of a ghost. She moved around till she found a place she felt secure in the back and settled in for the rest of the journey.

***

The train suddenly came to a noisy, clanging, steam spewing stop. Emily jumped to her feet and listened. It wasn't long before she heard movement outside the car's loading door. She looked around and decided to climb into the dark rafter area above the opening. The heavy doors slid open and sunlight shot into the car, throwing huge geometric shadows against the back wall as Emily clung to the beams in the darkness above them. Two men came in and another stood just outside loudly screaming out orders and baggage numbers. The two men began rummaging through the items and quickly throwing baggage out the doors and collectively moving crates out. They just kept moving things out, more and more.

Emily began to panic. Was this was the end of the road? She heard one of the men say the train was actually going all the way to Bayfield Canada. This couldn't be true, but it was. Bayfield she had learned earlier from a map Isabeau had shown her was a port town, and just off the coast of Bayfield lay Prince

Edward Island.

Luggage was sparse during the final parts of her journey and each stop the train made, she hid herself in the rafters of the wooden train car and waited. The train seemed to make so many stops and each time the doors would open, it seemed they were being opened wider than the time before, and most of the stops were during the daytime. Finally after two more days, she heard the conductor announcing Bayfield in the next car. Emily looked at the cracks in the wood, it was at least another hour until dark. Emily worried the train would unload and load and leave before she could make her exit.

***

Emily hung there, her nails biting into the wood as she became more nervous the longer she was left waiting. The sun was setting. It seemed to be moving slower than the men who were working. They were close to being completed when, the shadows ran along outside the car. She could see the colors reflecting as the orange sky bled away to red as it worked to fade to a blessed black.

Without warning, the doors suddenly slid across their tracks and slammed shut.

"Wait, wait I'm in here." Emily screamed out, dropping from the rafters.

"Hello, hello, is someone in their?" a voice called out from beyond the door.

"Yes, Please I am in here."

The door came sliding open and Emily stood before at least six men—all staring at the young girl in the baggage car.

"Miss, can I help you? What are you doing in there?" one man asked.

"You were moving bags and boxes, and I, I just wanted to look inside," she said cutting her eyes coyly at the man.

"You're not supposed to be in there. Are you a passenger on this train?"

"Yes. No, well I was. I just came on it from New York," she said, her rangy mouth thinning out into a kind of grin she didn't really want to give.

"Well, all I can say is, you were lucky young lady that we heard you. You could have been locked in there, and we would have sent you right back home. Now, get on out and move along."

"Yes, sir," Emily said moving quickly to one side and down the loading platform away from the train station. The sun had set for the most part. The coast she found was still at least a few miles away and she moved quickly toward it. She needed to cross the strait tonight. The fog was rising from the coast, moving in on Emily like a tangible white darkness, shutting her in, like a great ship, tense and anxious, she groped her way toward the shore.

There was a break in the fog. She could see it, down the hill in front of her, the Northumberland strait. She was almost there. She quickened her pace as she made her way down the hill toward the coast, her eyes wet with the thrill of it all.

Out of the darkness it shot through the night, a hollow clang which sounded from beyond the fog. The clang of the Ferry Bell. It was leaving. Emily pulled at her dress and picked up her pace now running down the hill, almost losing her footing a couple of times from the great strides and uneven cobblestone streets. The closer she got to the coastline the thinner the fog became and now she could see the craft pulling from its berth.

"Wait, wait" she screamed in desperation. But the craft kept on moving.

"You will have to catch the next one, Miss," came a cry from within the fog.

Emily still running, tried slowing, but her body force pressed her onward, she found herself bouncing along her wonky legs moved about as her body adjusted to the new strides. Finally she came to a stop at the Ferry's gate. She leaned forward hands on her knees in an attempt to catch her breath, when she raised her eyes, taking in that first deep breath, she saw the sign: "Next Ferry 8:00 a.m."

"8:00 a.m. Jesus, really? 8:00 a.m. I can't wait til' then," she said in a breathy voice.

She paced for a few moments the fear and anguish overwhelming her. Walking off to her right she made her way through the edge of Bayfield then out along and above the shore line shore. Wondering how she was going to make it out to the island before daybreak. She stood looking out. Fog coated the strait, and a cold moist wind made her eyes water. Suddenly the fog shifted a bit and the end of the dock became clear for only an instant. But it was there, tied neatly at its end. Alone and waiting. A small white skiff.

Emily looked around and saw no one and quickly made her way to the end of the planks and climbed into the boat. She found the two oars and untied the small craft. She placed the oars into the rowlocks and slowly turned the boat so her back was facing where she thought the island was and began rowing. The tiny boat cut through the water but once the shore was no longer visible and with the fog so thick it was hard to tell if she were making progress or just moving down the coast.

The water was dark and her vision was anything but clear. Then she saw a light, like a beacon in the darkness. The island. She rowed a little faster as the night was waning. After a short while the fog lifted and she found she was moving in the right direction. She could see the island in the pre-dawn light, lit at the edges with a crown of stars. Emily slipped over the side of the small boat abandoning its attention and into the dark water. She porpoised her way slowly toward the shore. The excitement was building, but so was the fear. She was almost there. The water jumped and bounced and grew stronger as she grew closer. There in the darkness her shadow slowly rose from the tide and crept across the red beach, then climbed the short cliff and disappeared into the woods beyond.

28

The stones press against grounds filled of half-heard whispers, whispers that startle - ghosts of sounds long dead.

The figure ran lightly, streaking through the darkness, feet barely making a sound on the narrow forest path, ducking and twisting gracefully to avoid contact with the dense surrounding trees and shrubbery. It was as if a shadow were sweeping silently over the leaves vanishing under graceful arching trunks. A skeleton of birch tree branches stretched above, the last of the leaves pulled away fading into a star-filled sky. Her white gown made her seem like an apparition—gauzy and ethereal, not quite there. The cool air was sharp and her bare legs stung from the cold. Oddly these woods are familiar. Like she had been here as a child. That notion seems wrong, but this place feels right.

Blood roared through her body and the icy air burned as she pulled it into her lungs as she made her way down to the cliff on the jagged, uneven path alone, in darkness. Below her, in the wind-scraped blackness, the sea unfurled, nothing but the stars for company. She turned inland toward a great rise. She moved quietly as the stones around her wrapping her arms over her chest as she set off up the hill. The silence and the cold pressed down on her. The only movement was the stream of vapor as her breath hit the freezing air. She moved quickly as the planet spun toward dawn. She came to a clearing and stopped at the edge of a garden held captive by a great iron fence. The night was now windless and lit by a quarter moon. Her muscles ached, her breath steamed in the air around her head, and she was damp with sweat. The garden beyond the fence seemed cavernous in the moon's half-light and the night sky was just a thin strip between the trees high canopy. She lifted the latch and pulled on the great gate, and a gap opened just wide enough for her faint figure to slide through. Once inside it seemed as if it lightened up.

Now away from the woods, the air seemed colder, odorless, not like spring. In spring the heat stilled air was heavy with the sweet scent of balsam, and the locust would whirr in the birches, coaxing you out of the sun and under their boughs. Emily felt a throbbing hot circle of white pain stabbing at her back. She turned to see the sky began to glow brightly spangled with early light, the colors of pennies and rose petals. She opened her bag and pulled out the jacket and gloves, pulling on the bonnet hood making sure it was pulled forward and tied. She would have to go slow now, so as not to let her skirt ride up and expose her legs to the morning sun above her boots. With the low morning sun rising at her back her shadow grew as she walked, stretching out in front of her as if it were clawing at what was coming. She passed through rows of rough-hewn stones and barrows, with names and stylized figures so worn with age they were no longer legible. The pale light began to gather, deepening her view of the sloping garden and tangle of woods beyond. There in the feeble trembling light, the thought touched her. She felt the tug of blackness, a yawning chasm as vast as the sea. She was close—the feeling hardening to a kernel of certainty in her heart.

She stood there. The woods behind her remained silent and empty as the first specs of snow began to fall, twirling lazily to meet the ground. All combined to give the scene a feeling of dreamy unreality. She wasn't close. She was there.

29

She was there in the twilight long enough for the glimmer in the distance to take shape, but she couldn't tell if she were moving toward it or it was moving toward her. Then it became what it was, a house—a house encircled by a vast forest.

She felt so very small on the stone walkway, at the bottom of the steps that led up to the grand old house—the house in the woods. It was huge, an ancient beast of a building, ominous in the twilight's glow and one that seemed to beckon the unwary. The evening was advancing and dark clouds tumbled in, casting a pall over the structure. There was the distant flicker of lightning, a few moments later she heard the delayed rumble of thunder. The top corners of the house were like towers with crenellated turrets and gothic arched windows glowing dull orange in the stormy twilight. The color of the house looked as if at one time it had been bright and beautiful but now, had bled into a dull monotony that spoke more of sickness than anything else. As she stood there, the twilight began to harden around the walls of the old house, and a single light in the upper window began to bloom. From where she was standing, the house seemed vacant. There was a light, but she saw no movement, no figures pacing the windows' walk. The cold wind made dead leaves caper at her feet in the way small animals do around their masters, and it just added to her uneasiness. She moved forward, passing between the concrete monoliths flanking the entrance, feeling prickly and in turning a little claustrophobic by the large wrought iron fence that skirted the edge of the property. The clouds that had been smooth and gray earlier were suddenly coarse and in places, kettle black.

Emily crossed an arm under an elbow, her lips turned slightly upward. She could sense something, something in the air, something forbidden. Then as the sun flung itself upon the fringe of the world, spilling its dying light over the edge, they emerged, like insects from their nests and swarmed the night. They moved as a single organism, silent as the shadows across and above the giant white boulders that hugged the cliffs and bordered the sea. Living in the belly of Mother Earth, they arose from their womb-like caves at dusk, darkening the skies until it was black as sackcloth. Emily halted and stood on end for a moment, watching in wonder as they rose and fell in unison until they too faded into the blackness of night. She came to a large door and stared nervously. What bothered her more was the sense of subtle coercion, as though the space beyond beckoned her to unlock its secrets, so she would see for herself. Emily twirled her hair with her fingers, she sighed audibly and stepped forward.

The wind died with the day and a hush settled over the woods as Emily knocked. The dead, dull thud of the knocker against the wood seemed hollow and pointless. It just didn't appear to resonate enough noise to notify anyone in this enormous house. After a few moments of impatience, she reached out and turned the knob. The door opened, the subtle protest of the hinges carrying clearly to her in the stillness. The cold breath of the winter night flowed into the house as she stepped inside. Then she had that feeling again—the feeling that deep down inside, something was going to happen, and she couldn't stop it now. Something that would change her, and even though she may not want it to, there would now be a before, an after, a was, and a will be.

She stayed motionless like a cat scenting prey for a while, casting her eyes around yet she could see no one. The walls of the room were slate gray, the paint thick and filled with brush strokes. Whatever it was meant to cover was going to stay hidden. It was sparse, almost empty, with a grand staircase. Her footfalls echoed in the large space. The floor in the next room was mottled, but solid. It creaked though even under her slight weight as Emily walked into what appeared to be the main living area.

The first thing that caught her eye was a gorgeous ornate frame above the fireplace that held within its borders the beautiful figure of a woman. There was something about the eyes. It must be in the gift of the painter—it was a talent, a quality, that confounds, shifts shapes, invests a thing with a mysterious aura. Emily guessed it was the woman that had changed Isabeau. Perhaps, the former queen.

Her nerves were on edge, and she pulled off her gloves and flipped her hood back then squeezed her hand. It ached. The consideration and the nature of her decision to betray would be forever engraved on the stone of her soul as well as that damn scar. Why did everything else heal? She rubbed it between her thumb and forefinger. The memory came alive again as she lingered on it, then kneaded the horror from her mind. She shook it off and walked around the large room. It was well furnished, and she sat down in an overstuffed chair looking around. The light coming through the cracks in the curtains adorning the tall windows tinted the air with a sepia tiredness. Emily rose and walked over to the window, pulling the heavy curtain to one side. The soft moon's light blanched the wooden floorboards under the square window and moths beat their wings in retreat from their perches on the window sill and sashayed into the evening skies as she watched the darkness dilute the last of the light.

She stood there looking into the night, the candles reflection mirroring in the glass, and the memory of her father's death rooted and bloomed. She could almost feel its malevolence pressed against the window. She stood there fixedly, not remembering it all; she did though remember seeing the Incredible quantities of blood that poured out of him. The awkwardness of his head lolling, mouth dribbling blood and saliva onto his bloodied chest and groin while his eyes rolled back to show the whites. But the physical actions that brought him to that point were only a blur. Perhaps in the intensity of that first, subconscious feeding she literally lost consciousness as she was engulfed in the waves of fear, excitement, pride, even revenge. His shirt was crimson. Was it at this point that she ultimately became what she is and not Isabeau's bite? She wondered. Then the memory faded.

Suddenly she remembered the light. She had seen it outside in one of the upper windows. She pushed the curtain back to its previous position and returned to the foyer staring up at the winding staircase that now stood prominently before her. Then again she felt something; it wasn't the ominous feeling she had before. No, this was more of a pulling or a calling. She felt she was being drawn away from the stairs and walked down a hallway beside them. Soon she found herself traveling through a long cloister with the main wall of the house on one side and an arching colonnade open to the darkened landscape on the other. This in turn lead to a door that took her then through what appeared to be a roughly built addition that adjoined, taking her downward into the depths of the house. Dim light cast dusty white lines through the slats of the porous walls of the addition until she found herself walking in a finished hallway, one that took a slight downward fall away from her.

The walls were blood red, trimmed in fine wood and on both sides hung beautifully framed portraits— amazing paintings, the faces and attire all seemed hundreds of years old. The air in the passageway was musty and still, and smelled vaguely of mice. Emily's footsteps echoed along the corridors as she made her way deeper and deeper into the bowels of the house.

She stopped, silence fell, and a new scent wafted toward her assaulting her nostrils. She wrinkled her nose. A foulness that tinged the trapped air along with the mahogany scent of the woodwork. A malodorous odor, permeating, seemingly oozing from the walls. She begun to sense something was off-kilter, although this impression had yet to coalesce around anything specific. Then there in a darkened alcove she heard something moving. There was something there, something deep and primitive. She could hear as it made obscene little sucking noises as if it were drinking there in the darkness. She took a cautious step toward it, her hands forming useless little fists at her sides. Studying she could just make out Its slender long clawed fingers moving like a spider across its web. It was clinging onto something, caressing it, squeezing it. The blackness pulsed and throbbed as it suckled on the shadows. Then suddenly a sinister flash of teeth amid the blackness. She drew back, receding against the opposing wall, moving, sliding herself against the railings as she eased her way past. Then she turned and ran, her feet slapping against the wood floor as she raced down the hallway. Air swooshed behind her. A scream rose in her almost tearing itself from her throat.

After a short while she slowed and began easing down the hallway with quiet, deliberate steps. She walked for what seemed another hour, then she paused, thinking that she heard voices, muffled yes, but decisively voices. She was moving toward them; she could sense it from the changes in volume and pitch. She came to another alcove, and there she found a large double door. She placed an ear close and heard a confusing welter of noise, voices shouting over one another, the rasping sound of feet. Then the lock turned, she backed up as the doors creaked open, and a thick mist seeped into the hall and hovered like veiled ghosts. She walked into the inky blackness of the room.

30

These are all the things that walk in your nightmares.

It was more like a nave, filled with a backward congregation, for as soon as she entered the enclosure, Emily Marsh could sense a presence within its cold stone walls, and she knew immediately that it was not the presence of God. Her light played across a crowd of figures. There were dozens—some male, some female.

Her eyes slowly adjusted to the half-light. There was above them a line of smoke that extended from the ceiling down, just cradling their heads. Everyone turned in Emily's direction. They were all pale, and their eyes were bright and judgmental. Candles and torches were burning along the walls and tucked in alcoves around the room. At the far end, Emily could see what look like a stage with a lectern. Emily took another step, and the ones closest to her edged back out of her way. She watched as the rest backed away leaving a path for her that led right to the steps of the large centralized stage.

They walked toward her. She saw them only as a black simulacrum of men against the white glare of light, and she felt like a weightless scarecrow before their massive silhouettes. She trembled. Then as they moved and came fully within the candle's glow, Emily saw they weren't massive creatures as she had thought. No, they were imposing, but they were thin and white, grub-white, and she stared at them with a deep sense of awe. The torches along with the candlelight made their flesh seem almost transparent. She could see the layers of muscle, the elegant pattern of tendons, with dark sapphire veins softly pulsing giving life to the horrible hearts that beat within them. She did not breathe. Time slowed and pivoted, as her eyes now gravitated back to the large crowd around her. All the faces turned in her direction; all eyes were on her.

Her situation seemed fragile and capricious and she worried that things could turn sour in an instant. The scent of death was redolent in the air. She stood there—her spidery fingers nervously tapping as the air hummed with the roar of silence. The stage in front of her had been formed from an immense wall of granite. She could just make out a scattering of sculptures in the edge of the stage—rough cut granite forms with polished and somewhat sinister shapes emerging from the stone; faces, body forms, creatures beyond description. It then flattened out then rose again finally topping out on a long ridge before disappearing once again into jagged peaks and fissures beyond forming a backdrop of stupendous power and majesty. Then with a savage roar like that of a beast, a flash of angry amber flames leapt up, casting eerie, quick-moving shadows deep into the surrounding alcoves. Billowing amber blooms danced around the room from the torches and candles then suddenly the flickering stopped, and the room became frigid, almost blizzard cold. Emily's heart was pounded so hard it seemed to knock itself against her ribcage. She swore under her breath as she balled her frozen hands into fists and shoved them under her arms to warm them. Her fingers felt like ice that could snap off at any moment. A single chill sashayed up her back. Then the two stepped aside and there from the darkness, a form, a face—a face blanched white with death. Emily bit down on her lower lip as it moved toward her through the glowing haze of candle smoke. She felt a creeping sensation of heat in her face.

He who drew near emerged stepping into a pool of candlelight. He was beautiful, elegant and pale, with long black hair that cascaded down and over his shoulders.

He was dressed entirely in black with a coat that reached and stretched toward the floor. There was something absolutely foreign about him and yet, at the same time strangely familiar. He walked forward and reached out a white hand and took Emily's in his. It made Emily's arm tingle, as if a gentle current were passing through. His fingers were cold, long and well-tended, and his grip firm as he pulled her closer staring at her intently. His eyes filled with sage were blue as the dusk that swallows the edge of the sky. Emily's eyes before him showed the same vulnerable intelligence as before she had even been bitten.

He inhaled deeply then his words came forth in a breath of smoke.

"Welcome sister. I am Ramear, son of Ressa— I am your brother."

Emily's lips parted as if to speak, but a shiver silenced her. She wrapped her arms around her torso, her eyes darting around the room. Then her eyes narrowed.

"My Brother?"

"Yes, brother. And I welcome you," Ramear said turning. "We all do. But, where is the one we contacted? The one called Isabeau?"

Emily paused her face hardened and her brow furrowed. There was an odd dalliance to her answer. She thought of Isabeau and what she had done to her. She thought of how at one time she would have cared. Now, there was nothing in her that even came close to it. The animal was here and the fear was gone. There arose a sound of a great sigh from the many faces that held the eyes that were upon her.

Emily blinked. "She is dead."

"Dead? How did she die sister?"

Emily blinked again but said nothing.

Ramear cleared his throat audibly. "How did she die?"

"What does that matter, she's gone, and I am here."

"It matters. It is against our laws for one vampire to kill another. So I ask you again sister," he said moving closer, his natural sternness twitching with anxiety. "How did she die? Did you kill her?"

The bluntness of the question was so strong and so sudden that it knocked the breath out of her lungs. There was an undefinable whisper of warning from deep within. Her next statement had to be the right one. If they could indeed read her mind, as Isabeau had once told her some could, then they already knew and if not, then perhaps she should deny it. Emily drew in a quick breath and then there was no sound in the room. She looked around.

Ramear shifted his weight, folded his arms, his cold blue eyes never leaving her face. Emily's gray gaze, as unblinking as Ramear's darker stare and already chilly, grew noticeably chillier. A silence ensued. It stretched into a minute, two minutes. Finally Emily with her downturned doll eyes searched for an answer, framing it carefully, then she raised them to Ramear her posture buckling just a bit as she tilted her head and in delicate tones said, "No, No I didn't kill her, brother."

Ramear lifted his head and stared at Emily, eyes stiller than death.

"Very well then, there is nothing to worry about then, is there?"

He asked probably trying to allay her fears, but she only blinked there in the gray smoke filled room. She felt his words were more of a poke at her rather than a question with any real objective.

Ramear, then turned, pulling Emily's hand guiding her as they faced the faction together.

"Brothers, Sisters we welcome her, she who will be our new Queen."

There was not the cheer that she had desired,

needed, and or expected. No, just a thousand glares above hideous smiles without a sound. Ramear released her hand moved back and pulled aside a large curtain from the back, and there it stood, in all its dark glory. The vampire throne.

It was beautifully horrible in design. An architecture arrangement of what appeared to be a weaving of thorn and bone. Long gnarled vines encrusted with thorns like the crown of Christ—knotted, twisted, visceral, flickering there in the shadows. The back ascended upward, cambering forward like an umbrella above the osseous sable seat flourishing at its crown. Obsidian, a raven black that it seemed to swallow the light and within its branches mire brutality and evil, those changes that wrought in us through experience in contrast to those that occur through simple growth. Emily looked on it and knew, she who would now be seated there would now be moving from childhood into adulthood even when the former was stolen rather than discarded. Then she saw it; the crown, it lay cradled within its seat. She hoisted her head and took an immodest step forward.

Ramear raised a hand. "Wait."

Emily turned toward him, her eyes narrowing to a point.

"We do have rituals, my dear sister. It is not as simple as that. First, you must accept the gift from the entire faction."

Suddenly a scream, dire, radiated from the darkness. Emily turned, searching. Then again the mournful cry echoed through the massive chamber causing a great stirring in the group. Backlit, a mere silhouette formed in the mist across a riser. It jerked and twisted within the haze until it too took form. It was one of the pale that she had seen earlier, pulling on a leash. She followed its leathery serpentine lead with her eyes and at the end of the tether screaming and tugging was a meager child. A male child maybe seven to eight years of age. Its eyes wide rimmed in red, somewhat plump in appearance—ripe, and whimpering.

"Please sister," Ramear said offering up the child.

Emily looked at Ramear then out at the crowd. Did they want her to feed on this child, here in front of everyone? The congregation below her was getting agitated, she could see it in their eyes, in their movements. Emily looked back at the small child, and she closed her eyes and smiled.

Her body suddenly lurched forward, and she growled with pain, her eyes dilated growing a darkened silver as if the moon had given her the color. Stretching she flung her arms out to her sides and claws sprouted pulling and ripping the skin as they ran from her elongated fingertips. Her head shook, the mane of crimson hair haloing her face evolving, augmenting now to a raven black. She could feel her bones shifting inside of her as her shoulders widened, and the agony of her spine popping and ratcheting as it rearranged and grew in length. She opened her maw as the bottom jaw joint thrust and cracked lengthening as well as her teeth. Blood ran as they pushed themselves through her gums. Her throat and mind dragging her through the fire, yet keeping her alive and conscious to endure every second. Her back arched as she pulled, her claws ripping the tightening cloth from her frame, freeing her body to move and grow. She threw out her chest as it broadened, her breasts widened and expanded becoming more muscular yet still feminine. Slowly her form became more anthropomorphic than human, the blood-sucking beast inside her reaching fulfillment.

Then there before them, naked in all her glory, nearly eight feet in height, she threw her arms back, and she screamed so loud that It shook the forest and even the mountain the forest mantled. Her eyes now faded to a steel gray as she looked down on the collective before her, and she smiled, blood and saliva dripping from her maw. Then she turned glancing down, her silvery eyes fixed on the child still being held on its leash blanched white with fear—his eyes wide, his body a constant quiver and not even able to scream. She took a single rangy step toward him, his eyes rising to her then she lurched forward snatching the wide-eyed boy before even a whimper could pass his lips, tearing into his flesh like a starving wild animal. First grabbing the child, a leg in one clawed hand and his head in the other, pulling it in two different directions, bending his head away from the shoulder before her bone-snapping bite came down on his small neck almost decapitating the youth. The sounds of tearing bone and flesh, the sounds of feeding, sucking radiated through the cathedral-like room as blood burst from the little body pouring down her naked form. Huge tendrils of steam rose from the warm liquid as she gorged herself moving his little frame around, his limbs becoming pliant, flopping about as she squeezed it, and flipped it, trying to get as much of his blood a possible. She then stood up tall gasping for air and raised her head, stretched her neck, back and forth allowing the liquid to run down her throat as flesh and blood run dripping from her lips and teeth. The child's lifeless frame gripped in one claw lying torn and dangling against the floor. She smiled as she flung the imbrued waste to the ravenous crowd below her, watching as a fight began when a few lept to be the first to taste her gift.

She then turned, overlooking them all, naked before them, steam still radiating from her blood-soaked frame. She just stood there, for a long time smiling, drunk with blood, her vampire body imbued in the crimson from the child. Then Emily turned and walked boldly without any fear before the throne. She reached down a clawed hand lifting the crown of thorns from its seat, watching suspiciously, eyes darting for anyone who would dare defy her at this moment. Her moment. Then she smiled and placed it firmly on her head. Her eyes no longer gray and troubled, looked out upon the beasts of darkness before her as she raised her head high, proud and strong, staring straight out at the congregation.

"I am Neera," she announced as she took her rightful place upon the throne of evil.

To be continued:

These and more are available at

Amazon.com, Barnes and Noble or your local bookstore.

Titles by D.B. Martin

HORRIBLE SANITY – Dark Tales - Brown

FEEDER – Book I of the Blood Chronicles

MOTHER – Book II of the Blood Chronicles

TERROR TALES – Vol I

Collective Works

World of Pirates

31 Days of October

CAW Telling Stories Vol I

Look for these titles coming soon

Goody

Terror Tales – Vol II

Noah – Book III of the Blood Chronicles

CAW Telling Stories Vol II

www.ingramcontent.com/pod-product-compliance
Lightning Source LLC
Chambersburg PA
CBHW062025170626
46813CB00001B/290